CHAPTER 1

*L*ondon
June 1818

"It was nothing," Savannah Raeni Shaw insisted, for the dozenth or more time in three days. No one listened. She stubbornly held her sister's gaze, even as Lyneé rolled her eyes and muttered uncomplimentary things about her sanity beneath her breath.

Or not so beneath her breath.

Savannah sniffed—a mistake, given they stood beside the overflowing gutter. The sun barely dented the crowded, cramped alleyways of the rookery, preferring to take its light and warmth anywhere else. Still, Savannah stayed.

Someone had to.

"Savannah." Lyneé gritted her teeth and spoke with exaggerated patience. "Someone tried to kill you."

"*Pfft.*" It was a weak retort, but they'd had this argument every day for three days. All it did was go round and round with no solution. She was tired of arguing about this. "I'm sure they did not. I'm perfectly unharmed, nothing else has happened, and even Dem hadn't heard anything after the incident."

"Incident" was the term she'd decided on when Dem, her self-proclaimed bodyguard and leader of Denmark Street, let slip what happened when he'd escorted her to her carriage. He'd made an offhanded comment to Browne, her footman. Browne, who took his position in the household *extremely* seriously, then informed her father.

Whoever had thrown the dagger had missed, and by quite a lot. Though the force of the throw had embedded it into the wall beside her.

The dagger in question was now in the Shaw house, as if it might offer any answers. But thus far, it had refused. The nondescript knife, with a plain wooden handle and an expertly sharpened blade, looked like a hundred other knives.

Lyneé gave her a disbelieving look and deliberately cleared her throat.

"I'm certain I'm in no danger," Savannah added.

Probably in no danger—not from that, at least. The odds that it had been anything other than an accident were incredibly slim. So slim, she'd dismissed it immediately as nothing more than idiot boys playing around. Gangs roamed St. Giles Rookery, looking for anyone weaker than they.

She'd never had a problem with them before. Dem kept them at bay, and they knew better than to harass the person who kept them alive. And surely, if someone had meant her dead *and missed*, they'd have tried again. It wasn't as if Savannah weren't noticeable. As the only healer consistently on the street, she was conspicuous enough. As a Black woman with vast resources at her fingertips, everyone knew her name.

"And the dead man?" Lyneé demanded.

That, on the other hand, was harder to dismiss. Certainly for the poor man who had been killed. She hadn't known him No

THE LADY'S COURTSHIP

A SECOND CHANCE REGENCY ROMANCE

CONRAD LEGACY
BOOK-FIVE

C.K. MACKENZIE

This is a work of fiction. Names, characters, places, and incidents are either the product of the author's imagination or are used fictitiously, and any resemblance to actual persons living or dead, business establishments, events, or locales, is entirely coincidental.

The Lady's Courtship
A Second Chance Regency Romance
Conrad Legacy Book 5

COPYRIGHT © 2024 by Emelia Publishers LLC and C.K. Mackenzie

All rights reserved. No part of this book may be used or reproduced in any manner whatsoever without written permission of the author except in the case of brief quotations embodied in critical articles or reviews.

Contact Information: ckmackenzieauthor@gmail.com

Cover Art by Graziana Masneri

Publishing History
First Edition, 2024
Paperback ISBN 979-8-9901599-1-4
Published in the United States of America

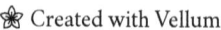 Created with Vellum

ACKNOWLEDEMENT

I have a lot of people to thank for this story. People who listened and encouraged me throughout this process. Thank you all, your support means the world to me.

one had. It wasn't, unfortunately, the first time she'd seen a dead body.

It was, however, the first time she'd witnessed an actual murder.

"Someone clearly aimed for him," Savannah insisted, confident in that. "You don't accidentally shoot someone with such precision."

The shot had killed the stranger standing beside her. A single shot through the man's temple. Fast, deliberate, and messy. Even now, Savannah, who had helped her mother and grandmother in midwifery and healing from the time she could walk, swallowed hard against the bile rising at the memory. She'd seen dead bodies before, unfortunately; every healer did. But that had been her first time witnessing a murder.

However, the chances of that shot being aimed at her specifically were slim. Pistols, rifles, musket balls, and gunpowder weren't terribly hard to come by, what with the sheer number of soldiers passing through. A quick hand, a carelessly unattended wagon.

That shot had been aimed at the man alone. It was too precise for anything else.

"All I ask is that you stop coming here for a few days," Lyneé insisted, exasperated.

"On the off chance someone purposely threw the dagger at me *and missed*," she stressed, "a couple days won't matter. It's best I remain here with my work. Besides," she added as Lyneé rolled her eyes again, "wouldn't they have tried again? Given it's been three days with no further incident, I think you're mistaken."

Savannah didn't take her safety lightly, however. She carried her own dagger, which now lay within easy reach in a specially made pocket of her dress. She'd also enlisted Dem's gang as additional guards and informants, and she had seriously debated asking some of the dockworkers who worked for her family for protection as well. Just in case.

She'd dismissed that as being overly cautious, paranoid even.

"At least let Browne accompany you instead of keeping him guarding the carriage," Lyneé argued. She looked around the street, but no one bothered them, not that Savannah expected anything else. Most of those living here respected her too much to eavesdrop.

"These women trust me. *Me*. They accept Browne when he delivers food, but it ends there." They'd never openly speak with Savannah if her footman stood in their cramped room, looming over them. It'd taken her weeks before they trusted her as it was.

"Do I ask so much that you can't stay home for a few days? A week?" Lyneé muttered under her breath again, but Savannah didn't miss her disparaging words.

Yes, it was too much. She couldn't stay home. She hadn't been able to stay still for years. Working, moving, exhausting herself was by far the better option than sitting and remembering. Or wallowing.

"At least let's ask Uncle James for more protection…"

Lyneé trailed off, staring wide-eyed over her sister's shoulder. Savannah's heart skipped, and her stomach dropped. Spine straight, her gaze flew to her sister's, but Lyneé didn't say a word. She didn't have to.

Standing beside the foulest gutter she could have chosen, tired, annoyed, and worn down, Savannah hoped it might be her father with the armed guard he'd threatened to hire. Or her Uncle James and a platoon of men. She grasped for any other options—perhaps her family had hired someone, such as a former soldier, to follow her around.

It didn't work. She couldn't lie to herself. She knew who walked behind her. That knowledge shot down her spine, making her skin tingle like a caress. Or a warning.

Her feet turned her body around, even as her brain screamed at her to run. She never listened to her brain, only her foolish, traitorous heart. Which brought her around, one inexorable step at a time, until she saw him.

Because of course she saw him. Of course he was there. Of course, of all the imaginable days and times, he'd decided on today. Her appetite fled.

So, too, did her common sense.

Savannah's heart skidded to a stop, then galloped far too fast. He looked the same. Tall and confident with that stupidly wide smile and sparkling blue-green eyes. His hair curled over his collar, longer than the last time she'd seen him. The last time she'd run her fingers through his soft, dark curls as they laughed together in bed.

This moment might've been better, Savannah thought, if he'd grown ugly or lost his hair, as inexplicable as that would have been. She hadn't fallen in love with his looks. The way he made her laugh, yes. The way he listened, definitely. Savannah had loved the way he devoted his entire person to simply being with her. Or had, once upon a time.

Before he'd left her.

He held something, but she couldn't concentrate on what. No, she saw only him. No matter how much she wished to run in the opposite direction, instead she walked forward, drawn to him, as she had been since the first time she saw him, aged five.

"Tristan Conrad." His name flowed from her tongue, though it had been three years since she'd seen him, since she said his name, since she dared think of this meeting.

When he left her, she banished him from her mind and her heart. She banished his name from the house she lived in with her parents and three younger siblings. No one mentioned his name. Ever. Not even when the Conrads visited, or that single time afterward she'd traveled to Hertfordshire to visit their grandmother. Who, of course, lived at Nelda Hall with the Conrads.

Never. Ever.

Until today.

The past three years' heartache rushed back in a blink, stealing her breath and crushing her chest. The din of the street faded as muted as the sunlight. As if the sun shone solely for him, only the man approaching her made any sense. Except he didn't, because he'd abandoned her.

"Savannah." She heard Lyneé's voice, a distant echo. Her gaze remained on Tristan.

She didn't know what she expected. A laugh, perhaps, with that wink that always made her smile. A joke about her missing him. Honestly, she'd stopped imagining—dreaming—about this reunion two years and eleven months ago.

Tristan smiled, that soft, intimate smile she knew better than her own. He stopped just out of reach, which was probably a good idea since Savannah couldn't decide whether to kiss him or slap him.

"Hello, love."

Her arm shot out, and her hand connected with his cheek.

Clearly, the urge to slap won out.

HE DESERVED THAT.

Tristan didn't even bother to cover his now throbbing cheek. Perhaps their first conversation in three years shouldn't have started with *Hello, love*, but it'd slipped out, as natural as breathing.

"And here I brought you a gift." He worked his jaw slightly and grimaced. She'd always had a terrific arm.

Her beautiful brown eyes narrowed, and as foolish as it seemed, he wanted to kiss her. He always wanted to kiss her. He

THE LADY'S COURTSHIP

wouldn't—even he wasn't that stupid—but the instinct pulled him forward.

"You hired him?" Savannah's hand shot out, her finger jabbing him in the chest, as she whipped her head around to accuse her sister.

He shifted his sack away from her anger. Obviously, she and Lyneé had been in the middle of a conversation. He hadn't expected to see Lyneé, but then, the sisters had always been close. For all the ways he'd envisioned this reunion with Savannah, her jabbing at his chest hadn't been on the list.

Unfortunately, the slap definitely had been.

"Hired me?" he repeated, somewhat bewildered. No one knew he'd returned. He'd put to port only on the morning tide. However, he masked his confusion and looked between her and Lyneé, who held up her hands.

"I did not," Lyneé insisted. She composed her face into an impassive look, though her eyes couldn't mask the fire she shot at him. "Papa wouldn't have either. Not him. Never *him*," she added with enough force to shoot a cannonball. "Though you do need protection, Savannah."

Savannah whirled around and glared at him once more. "Why?" she demanded, jaw clenched. Her hands fisted at her sides, and she raised her chin.

"Why the present?" he asked, lifting the sack. "Why am I back?" He thought that was obvious. Still, he rocked back on his heels, ready to dodge another slap.

"Yes," she spat.

Oh, but Tristan knew her better than that. She had more words she wanted to spit at him. He knew she also didn't want to be anywhere near him, but here they were.

Fate did like to laugh at him.

"Would you like to meet Jiesha?"

She stilled and sucked in a sharp breath, her gaze roaming the area behind him. Tristan mentally rolled his eyes at himself.

Idiot. He used to be so good at talking with her. Flirting with her, seducing her—being seduced by her, for that matter. Apparently not any longer. Three years couldn't have addled his brain that much. Given how wrong he'd been to leave her in the first place, perhaps it had.

Of course, she thought he meant a lover or—heaven forbid—a wife. As if anyone compared to her. Carefully maneuvering his canvas sack, he kept his gaze on hers, lest she strike again. Then he lifted the flap and gently took out the rabbit, a soft white with black spots.

Savannah hadn't reached for her dagger, which was a definite plus. Lyneé had uttered a disgruntled sound and melted into the background, smart woman that she was. Savannah's gaze flicked to the rabbit and back to him, then focused on Jiesha.

"Oh," she said softly. "She's beautiful." Her gaze remained on the rabbit as she reached for her. "Where did you find her?"

"A merchant." He'd stolen her from a rather abusive merchant in Antwerp, but that was a story for another time. "'Jiesha' means 'beautiful rain.' Or so I've been told."

The merchant could've made it up; he wasn't exactly what anyone would call honest. However, Jiesha was a beautiful name no matter the meaning.

"She's lovely." Her head jerked up, and her eyes rained fire. "This doesn't mean I forgive you."

"I didn't think it would," he said honestly. He reached out and ran a finger down the back of Jiesha's head. She looked at him, eyes large and scared. "She's been through a lot," he added, dropping his hand. "She's skittish."

Savannah cuddled the rabbit against her chest. "Why did you return?"

His eyebrows shot up. "In general, or today?"

Lips pressed tight, she looked like she might hit him. Again.

He wondered what she'd expected. What he'd expected, for that matter.

She carefully petted the rabbit's head, head tilted as she watched him cautiously. When she spoke, her words barely dented the busy street. "I never thought I'd see you again."

For three years, all he'd thought about was seeing her again. About the last time they spoke, right before he left when he very foolishly didn't ask her to join him. When he left her, and his heart, and boarded his ship, setting off on his own adventure.

Alone.

"I arrived on the morning tide," he admitted. It didn't escape his notice that the crowded street gave them a wide berth.. "One of your father's secretaries let slip where I could find you."

"I'll have words with him," Savannah muttered. She sniffed, wrinkled her nose, and raised her head. "Why bother? You could've arrived and left for Nelda Hall, or your next grand adventure, or whatever you chose." She blinked against the wind, though he swore he saw tears in her eyes. "Alone," she added without inflection. "Why seek me out?"

He missed her. He ached for her. He had a hundred thousand apologies on his tongue, none of which were good enough. He missed her laugh, her smile, the sound of her voice as they walked the wharves and talked about their future. His fingers ached to feel hers around his. Tristan longed to kiss her again, taste her skin as they made love. Hold her close.

"Why are you in St. Giles?" he asked instead, gesturing around the cramped, filthy, derelict street.

He noticed the man then. Tristan knew he hadn't been there a moment ago, but had appeared silently, stealthily. He looked as if he usually stood there, just out of earshot, three paces behind Savannah. A guard? Hadn't she said something about that? About her father hiring someone? Why?

The wind whipped down the street, sending rubbish skipping through the gutters and stirring up a truly foul stench.

When Arnault, his first mate and closest friend, had informed Tristan that Savannah visited St. Giles daily, he hadn't believed him. Yet here she stood, wearing an old gown, glaring daggers at him.

He knew why her sister glared. However, the mystery of why Savannah was standing in St. Giles confused him. Lyneé mumbled something about the carriage and disappeared into the crowd.

"I choose to be here." The words shot out, almost as if she'd memorized them. "This is where I chose to pursue my future."

"Chose—" He swallowed the rest of his words. She didn't have to say more. After he left, she meant. Tristan nodded, a slow movement. She'd kept her voice even, but he knew hurt lay beneath the surface, waiting to explode at him.

The man behind her hadn't moved, watching him with a wariness Tristan appreciated, even if that wariness was aimed at him. With an impatient grunt, he pushed the man's presence to the back of his mind. Savannah had to know he was there; she had always been highly aware of her surroundings.

"You have no right to question me, Tristan Conrad." Savannah's cold gaze met his, and he once more wondered just what he'd expected from this meeting.

For her to fall into his arms? That was not the woman he loved. A quick and easy forgiveness? Ha, that hadn't even crossed his mind. Tristan had simply wanted to see her again. Start over, mend the rift he'd caused.

Such a tame word for what he'd done.

"I'm not questioning you." He kept his voice steady, though a flare of annoyance crept in. "I'm asking why you're *here*. I expected you in the offices."

Something passed over her face, he couldn't tell what. He knew her so well, or once had. Now, he had only more questions.

"I never expected to see you again." The bite in her voice

THE LADY'S COURTSHIP

chilled him. She stepped back. "We're talking in circles. Thank you for Jiesha. I shall take care of her. Don't come round again."

So saying, she stepped around him, no doubt toward the carriage Lyneé had mentioned. Her guard followed.

"Who's your guard, then?" Her earlier words about hiring a guard echoed in his mind. "I thought you didn't need one."

"Dem isn't my guard." Though she kept her voice low, the heat of her anger boiled hot enough to singe him.

"No, but you need one. Are you going to tell me why?" He watched as the street cleared for her, people moving around her as she strode toward the church. "What happened that has Lyneé so worried?"

"Nothing."

"Savannah." He stopped her with a light hand on her arm. Beneath his touch, her taut muscles quivered with anger. "Lyneé doesn't worry easily. Neither do you."

"A misunderstanding about certain circumstances." She shot him a withering look. "Once again, it has nothing to do with you."

His mind raced with questions about what the misunderstanding might be. What could be dangerous enough that both her father and sister insisted she needed an armed guard?

"Did someone accost you?" Tristan searched her face, but it gave away nothing. "Try to harm you or—"

"I forgot how meddlesome you could be," she muttered, but she didn't move away.

"I'm not meddlesome," he insisted, offended at the very thought. "I'm worried."

"Tristan, I'm tired. I have an afternoon engagement, and now I need to find food for Jiesha. Whatever you think you know, you do not. Whatever you think you want to know, I do not care. My life is no longer any concern of yours."

Afternoon engagement? Jealousy burned through him. It didn't matter how many years had passed or what happened between them. Time hadn't changed his feelings for her. She was right, of course— strictly speaking, it wasn't any concern of his. But his jealousy threatened to have him spouting words he probably shouldn't.

"Be that as it may," he finally managed. His tone wasn't exactly even, and Savannah's narrowed gaze told him just how much she appreciated that. "I care for you, and I want to see you safe."

"I've seen to my own safety for the last three years without you, thank you very much," she snapped.

"I deserve that." Would her afternoon engagement keep her safe? Or even know how to?

"Your acknowledging what you do or do not deserve doesn't make anything better or right."

"I didn't say it did," he insisted, his control slipping further. "I owe you more than an apology; I owe you explanations and atonement."

She flinched then. It was slight but clear as day to him. "Tristan." She sounded weary now. "Please don't. Whatever happened three days ago is no concern of yours. As I said, a misunderstanding. My family is overreacting because they worry."

Tristan let loose a string of curses. How thick was he? "Someone tried to hurt you."

"No." Her weariness dissipated with that harsh word. "I witnessed a murder, that's all."

"Witnessed a murder," he repeated, but his anger and fear for her safety simmered beneath his skin. "That's all." She made it sound so blasé that Tristan could only blink at her in disbelief. "And you think your family is overreacting?"

"Things happen here. Murders, violence, especially amongst the women. I can watch over myself."

"Damn it, Savannah!" The words exploded from him. His control vanished. "Someone tried to kill you!"

CHAPTER 2

"I don't want your help," Savannah seethed. Hot anger flushed through her but did little to warm her. Despite the beautiful June day, the tall, cramped buildings hid whatever sunlight warmed the day. Certainly, no warmth thawed the streets. Or her fingers where they locked around the rabbit. "And I certainly don't need it."

His lips pressed together and his gaze flicked around the street.

So many emotions raced through her, she didn't know which one to grab first. Anger. Anger worked. Anger had sustained her; it gave her something to hold on to when she thought she'd drift away from heartache, drown in anguish. Anger gave her a means to stand tall in the face of gossip and those horribly pitying looks.

A broken engagement, abandonment. The scandal that had accompanied all that. His family had tried to contact her, of course, but Savannah hadn't wanted anything to do with the Conrads. Unfortunately, their families were far too intertwined to sever all ties.

However, Savannah had tried. She'd cut off all contact with

Tristan's siblings, though she'd once been close with them. She'd stopped visiting Hertfordshire where her grandmother lived with the Conrads, even though the long trip from there to London made her grandmother ill.

"Someone tried to kill you," Tristan said in such a reasonable tone that she wanted to slap him again. Unfortunately, she knew him far too well, despite the pain and heartbreak and three years' separation.

Fear. It lurked beneath his reasonable tone, thick and heavy between them. She struggled with that. His fear for her, that something might happen to her. He had no right.

"Why do you care?" She shoved away whatever feeling she had at realizing he still cared for her and grabbed onto that anger again. It buoyed her in this new storm she found herself wading through. "You have no right, waltzing back into my life and acting as if you care."

As if three years hadn't passed. As if he had any say in how she lived her life now. Lifting her chin and holding his gaze, Savannah shoved down her heartache, that persistent longing for his arms around her. At the moment, it was all she had. The rabbit squirmed in her arms, and Savannah loosened her hold. Bringing Jiesha closer, she gathered her strength and stood her ground.

"Of course I care, Savannah—"

"No. Whatever happened three days ago won't happen again. Things happen in St. Giles, you know that." Her words belied the prickling down her back, as if someone was watching her. Which was ridiculous. No one did. Well, perhaps some onlookers gawked because of this very public argument, but not for any other reason.

"I know your family isn't prone to overreaction. If Lyneé suggested a guard, there's a reason." He stepped closer, and Savannah had the absurd feeling that she should hold up the poor rabbit as some sort of ward against Tristan.

No. Never. She wouldn't back down or show him any weakness. Never again.

"Whatever the reason for that man's death, I'm not involved. Whatever happened, it no longer concerns you." Savannah ran a comforting hand down Jiesha's soft fur and wondered again how the rabbit had come into Tristan's possession. She held back her curiosity. "You left. Our engagement is broken. We have no attachments any longer."

Her throat ached with those words, words she never thought she'd speak aloud. Tristan paused, his only reaction the slight widening of his eyes.

"Goodbye, Tristan." She spoke the words she hadn't been able to say when he'd abruptly announced his departure, through a letter of all things. When she'd thought, for one wild moment as she read his laughingly brief letter, that of course she'd accompany him.

They'd done everything together from the moment they met. Learned their families' businesses, learned to ride and dance and read together, explored London and the wharves and the grounds of his family's estate. Learned each other's bodies. Nauseous now, Savannah wondered if he'd taken other lovers while he was out exploring.

Her throat closed with that staggering realization, and she turned and left. Tears blurred her vision, and she angrily blinked them away. Until this moment, that thought had truly never occurred to her. Fool that she was.

She already knew she was a fool when it came to Tristan Conrad. She didn't need her own internal voice reminding her over and over.

He didn't follow her. Savannah knew that without looking around. Then again, she always knew where Tristan stood, felt his presence as keenly as she did the breeze over her face.

No, he hadn't followed her, and she had no idea what emotions that evoked.

Her path cleared as she strode toward St. Giles in the Fields, the church where her carriage always waited to take her home. Lyneé was nowhere to be seen, the traitor, leaving her alone with Tristan. Closing her eyes for a moment, Savannah pushed that aside. Lyneé had no doubt returned to her errands in her own carriage. She knew the dangers in the area. On any street, for that matter.

Nodding at Browne as he held open the door, Savannah wordlessly climbed inside. She needed a moment, one single moment of privacy, but she couldn't foresee that happening. Not in St. Giles, where so many knew her. Not in the carriage, where any crying or screaming she indulged in would be heard by the staff. Not even her family home. Given what happened three days ago, she might never have a moment alone again, and she needed one now more than ever.

The rabbit burrowed into her lap, seemingly content.

At least one of them was.

"What am I supposed to do with you?" Savannah asked her, throat tight with too much emotion. Anger and grief and even tears, though she'd never shed them. Jiesha's large dark eyes looked up at her, her little nose working up and down, and Savannah melted. "Oh, all right." She rested her hand along her furry back. "You're adorable, you are. But I've no idea how to care for a rabbit."

Leaning her head back against the wall of the carriage, she closed her eyes and blocked out her thoughts. Or tried to. They whirled around and around, jumping from the murder she witnessed to the dagger embedded inches from her head.

Tristan's sudden arrival mixed up everything, and Savannah had no idea what to make of that. Then again, whatever he'd expected from his gift-bearing return, it probably wasn't an argument about whether she needed protection.

As the carriage made the final turn that would bring her onto her street, Savannah tried to remember the exact order of events from three days ago. She'd been talking with Dem, who said some of the gin houses had closed, she remembered that now. Was that important to what came after? She didn't think so, but then, with all the fuss over her safety—and her own dismissal of that concern—Savannah no longer knew.

The man had fallen dead from a rifle shot, and then the knife had embedded itself in the wall beside her. She was positive it happened in that order. The problem was no one knew who the dead man was. Not necessarily an oddity in the rookery, where people appeared and disappeared with a rapidity that made keeping track of the populace difficult. If someone could identify him, perhaps a magistrate might be able to learn something.

Savannah sighed at her own naivety. Given the location, any investigation would most likely be terminated before it truly began. Still, strange that he'd been right beside her when he died.

No matter how she tried to dismiss that as coincidence, Savannah didn't quite believe it.

Perhaps she didn't need a guard. Perhaps that incident had been wholly unrelated, as most things were. However, the unease that slithered down her spine told her not to take this lightly.

"I definitely don't need Tristan," she grumbled to Jiesha as Browne opened the carriage door onto the spotless street near Grosvenor Square. "Thank you," she smiled at the footman as he eyed Jiesha suspiciously.

Head high and carrying her new rabbit, Savannah walked toward her family's townhouse and had no idea what she might say to them Dealing with a nameless dead man and a possible attempt on her life was one thing. But dealing with her returned fiancé?

Former fiancé. There was a definite difference there.

Semantics aside, Savannah had no idea what to do about that.

Tristan hadn't sent word of his arrival in London.

He could've traveled to Nelda Hall, where his eldest brother and his family lived. Or Regent's Park, where his oldest sister and her husband resided. At the moment, Tristan had no idea where his parents lived. After they'd handed over Nelda Hall and control of Conrad Shipping to Grayson, they liked to travel around the country, visiting their grandchildren.

The last he knew of his other sister, she and her husband lived on a vast estate with more animals than blades of grass. As for Philip, as far as Tristan knew, he had planned on sailing for Egypt, but Tristan didn't know if he had returned or where he might live now.

Three years at sea, visiting a dozen ports and expanding the Conrad Shipping domain, had left him richer and more experienced with the world. Wiser, he hoped, in what truly mattered. He'd seen places he'd only ever imagined, and he wouldn't change those experiences for anything. However, the price was higher than he'd expected.

Losing Savannah. Losing touch with his siblings and their families. Not even knowing where his parents currently lived.

Which now left him in the unenviable position of knocking on his aunt's door with a single bag of his belongings, a charming grin, and the hope she wouldn't turn him away. As he waited for the door to open, Tristan let his gaze wander five houses down the street to the Shaw's home.

No one stood on the street, no carriages or horses or foot traffic. Tristan glanced at the neighbor's house, but Mrs. Hawthorne, the gossipy neighbor who knew everything and everyone on the street, had died years ago. The new occupants barely spent any time here, or hadn't when he left, and were certainly not the gossip Mrs. Hawthorne had been.

"Ah, Mr. Tristan."

"Hello, Alans." Tristan quickly faced the butler and stepped into his aunt's foyer. "Is Aunt Nadia home?"

"I'll let Mrs. St. Clair know you're here," Alans said with a nearly imperceptible side-eye. He'd taken over from Martin, Aunt Nadia's previous butler, only a few years before Tristan left. Now, as Alans watched him with far more scrutiny than Tristan was used to, he wondered how Martin fared. Alans gestured for the front parlor, and silently disappeared.

Unsettled, Tristan paced the room where he used to spy on the street on a child. He couldn't have said what he expected upon his return. He'd thought about it for three years, almost from the instant he set sail. Tristan should have guessed Savannah's reaction—he'd hurt her badly, all for a chance at adventure.

When he arrived in port well before dawn, all he'd thought of was finding Savannah. Tristan had no idea how to overcome any of it, and he hadn't any more answers by the time Aunt Nadia entered the room.

"Tristan." Arms wide open, she hugged him tight and kissed both cheeks. "I heard you'd returned."

Pulling back, he blinked at her. "Already?" He shook his head before her look, which told him obviously she had, translated into words. "Never mind. Of course."

Savannah's mother, Sophia, was Nadia's closest friend. Of course she'd heard. Of course, word of his return had spread faster than wildfire. His aunt, not by blood but by the unwavering friendship Nadia shared with his own parents, didn't even bother to answer him.

"Are you passing through on your way to Nelda Hall?" Nadia asked in such a sincere yet somehow offhand manner, Tristan didn't wonder how she'd survived the Russian Tsarina's court for so long. She never asked a question unless she already knew the answer.

"Did you know someone tried to kill Savanah?" he asked rather than answer his aunt's obvious question.

Just then, Alans wheeled in the tea tray, piled with biscuits, marzipan, and coffee cups. Behind him came a second tray with already warm kanakas for their coffee. Tristan waited while Aunt Nadia thanked the butler and poured the coffee.

"I know Hugh and Sophia believe someone did," Nadia said as she sat on the settee. Her dark eyes held his as she watched him over her cup. "And that Savannah doesn't believe so."

Tristan snorted and paced the parlor, ignoring his own coffee. Savannah's words haunted his every step. He'd chosen adventure over their engagement and hadn't any right to get involved. But right had no control over worry, and Tristan worried. He loved Savannah, always had. He'd mistakenly believed sailing was the adventure he craved, but he'd been wrong. Savannah was what mattered. Worry for her gnawed at his gut, taunting him to act.

"Why are you concerned?" Aunt Nadia's voice stopped him in his tracks.

"Of course I'm concerned," he snapped, drinking his hot coffee as if it were cool carob juice instead. It burned his mouth, but he only set the cup in the saucer with a decisive click. "Why aren't you?"

"I am." She glared at him, that haughty look he so admired but couldn't quite emulate. "We all are, but—and I shouldn't need to remind you—you left her."

"I know," he snapped again. She merely raised an eyebrow. This was not the welcome he'd hoped for. His cheek still stung from Savannah's slap. "I know," he said again, in a quieter, but not calmer, voice.

Before he snapped the fine porcelain, he set the cup and saucer on the tray and once more paced to the windows overlooking the street. He'd spent so much time in this house, growing up beside Nadia's children, walking down to the Shaw household whenever he wished and spending time with Savannah.

Standing here, in a room he'd spent so much time in—or, rather, racing through—Tristan felt more like an outsider than he had those first months on his ship.

"Why have you returned, Tristan?" His aunt stood beside him and watched him with a look that once again said she already knew the answers. She held up a hand before he gathered his thoughts. "I don't mean I'm not thrilled to see you, *malenkoye solnysh*."

Little sun. Tristan smiled at the endearment. "I'm thrilled to see you, too, *Tetya* Nadia."

She returned his smile and leaned her head on his shoulder, squeezing his arm as they both looked onto the street below. "I'm happy you've returned safely. I simply wish to know what you expected from Savannah."

"I don't know," he admitted. It was the first time he'd voiced that. For three years, he'd wondered if he could have done something differently. A simple question would have changed everything. But adventure called, the tempting what-if he and Philip, his elder brother, had talked of so often.

"Perhaps you should reason that out before you try talking with Savannah."

"What—" He cut himself off. He'd ask Savannah what happened, though at this point he doubted she'd answer.

She'd be right to stay silent. Strictly speaking, he hadn't broken their engagement, but of course that was what the scandals would whisper. What right did he have to anything? Her time, her answers, her forgiveness? That last, no matter what, he needed. Though Tristan doubted he deserved it.

"Can I stay here, *Tetya*?" He kissed the top of her head.

"Will you stay away from Savannah?"

"No."

"Tristan," she sighed, clearly annoyed. She muttered several uncomplimentary names in Russian beneath her breath. "She's been through a lot. You left her."

He did not need that persistent reminder, thank you. He needed—her. And while Tristan had no idea how to go about getting her, he'd at least keep her safe.

"I'm not trying to win her back." A bald-faced lie if ever he'd uttered one. Clearly, Aunt Nadia didn't believe him. "I'm trying to keep her safe."

Nadia snorted. "Safe?" She laughed. "You think she can't do that?"

He offered a weak, rueful smile. "I know she can."

His mother believed everyone had the right to defend themselves—man, woman, child, it didn't matter. So she'd taken it upon herself to train half the County, and anyone else who wished to learn. It was a dangerous world, she always said. Best be prepared.

"Her choice is hers, *malenkoye solnysh.*" Nadia kissed Tristan's cheek and turned from the window. "Abide by it."

"Yes, *Tetya.*" He didn't roll his eyes in exasperation. He would respect her choice. He'd hurt her enough. Still, he wanted a chance to apologize—preferably without the slap. A chance to talk. She owed him nothing, but he owed her that.

He'd missed her these last three years, with an ache that haunted him. Was he a fool for leaving the way he had? More than. Would he do it again? Only if she accompanied him. Right now, all he wanted was the chance to make things right.

"Come into the study, and you can tell me of your travels while I read over the manifests." She eyed him again but softened. "I'll send word to James. He's at the taverns, overseeing the shipments."

"You have people for that." Tristan shook his head. "You always do too much yourselves."

"There are still rumors about uprisings and turmoil that

might affect us. He likes to keep abreast of such things." She grinned now. "He likes to be involved. Keeps him busy."

Laughing, Tristan offered his arm and escorted her from the parlor. "And out of your hair?"

"We share a great many interests, *malenkoye solnysh*. Now that's he's retired from the army, he needs a diversion." Nadia sighed again but grinned. "Your uncle is many things; idle isn't one of them."

"I'll wait until he arrives, then. I've heard rumors of unrest in Flanders."

CHAPTER 3

The next morning, having slept fitfully, tossing and turning and cursing Tristan with every movement, Savannah dressed in one of her older gowns. She'd promised Ailene, Dem's sister, she'd visit and check on her and the babe. While there, she'd meet with Dem again, discover what, if anything, he had learned about the stranger's murder.

She hadn't much hope. Three days in the rookery and no answers thus far only meant no answers ever. The rookery swallowed its secrets, kept them buried from the outside world.

And she'd do everything in her power to avoid Tristan.

Savannah walked into the morning room, where the family usually breakfasted. They ate earlier than most, usually just after dawn so her father could oversee any ships arriving on the early tides, but her mother insisted they try and eat at least one meal together. Studiously avoiding her parents' and Lyneé's piercing gazes, she sat in her usual seat. Lucky for her, her brother was on one of their merchant vessels to Copenhagen, and her youngest sister was visiting their grandmother.

Coincidently, at the Conrad estate.

"I'm not talking about him." She looked up, met three concerned gazes, and returned to her paper. The words blurred together, but they didn't seem important. "He's not worth my breath."

He wasn't worth her sleepless night, either, but here she was, tired and tetchy. Her toast and jam tasted like ash, the coffee held no flavor despite the cardamom, and Savannah had absolutely no idea what she'd just read. Undeterred, she continued reading and eating.

"Hmm," her mother said, clearly unconvinced. "I'm not disagreeing," she continued, her voice soft and flowing over the utterly silent table. Savannah did not look up but sipped her coffee. "How do you plan on avoiding him?"

"You could stab him," Lyneé offered.

She merely glared at her sister. Her sister, who had left her alone with Tristan yesterday. The traitor.

"You could," her mother added. "But, darling, please don't do so here. His parents are good friends, and I'd feel obligated to sew him up."

Savannah snorted and met her mother's gaze. Sophia Shaw watched her carefully, her dark eyes serious over her teacup. She'd never developed a taste for coffee and preferred the tea they imported. For one beautiful moment, Savannah let her mother's support wash over her, and she nearly smiled. Then, before those twisting emotions of yesterday flooded her, before she lost all sense of herself in the myriad chasms that had opened beneath her feet, Savannah returned her gaze to her paper.

Swallowing hard around a bite of egg, she took a moment to rebuild the walls that had kept her sane these last three years. Burying her anger and pain and grief deep within her, which probably wasn't at all healthy, she finished her toast and set down her paper.

"I shan't stab him," she promised. She wouldn't cry, either, though emotion closed her throat for a too-long moment. "I won't be seeing him again at all."

Her father even snorted at the falsehood, but Savannah defiantly met his gaze.

Hugh merely rolled his eyes. "How about we discuss the other thing?" he said in a gruff voice. "The fact that someone tried to kill you."

She hadn't a defense against that. Savannah had spent the previous hours focusing on the problem of Tristan. She hadn't *forgotten*, per se, about the most likely nonexistent attempt on her life. Instead, she'd merely shoved it aside.

There were only so many things she could handle at once.

"No one tried to kill me," she said dryly. Still, she imagined all too clearly the image of that knife embedded on the wall beside her. "I promise I'll be on guard, spend less time there, but I won't abandon the women."

Her father's face darkened. "I resisted hiring a guard for you, or having additional footmen accompany you. There's no rumor about anything on the wharves. Most of the men there were as surprised as I was at the news."

She lifted her chin and forced herself to eat another bite of egg. "That only reinforces my position. Nothing happened."

"Something did." Her father didn't raise his voice; he rarely did. His tone had hardened, however. Flattened. He hadn't become a rich shipping magnate by vacillating. "What's more important, Savannah? I'm betting on your life."

She snapped her mouth closed. He didn't lay on the guilt often. Her parents had raised her and her siblings to be strong, independent people who forged their own paths. Savannah had studied midwifery and healing under her mother, who had learned from her mother, who had learned from hers.

It hadn't, however, been her first choice for a life path.

"I already have Browne," she said. Part of her was obstinate about this, and part of her acknowledged that additional protection was never a bad idea no matter where one worked. Doubly so in St. Giles. "And Dem and his gang will be on the lookout."

Savannah pushed both her unread paper and her nearly full plate away. A small piece of the walls that surrounded her broke away, and a single well-aimed arrow could easily pierce her heart.

"He appreciates what I've done for his sister and the babe." She pressed her lips together and wondered if a second cup of coffee would help wake her or merely upset her stomach more than it already was.

"Dem is also trying to expand his influence," Hugh pointed out with a reasonableness that made most people agree to whatever terms he offered. "He's more concerned with that than keeping you safe. Although—"

"Although"—Savannah latched on to the segue with both hands—"with the right incentive, he could be a powerful ally. Increase his sway in the area as well as keep me safe."

She had a feeling Dem truly liked her. Not only for what she'd done for his sister, but because she cared. She visited the rookery several times a week, staying hours on end in order to see people who needed her knowledge of the old remedies or how to sew a wound and keep it from becoming infected. Most importantly, she never asked for anything in return.

"I think it's time to call in those favors," she added.

Pushing away from the table before they could discuss her life any further, Savannah nodded at her family and strode out of the hall. They loved her, worried for her, she knew that. But right now, that caring and affection stifled her.

She needed a good ride across the fields with nothing around for miles. The wind on her skin, the sun shining warmly on her back. Half tempted to saddle her horse and ride far out of London, Savannah—

The scream stopped her dead in her tracks. In the next

breath, she sprinted up the stairs and for her rooms. Behind her, the clatter of shoved chairs echoed along the hall.

"What's happened?" She burst through her bedroom door and stared at Anna, the upstairs maid. "Anna, what's wrong?"

Eyes wide, cheeks pale, Anna merely pointed at a corner. As Savannah moved around the bed, a dozen thoughts raced through her mind. No one could've entered. Not her bedroom, not this house. They were too well protected and had been since she could remember. Not everyone appreciated people of their race or class building their stellar reputation.

Had whoever killed the stranger sent a message, one that had somehow bypassed all their footmen and locked windows?

"Jiesha?" Savannah stared at the rabbit, whose back was against the corner, her eyes darting around the room, her nose twitching rapidly. Jiesha stared at Savannah and Anna as if they were the intruders, even as she shrank into herself, clearly more terrified of Anna than Anna was of her.

"What's happened?" Hugh demanded as he burst into the room, pistol at the ready.

"Why is there a rabbit in your bedroom?" Sophia asked over him, her own dagger drawn.

Sighing, Savannah cautiously stepped for the corner and scooped up a frightened Jiesha. Surprised the rabbit hadn't sprinted beneath the bed and as far from Anna as possible, Savannah was nonetheless gratified that Jiesha allowed her to hold her. Cuddling the poor thing close, Savannah cursed Tristan anew. How dare he bring her a pet she instantly loved!

The rabbit shook in her arms, clearly terrified, but Savannah didn't know if that was from picking her up, from Anna's screaming, or the numerous people now invading her bedroom.

"Jiesha startled Anna," she said, as if it were an everyday occurrence.

"Jiesha?" Sophia eyed the rabbit. "You have a rabbit named Jiesha?"

"Tristan," she sighed, exasperated. "It was a gift."

"A gift." Hugh shook his head and left, back to his breakfast and cargo manifests, no doubt.

Lyneé merely laughed and disappeared to her own activities, leaving only Savannah, Anna, and Sophia in the room.

"I don't want to talk about it," Savannah blurted. Cursing herself for that slip, her loss of control, she held Jiesha tighter. "I don't even know what there is to talk about."

Sophia nodded and closed the distance between them. She reached out and ran a finger down Jiesha's back, but the rabbit didn't move. Only trembled harder in Savannah's arms. "At least talk to him, darling." She kissed Savannah's cheek. "I think you two have a lot to work through."

The only thing she had to work through with Tristan was how he came into possession of Jiesha. Nothing else mattered. Not anymore.

TRISTAN DIDN'T WAIT for her at the end of their street. That would've been unseemly. Ungentlemanly. Unnerving, even. Tempted as he was to follow her, he didn't do that, either. She knew how to use a dagger, and he'd be her first target.

Instead, he returned to the scene of the crime, so to speak. Whatever that crime had been, whether Savannah had been the target or not, someone had murdered a man right beside her. Tristan didn't necessarily believe the man had gotten in the way and been killed in her place. According to Aunt Nadia and Uncle James, that stranger had been killed with a more expensive rifle shot and powder as opposed to an easily concealed dagger.

Rifles boasted a distance and precision nothing else could. No need to stand beside a man while you killed him; you could do it from a three hundred yards or so.

The knife worried him far more. Uncle James had dropped that news at dinner last evening. Given he once worked for the Intelligence Department of Horse Guards Tristan had a feeling that piece of information had not been a slip of the tongue.

The towering buildings that lined the streets near the church blocked most of the sunlight and cast a chill over the day. Tristan ignored the darkness and the stench of stale gin as he strode to the spot on Denmark Street where he'd met Savannah yesterday.

Where she was now.

He grinned. He'd thought he might find her here.

Once the thrill of adventure wore off, within a week after he left, Tristan found he missed knowing where she'd be. Missed her constant presence and knowing what he thought. He missed the feel of her body pressed close, her hand in his.

Now, stopping on the corner, he clasped his hands behind his back and most certainly did not reach for Savannah. Even if his fingers itched for the feel of her.

Tristan didn't know exactly where the man had been shot. His dead body was long gone, no doubt sent to a pauper's grave, any possessions looted. Tristan wondered if Savannah knew what had been taken from him. One of the street urchins would, but they wouldn't trust him with that information. Not yet.

As he looked around the area, nothing stood out as unusual, though he certainly had never frequented a rookery enough to judge.

"What are you doing here?" Savannah demanded, her voice low and harsh. Cold enough to chill even the warm June day.

"Savannah." He bowed low, grinning at her.

As beautiful as ever, he thought, once more committing her face to memory. The miniature portrait he carried in his breast pocket lay heavy against his heart. It didn't do her justice. Three years didn't seem like a long time, yet she'd changed.

She held herself stiffer, as if balancing the weight of the

world on her shoulders. Her face set, unwilling to give away any hint of her emotions, unlike before when he so easily knew everything she felt. Even her movements had changed, shorter now, not as expressive. Did she still dance?

"Who's your friend, Miss Savannah?" the man beside her asked. Tall and thin, with suspicious blue eyes that glared at Tristan, he looked about as trusting as anyone here. The man from yesterday, who'd guarded Savannah without a word.

"He's not my friend." Savannah glanced at the man quickly. "He used to be my fiancé." She grimaced at that no doubt reluctant admission and narrowed her eyes further.

"Tristan Conrad." He nodded at the man who stood guard over Savannah. As grateful as Tristan was for the protection the man offered, he should be the one guarding Savannah. But he'd failed in that, too.

"Dem," the man grunted.

"Dem." Savannah didn't look away from Tristan but softened her tone. "Ailene will be better in a few days." She turned then, thoroughly ignoring Tristan. "I'll send round a basket of food. I don't care what she thinks of it, she's to eat everything in there."

"All right. You need an escort, Miss Savannah?" Dem asked, not bothering to lower his voice.

"No." She forced a smile, there and gone in a heartbeat. Another change—Savannah used to smile all the time. "Thank you. Get back to Ailene."

Dem didn't look convinced. However, he nodded at Savannah, glared at Tristan, and disappeared into the crowd. The same crowd that gave Savannah a wide berth, keeping out of her way. Or Dem's, perhaps.

"I thought you didn't want a guard," Tristan said casually. A small stab of jealousy wormed its way into his heart no matter how he reminded himself he had no right to feel it. He wished his heart would remember that.

"Dem protects me while I'm here." She hadn't moved but watched him carefully. Her back remained rigid, her gaze wary.

Unbidden, memories of him and Savannah together in bed forced themselves from behind the wall he'd built over the years. Her body pliant beneath his hands as he tasted her, glorious as she straddled his hips, taking him deep inside her.

"One of a gang?" He had no idea what he was saying. No matter how he blinked, the memories refused to dissipate. His fingertips tingled with the clearly remembered feel of her skin beneath his touch.

"He's the leader of Denmark Street," she reluctantly conceded, her voice dropping. "Hence his name. Why are you here? I thought you were done with—"

Her. Done with her.

"I'm worried about you." Which wasn't what he'd wanted to say. This corner, with its filth and stench and barely visible sunlight, was not the place for such confessions. Tristan owed her far more than an apology in the St. Giles Rookery. He owed her the world. "Someone tried to kill you."

"Once more, I fail to see how that affects you in the slightest." She stepped forward, the movement as stiff as her back, but her glare burned through him. "And Lyneé is wrong."

"I doubt she'd make such a mistake," he scoffed. Tristan resisted mentioning that Aunt Nadia and Uncle James also believed someone had tried to at least harm her, if not kill her.

"Regardless, it still does not affect you." She stepped around him without another glance and walked toward the church.

"Savannah—you're right." Tristan fell into step beside her. Even without her guard, people stepped out of her way. They knew her here, he realized. Respected her.

"Then why are you here?"

"Curiosity. I'm curious about the dead man." Not the entire truth, but not a lie either. "Who wanted him dead, and why? What had he done, if anything?"

"Please." She snorted and stopped in a rare patch of sunlight. It glowed off her skin and sparkled in her eyes. "He could've looked at a man the wrong way. Talked up the wrong woman. Stolen from a street urchin or one of the gin houses."

"Normally, I'd agree with you. Except for the rifle shot." He paused and looked around. Considering the mass of people living here, they were strangely alone. Unease slithered down his spine. She didn't notice or had grown used to people keeping their distance. "Why throw a knife at someone after you've gone to the trouble and expense of shooting them?"

Her lips pursed so hard he thought she might crack her jaw. She agreed with him. Tristan didn't feel any sense of triumph, merely the icy hand of fear. She'd already thought of that and had retuned anyway.

"Why did you come back here?" He kept his voice low, mostly in hopes of keeping his anger at bay—a futile hope. But at least no one overheard them.

"This isn't the place or time," she snapped. "And I owe you no explanation."

"You don't," he agreed. It came out sharper than he intended. "But I only want you safe." Another partial truth. He did, of course, want her safe. He also wanted her. Period, end of story.

"Hmph." She eyed him, and her shoulders relaxed just the slightest as she stepped forward.

Which was, of course, when a wild shout echoed through the crowded street.

For one single breath, Tristan stilled. His instinct was to jump into action, but Savannah's safety kept him at her side. *Protect her.* The disbelieving look on Savannah's face told him exactly what she thought, but they both knew he had nothing to do with the scream or the mob who descended on the scene like someone was giving away free gin. Or tossing guineas into the crowd.

With another glare, she pushed past him. He cut her off,

stepping in front of her and taking her arm. Tristan shoved a man running toward the scene out of his way and ignored the curses the man spewed at him.

"Savannah." He pulled her toward an abandoned doorway.

"This has nothing to do with me," she insisted, voice low and angry, gaze hard and unyielding. She jerked her arm from his grasp. "Shove off, Tristan. I have work to do." So saying, she stepped around him and walked confidently into the crowd.

He started after her, no more than a step behind. Several inches taller than most of the people here, and far more determined, he easily kept up. Three years might've been a long time, but several lifetimes wouldn't be long enough for him to forget her stubborn streak.

Glaring at an opportunistic pickpocket until the boy slithered away, he stalked after Savannah.

The crowd parted for her, murmuring "Miss Savannah." A few even bowed or curtsied. Though Tristan was of the firm opinion that *everyone* should bow before her, he did wonder what she'd done to earn such respect in so poor a place.

She cared. Of course. Foolish of him to think it took anything else.

She cared about these people, not because it was fashionable or an easy way to prove devoutness, but because she truly did. They respected her for that sincerity.

While he glared at the crowd, who clearly had no ill intention toward her, she talked with people.

"Find me a cloth, Betty. Press tight, Robbie." And so on.

She knelt beside a woman on the ground, one they both knew was close to death. She clutched her belly tight beneath the thin, torn cloth of her dress, struggling with each breath. Tristan stepped closer. Another look showed no one watching Savannah in particular, only the scene itself. The crowd swelled closer, then back, allowing him access to her.

"Do you know who stabbed you?" Savannah asked, leaning

close, one hand on the woman's cheek. "Nell, do you know who did this?"

Tristan knelt beside Savannah but could offer nothing except silent support. She leaned against him, just the slightest. She knew this woman; her compassion wasn't for a mere stranger, but someone she knew by name. Nell's gaze flicked from Savannah to him and back, but she didn't say a word.

"I'm sorry," Savannah whispered as Nell's last breath rattled out. "I'm so sorry, Nell."

Tristan placed his hand over Savannah's. She looked up, calm, quiet, as steady as her hands. Only he saw the heartbreak in her gaze, heard the shift in her breathing. Tristan rested his hand on the small of her back and hoped she'd accept his support. In this, at least.

"Robbie." Savannah's voice cracked. She paused and cleared her throat. "Find Mr. Christie." Robbie jumped up and did as instructed, but Savannah didn't watch him leave. She turned to Tristan instead.

"Thank you," she said quietly.

"I'll take you home, Savannah." He held out his hand, waiting until she placed hers in his, and stood. "Mr. Christie will see to this?"

She rummaged in her basket and wiped her hands on a cloth, cleaning them as best she could.

"He's the vicar at St. Giles in the Fields. He and his wife will take care of Nell." Savannah paused as if she had more to add, but then she merely shook her head. "She was a sweetmeat seller at the theater houses. Wanted to be an actress."

"Betty, was it?" Tristan also helped up the woman next to Savannah, waiting until she steadied herself. "I'm taking Miss Savannah home. See that Dem knows of this."

Savannah snorted. "Catch on quick, you do," she muttered. Louder, she said, "Betty, if anyone has information, they're to tell Dem." Then her voice lowered, hardened. "I want to know who did this."

Betty offered a quick bob and disappeared into the crowd. No one touched the body, didn't rifle through pockets for a bit of coin or a charm. Savannah watched over Nell with a ferocity that kept everyone else away. Tristan didn't watch Betty leave, just stood guard with Savannah over Nell's body until Robbie and Mr. Christie returned. Things moved fast here.

"Miss Savannah." The vicar nodded with a sorrowful glance at the body. "I'll see she's taken care of."

"Thank you, Mr. Christie. A proper burial, if you please." Then she turned toward Tristan, watching him with dark, tired eyes. "Browne is waiting at the church with the carriage."

Tristan nodded so she wouldn't see his confusion. Why would Browne, who would fight to the death for any one of the Shaws, stay by the carriage instead by Savannah?

"Let's go." He didn't take her hand, though he wanted to, the reflex so natural and innate. Instead, he took the basket she carried, with her herbs and poultices, and placed his hand on the small of her back.

"I don't need protection," she insisted as they stepped away from the crowd. "I need to know who's killing the women of St. Giles Rookery." Savannah met his startled gaze. "And I want your help to find out."

CHAPTER 4

~~~

Savannah didn't know what made her admit that. Offering to work together sounded a far sight tamer than asking for the protection she didn't feel she needed. Her sheathed dagger sat heavy in her pocket, within easy reach at any moment.

She used to wear it on her waist, but that was far too tempting for a pickpocket. Given the last few days, perhaps she ought to reconsider. Reaching for the handle in her specially made pocket took several seconds longer than at her hip. Those several seconds might mean the difference between life and death. Hers.

Perhaps she ought to reconsider a few things. Like the longing that burrowed beneath her skin, tempting her to lean over and kiss Tristan. Taste his lips and feel his skin beneath her fingertips.

Savannah had thought she'd banished such longing once and for all when she'd locked away the memory of her life with Tristan. Obviously not, given the way her body reacted to his. But Tristan, blast him, showed no such feelings toward her. He walked easily by her side, as if they were naught more than old friends out for a stroll.

She angrily shoved aside that ridiculous feeling, that temptation she had no business being tempted by.

"Someone is killing the women?" Tristan's head tilted. The wind blew gently over his hair, ruffling the curls. Damn him and this compulsion to feel those strands beneath her fingers! She used to love running her fingers through his curls.

His eyes narrowed, and Savannah couldn't quite make out his expression. "What does that have to do with the attempt on your life?"

"Let's retire to the church. Mr. Christie has a small office I sometimes use."

"Savannah…" But his gaze flicked around the street, and he nodded. "All right."

"This doesn't mean I forgive you." She had no idea what it meant, truthfully. Her mother's words echoed in her head—*a lot to work through*. Savannah supposed she and Tristan should talk, though in all fairness, she had no real desire to do that. Ignoring the situation and being done with him sounded much better, if not at all feasible. "It simply means you might be of help in this matter."

From the corner of her eye, she watched him nod solemnly. "I understand."

She doubted that. Doubted she understood either, but the church loomed at the end of the street, and she needed help. Savannah could ask her family; Lyneé would be more than willing to help. Papa, too, of course—she wasn't without resources. Dem would've rounded up every member of his gang for a good fight if she asked, but she certainly didn't need a fight.

She needed answers.

The simple truth was, she didn't want her sister involved. And while she trusted Dem, he was chasing after greater power on the street. He'd been open about wanting to secure his place as head of the most powerful gang in the rookery. There were others, of course, who'd offer their help. She only had to ask.

"How long have you worked the street?" Tristan asked.

She glared at him like any lady would.

He sighed, looking upward. "I didn't mean it like that," he muttered.

Savannah pressed her lips together so they wouldn't curve into a smile, but she couldn't control that slight twitch. Annoyed he'd made her smile, had broken through her walls, she clenched her hands into fists as they exited Denmark Street and came upon the square where the church sat.

"I meant how long have you…helped out here," he corrected ruefully.

"Two years and ten months." She paused again, struggling with her own feelings on the matter. Unfortunately, the short walk offered no answers. Instead, she faced him. "I chose to make myself a resource here, where people were forgotten. Like I was."

Tristan flinched, and she felt a bolt of satisfaction at that, short-lived though it was.

"I deserved that." He took her arm as they crossed the street, his hand warm through the plain linen of her gown. "I deserve a lot more," he admitted before she could retort.

Savannah shook off his arm. She didn't like understanding Tristan, though he always knew what to say in apology. He always meant it, too. Or she thought he had.

They walked around the side of the church and into the sunlight. Savannah took a moment and let the warmth thaw the ice around her heart.

"Why are you here?" she asked again. The words came out tired, drained. Her anger simmered in her heart, but she hadn't the strength to fight, not after Nell. His answer yesterday barely scratched the surface. "You could've returned to Nelda Hall. Or to any of your siblings. Do your parents even know you've returned?"

"No." His gaze scanned the area.

She knew he'd prefer his back to be against the church wall; she'd also prefer to keep anyone from sneaking up on them. But, petty though it was, Savannah wasn't in a conciliatory mood.

"I stayed at *Tetya* Nadia's last night."

The sun couldn't melt the ice that suddenly ran through her veins. He'd slept down the street? Of course he had—foolish of her to think otherwise. Where else would he have slept? Regent's Park, perhaps, with Esme and her family, or onboard his ship. But no, he'd slept a mere five houses from her. Where he always stayed when in London. She should've guessed.

"Let's get inside." Savannah shoved aside this new revelation and pulled out the key for the office. She didn't look at him as she unlocked the small side door, entering the newly renovated cupboard.

It wasn't large enough to be called anything else. She didn't bother to light a candle; the sunlight that streamed through the small, round windows lit the room enough for her purposes. She used this office mostly for quiet moments after visiting the street. The sheer poverty of the area weighed on her, and she knew no matter how she helped, it'd never be enough.

Tristan leaned against the secretary desk Savannah rarely used. She had no need of letter writing here, and any accounts that needed reconciling were done on the street.

"This isn't anything more than an investigation." She glared at his relaxed pose, annoyed by it when she felt as if a thousand needles pricked her skin and an iron rod had been strapped along her spine. How was he so calm and collected around her?

Oh. Oh, stupid, stupid Savannah.

He didn't love her anymore. He had, after all, left her with barely a word. He'd sailed around the world for three years and took who knew how many lovers. That didn't explain why he'd shown up in her life immediately after making port and with an adorable rabbit. However, knowing he no longer loved her made things easier.

Except her heart ached with every beat, and nausea welled in her throat. Curling her fingers into her skirts, Savannah backed away from him until she hit the opposite wall. Distance did not help. The room closed in on her, but she raised her chin and met his gaze as if nothing happened.

Nothing happened.

"You're the smartest person I know, and the most observant." Her voice cracked, but Savannah sniffed and forged ahead. Emotions had no place here. Even if they clawed at her throat and pounded through her veins with every beat of her heart.

Not as over him as she told everyone she was. But then, Savannah knew she'd lied each and every time.

"Considering the brilliance of your family, I'll take that as a compliment." He nodded in appreciation and crossed his arms over his chest. He never boasted of his intelligence, no matter how brilliant he truly was. "What makes you think someone is targeting the women of Denmark Street specifically?" His head tilted, and in the faint light his face remained in shadow.

"Nell isn't the first one." Savannah held up a hand. "I know people die with unmatched frequency here. This is different. Ailene, Dem's sister, was attacked." She paused and whispered, "Violated."

Tristan growled. "Do you know who did it?"

She shook her head. "No. It was late, the gin houses were overflowing, the gaming hells full to capacity. That's where she works. Worked. She has a son now."

"I'm sorry. Has she food, shelter?"

Damn him for being so caring. As if it never occurred to him to think otherwise.

"Yes. Dem cares for her; he's determined to discover the culprit and have his justice." She didn't blame him. If someone had done the same to her two sisters, Savannah would do all in her power to find them and see they paid.

"She wasn't the only woman violated?"

Savannah shook her head. "No one knows the culprit." She licked her lips and told her ex-fiancé, her former lover, what she hadn't told anyone else. Trust was a strange, finicky thing. "A few of Dem's people saw a group. Three or four men. But there aren't any candles lighting the street, let alone an Argand lamp."

Tristan merely nodded at her weak attempt at a joke. "This group attacked others?"

"Yes. It escalated." Savannah closed her eyes and focused entirely on this. On what happened to these women, on how to stop the attacks. "Several more were attacked, then they just… stopped." She met his gaze again. "Someone killed Nora three days ago. That attack surprised me."

"Because she was murdered." Tristan nodded, easily following along.

That was why she'd confided in him. He easily followed any line of thought to its natural conclusion, and faster than anyone Savannah knew. He'd planned to go to Oxford, to study law and natural history.

After Harrow, he'd returned to her instead, and they'd planned on marrying.

Stop it! She swallowed hard, but the memories crowded her mind, refusing to let her be. They filled her heart until it beat too fast. The letters they'd exchanged over the years while he was at Harrow. The summers they spent together. The promises they'd made.

"Could it be someone copying the crime? Different people but the same crime? What do these women have to do with the man who was murdered?"

Annoyed at her own thoughts and Tristan's insistence on bringing that up again, Savannah growled, "Nothing. I keep telling everyone that. That man's death has nothing whatsoever to do with me or the dead women."

"People don't waste rifle shots, Savannah." He watched her, but she still couldn't make out his expression.

"Indeed, they do not," she snapped, hating the way his voice caressed her name. "Therefore, he was clearly the intended target."

"And the knife? Why shoot someone, then throw a knife at them?"

She still had no real answer for that. "Maybe he was one of that gang who attacked Ailene. Maybe he was searching for his own thief." She closed her eyes. "It doesn't matter in this instance."

"I think it does," he corrected, smooth and fast. As if they debated something far more mundane than a killer. "However, for the moment, let's assume whoever has been killing—is it always the same?"

"The method?" He nodded, and she continued, "Yes, both Nora and Nell were killed by a knife. Sliced across the abdomen. Deep and quick."

"Takes strength for that. Precision. Close proximity." He paused, and she waited, letting him think.

Savannah did not think. She purposely blanked her mind and watched the dust motes dance in the scant sunlight. Fate laughed at her.

"Dem. How much do you trust him?"

Surprised by the question, she blinked at Tristan. "Enough that I know he'll find who did this."

"You're certain he's not responsible?"

"I am. He and Ailene are extremely close. She raised him after their father abandoned the family and their mother fell in with the gin houses." Ailene had kept them both clean—no drinking, no opium. Savannah respected that. She considered

Ailene a close acquaintance, Dem more a partner, though she knew his place here and respected it.

"And he doesn't know who's responsible?"

"Which is unusual, I agree." She pushed off the wall and paced a few steps. Nerves and memories and anticipation danced just below her skin. "That's why I think whoever is responsible isn't from the rookery."

TRISTAN TILTED HIS HEAD AGAIN, mostly so he looked like he was following Savannah's very logical line of thought. In truth, he was trying to catch a glint of her dark eyes in the few rays of sunlight.

He loved to watch her eyes when she thought through a problem. They always crinkled at the corners, their deep brown sparkling with determination.

Questions about her time here clamored around his brain, but Tristan kept on the subject. She'd made it abundantly clear she didn't wish to talk about anything other than these murdered women, and he'd respect that. If it meant he could spend more time with her, that he'd have more opportunities to apologize and explain how he felt, he'd take whatever time she offered.

More importantly, he'd do whatever was necessary to keep her safe. Tristan didn't care if she liked it or wanted it. He had three years to make up for, and he wasn't backing down.

"Was that man's murder a ruse? A distraction, perhaps?" He shook his head, not sure how that could even be. "He's dead either way. Did he have anything on him? Money, a watch, even a knife we might trace?"

"Nothing." Savannah stood closer to him now.

If he were a betting man, Tristan would wager she didn't

realize it. Ah, there were her beautiful eyes, and yes, they sparkled in thought.

"Literally only the clothes on his back," she continued. "Not unusual here. Nora was simply murdered." She grimaced, shaking her head. "If such a word as 'simply' could be used." She pinched the bridge of her nose. "Like Nell just now. Exactly like her, though late at night, when the gin houses were full."

"We'll return tonight," he agreed, as if Savannah had spoken that plan aloud. No, three years hadn't changed his understanding of her. "I know what you're thinking, Savannah, and I'm not letting you return here alone at night."

She glared, her chin tilted just enough to show him how little she thought of his statement. "I asked for your help because I know you'll offer it. I didn't suggest it so I could listen to your lectures."

Of course he'd help, and it galled him that she might think otherwise. Tristan didn't move from his negligent position on the small desk. In fact, he swung his leg absently, as if he hadn't a care in the world. In truth, he wanted to shake her, though he knew that'd only earn him another slap. Kissing her was also an option, unfortunately with the same outcome. Savannah narrowed her eyes at him, and he nearly smiled.

This pose might have fooled nearly everyone else, but it wouldn't fool her. Never her.

"What makes you think there's more to these murders than drunken idiots with daggers?"

"A feeling," she admitted quietly. "Drunken idiots with daggers don't disappear into the night—or day in Nora's case—without a trace. Nothing was taken from either Nora or Nell. Not their clothing, whatever coin they carried. Nothing. Ailene wasn't the first woman violated, but she was the last. After her, those attacks seemed to stop."

"Almost as if this group, whoever they are, had their fill of such distasteful things?" He scrubbed a hand down his face. It didn't erase the surge of anger that choked him. The bile that coated his throat at the thought of what happened here. "They could've been a completely random group that someone saw and pointed a finger at. An easy target." That sparked another nagging thought. "If they are responsible, why? Why attack women? What's the connection, if any? Why stop the violations and start murdering them? The thrill of it?"

"I'd hardly say that's thrilling, but people will do anything for a lark. Or a coin." She sighed and rolled her shoulders. "I promised Papa I'd sup with him."

"He's worried about you being here." Tristan nodded and straightened, offering his arm. "I'll walk you."

"You aren't invited."

He threw back his head and laughed. "Whatever you think of me now, Savannah, I'm not that foolish."

A smile graced her lips, there and gone in a breath. Progress. Maybe. Enough that he felt confident she wouldn't literally stab him in the back as they left this cupboard of an office.

"Why do you need an office in the church?"

He waited, watching the street as she locked the door. The day hadn't necessarily warmed, but it had brightened. He watched the clouds race along the sky, small puffs dotting the blue. Not the same as over the sea, where he could watch the endless sky and barely make out a stretch of land.

Beautiful nonetheless, because this was home.

It'd taken him three years to realize that. Less to admit his mistake, the mistake his family had let him make even while they shook their heads at his folly.

"It's not far from home, but some days it all gets to be too much." She took his arm, almost without thinking, as they strolled around the front of the church where her carriage and footman waited. "There are so many who need help." That determination crept back into her voice. "I do what I can, but there's always more. Lyneé helps sometimes, but she has her suffragist meetings."

Suffragist meetings? That was new and intriguing. He'd ask about that another time. "You care, which is more than many can say."

"Hmm," she agreed, but he heard the wariness in her tone. She didn't believe what she did here helped—that it was enough.

"Enjoy your meal with Hugh." He handed her into the carriage, mindful of the glares from both footman and driver. Tristan almost waved at them cheekily but held back the impulse.

He hadn't left those childish impulses behind, but he'd learned to control them. Somewhat.

"I'll pick you up tonight, what time—nine?"

"All right." She watched him from the doorway, and Tristan knew she had second thoughts. "Tristan."

"I'll help you find them, Savannah," he promised. "Then we can talk."

She didn't answer, and he stepped back, closing and securing the door. Nodding at Browne, the footman who continued to glare at him, Tristan turned for the wharves. He hadn't taken a hackney from Grosvenor Square—too on edge for that when a good walk would help clear his mind.

But the two-mile walk only added to his questions. Why murder the poorest of poor women, other than for a game? A sick game, at that. He let the question turn over and over again.

The walk back at the wharves provided no answers. Once there, Tristan headed for the berth that held his ship.

"Ah, Tristan. Back already?"

"Arnault." He nodded at his first mate. Frederic Arnault towered over Tristan's own tall frame. With his shining blue eyes and thick, curly blond hair, he looked more like a Roman statue than a seaman.

"Alone, I see." Arnault clucked his tongue, his Flemish accent heavy with his disapproval. "I told you to bring flowers instead. Women love flowers." He nodded sagely. "Or cheese. You never listen."

"I'll keep the cheese in mind," Tristan promised. Savannah wasn't partial to cut flowers; she preferred walking through fields of them in the country. Cheese, on the other hand, she enjoyed very much. "However, Savannah took to Jiesha immediately."

He should've asked after the rabbit, but he'd been caught up in this new mystery surrounding Savannah. Tonight, on their way back to Denmark Street, they'd have plenty of time to talk. And he could apologize.

"The rabbit?" Arnault asked dubiously. "Flowers," he reiterated. "Tulips, roses, gladiolas. Something bright. Or perhaps white lilies, hyacinths even, or violets. Yes, violets. Something forgiving." He shook his head and folded his arms over his wide chest. "That cheese from the abbey, offer her that."

"I'm seeing her again tonight." Tristan looked over the deck of his ship, where his crew diligently worked at cleaning the exterior after her long voyage. They didn't watch him, though Arnault's voice boomed over the deck as a good first mate's ought.

"Good." Arnault nodded decisively. "You're taking her to a ball? You'll need fresh clothing."

"A ball?" Tristian shook his head and brought himself back to the present. "No, we're looking for a killer."

As soon as he said it, he realized how odd it sounded. Finding a killer wasn't a courtship. It wasn't even proper, he'd wager. Arnault believed Tristan was wooing Savannah, trying to win her back. Not track a killer in the St. Giles Rookery. Tristan pinched the bridge of his nose and closed his eyes. He already knew what Arnault was going to say.

"A killer? Bah." He huffed. "How is that pursuing her? Dancing. You need to take her dancing."

THE LADY'S COURTSHIP

Savannah loved dancing, loved the freedom of movement it offered. It didn't matter what the music was, she loved to move to the rhythm. When they were younger, Tristan had briefly debated learning the fiddle simply to watch her dance. But it hadn't taken him long to realize he'd rather dance with her than watch from the sidelines.

"I shall," he promised, not entirely certain how to go about that when the only reason she'd spoken to him was to ask for his help. Help in solving a murder. Not dancing, unfortunately.

"Good." Arnault nodded. "That's how you woo a lady."

"Someone is murdering women," he admitted, his voice low though he doubted anyone eavesdropped. It wouldn't matter if they did. He trusted his crew implicitly; all but two of them had sailed with him for three years. The two additions came from Antwerp, the last time they'd made port, when he'd stolen Jiesha and two abused footmen from that corrupt merchant, Van Zanten.

Arnault hummed and nodded slowly. "Perhaps spending time with her while investigating this is not a bad idea. She is passionate about these women?"

"Yes."

The entire street worshipped her. He'd seen that immediately. And he knew it wasn't because of Dem and his iron-fisted control. When he'd returned from his travels, Tristan had expected to find her in the offices, reading over manifests, seeing to other captains and cargo. Where she belonged, overseeing Shaw Shipping.

He'd been surprised when Arnault discovered her elsewhere.

"She's—" He didn't know how to explain Savannah's being in St. Giles. "Helping" sounded too tame. Many women helped, but usually with money or a donation of old clothing. Sometimes food, if it suited their image. "She *does*," he settled on, though that also sounded too insipid a phrase. "She sees what needs done and does it. She doesn't wait for others to make things happen."

She hadn't waited for him, and that small part of Tristan that thought she would deserved the sneering laughter and slap he'd gotten. Idiot.

Turning sharply on his heel, he strode across the deck and looked out over the wharves. The workers moved around, unloading and loading cargo, some laughing while they sat on crates.

He'd seen a dozen such wharves in the last three years, but none hit home quite like this one. Because no matter how he always searched for Savannah in every port, he knew he'd find her here.

"What did you think would happen when you returned?" Arnault leaned against the railing, hands clasped in front of him. He didn't look at Tristan, but at the vista below.

The slap, definitely. Perhaps a chance to speak with her, explain his actions. Though he supposed he could've done that the second he'd committed to leaving. Instead of instantly boarding the ship, he could've taken an hour. If they missed that tide, there was always another one.

"I'm staying at my aunt's house in Grosvenor Square," he said instead. He hadn't a real answer for his friend, anyway. And the confessions in his heart were for Savannah alone.

"What should I tell the men?" Arnault faced him, serious now, quiet. "Do we sail again, or are you staying?"

That was the question, wasn't it?

CHAPTER 5

Tristan walked from Aunt Nadia's to the Shaw household down the street. It hadn't changed in three years, though why he'd thought it would, he had no idea. He could've walked this short route in his sleep, he'd done it so often.

He'd spent more time at the Shaw house than at his own house in Hertfordshire, or even at Aunt Nadia and Uncle James's.

Now, the weight of his dagger on his hip and the knowledge that Savannah had put herself in danger made his steps heavier. He didn't much care about his reception when he knocked on her door. He cared that Savannah insisted on returning to Denmark Street, at night, and if he hadn't agreed to help, he knew she'd have done it alone.

"Walters." He nodded at the butler, who very much looked as if he didn't want to let Tristan cross the threshold. However, the man merely raised his chin in silent, if condemning, greeting and stepped back.

Tristan stepped into a foyer as familiar as his own. This

hadn't changed, either. Once again, he had no idea what he'd expected. A complete refurbishment? New décor? Not when that money could be spent on investments, and certainly nothing as wasteful as keeping up with the latest trends in upholstery.

"Miss Savannah will be ready momentarily." Walters retreated to the door like he was standing guard during one of the smuggling runs the families engaged in before Tristan was born.

What did the man expect? That Tristan would run off with the candelabra? Running off with Miss Savannah sounded more likely. Walters hadn't looked at him like that when he used to come round. Back then, he'd had a more affectionate, indulgent look on his face. Unlike now, when he looked as if he wanted to tackle Tristan, tie him up, and toss him overboard.

Tristan's lips twitched at the thought. He rocked back on his heels, hands clasped behind his back. Meeting Walters's unwavering gaze, he waited.

"Good." Savannah's clipped greeting echoed in the foyer. "Let's leave."

"As you wish." Tristan offered his arm, much to Walters's disbelievingly raised eyebrow and Savannah's annoyed huff. Or perhaps that huff contained a hint of amusement.

"We'll hire a hackney." She did not take his arm. "Thank you, Walters."

"Miss Savannah." He bowed, his voice thawing for his mistress.

"You look flushed." Tristan bit back the rest of that sentence. That he'd always adored the way her cheeks flushed when they kissed or made love. That he loved to hear her laughter echoing around them as they raced through the house or the gardens, her eyes sparkling with love and freedom, that happy flush on her cheeks.

"I'm sure I don't need to tell you that your return has set off quite the…conversation." She strode down the sidewalk, head high, her light summer pelisse swirling about her ankles. Her lovely, perfect ankles.

"I'm sure," he murmured. "Are we hiring a hackney so no one knows we're there?" He didn't offer his arm again but easily kept pace. No one followed them, but he knew that wouldn't last. Even dressed in old, informal clothing, a couple walking at night was a signal for any thief in a three-block radius.

Savannah paused, then nodded "Yes."

Eyes narrowing, he watched her as they drew closer to the corner. "And the other reason?"

She didn't answer immediately but sighed. At the corner, she met his gaze. "You aren't the most popular person in the household. Even amongst the servants. This is easier all around."

"And the additional protection Browne offers?" He held up a hand. "Not that I disagree. It's best a local hackney takes us around. Less suspicious that way."

"Are you suggesting you aren't up to the challenge?"

He laughed, refusing to take the bait in her biting words. "I expected no one would let you leave. In my company. Alone."

"There is that," she agreed. Savannah paused again, and he wondered just what sort of argument her family had engaged in before she joined him in the foyer. She held his gaze for another moment, but he couldn't read her thoughts.

"Despite my infamy, I'm equally certain the servants wouldn't leave you to your own defenses. Or mine."

"Browne and Peters are already on the street, waiting for our arrival," she admitted. "It's only a short walk, but we'll hire a hackney at the end of this row of taverns."

Tristan almost made a quip about which row, as most of these streets were lined with taverns and closed markets. Instead, he took Savannah's arm and kept her close. He didn't want her lost. Or worse.

"You've given this a lot of thought," he said instead as the evening crowd jostled them. The theaters hadn't yet let out, and the late crowd had already arrived fashionably late. Here the sellers hawked fruits and sweetmeats. "Why?"

"If you think I'm in the habit of sneaking out of the house, you should know better."

He did snort then. She had more freedom growing up than most women of her station and had never needed to sneak around. She merely did as she pleased. Mostly with him. "That's not what I meant, and you know it." Once more they walked in silence. At the next corner, he stilled her. "You're right, Savannah." Her gaze shot up and met his. He saw surprise there, but she immediately blinked it away. "I do know better. So why?"

She turned away, her gaze guarded once more. Tristan knew he was putting off his apologies, the talk she claimed she didn't want, the one he knew they needed. If for no other reason than to clear the air. Their families were too close not to. He loved her, wanted her. But he'd never force her. And this certainly wasn't the place. He'd work on earning her trust first.

"If you have to ask, you don't know me at all." With that, she hailed a hackney.

The driver had eyed them both dubiously, probably because Savannah had hailed the hackney rather than him, but he hadn't uttered a word. Now, with the cab pushing its way through traffic, Tristan settled in across from her. The cab itself smelled stale, as if the windows hadn't been open since its construction. Neither touched the rug that was folded beside Savannah.

"I realize I'm possibly the last person you want to help you." He'd ask her about that later, why she'd even suggested it. For now, he held her gaze. She sat straight and proud against the jostling of the carriage, shoulders rigid and chin tilted. "I simply wish to know why you've taken such an interest in a single street. It has nothing to do with helping them. This is more."

"Not everyone has the protection we're afforded," she said slowly. Her words rang of truth, but also hesitation. "I have the skills required of a midwife and a healer, and I've spent the last years earning the trust of those I help. Could I do more?" Her head tilted from left to right, but her voice remained quiet. "I think it's important I use my skills where they're needed. And it feels…good, productive. Invigorating, even. Knowing that I have helped others."

"Is that why you've made a pact with Dem? So you can help all the women you can?" He understood that need, the desire for more. It was what led him to leave, to find himself in a way he hadn't thought he could here.

"When I first started, Dem didn't have the power he does now," she admitted with a quick twist of her lips. "I required assistance and the respect that comes from people trusting me." She laughed, a quick, light sound. "Also, he thought he could bribe me into paying for protection."

Tristan laughed. A long, loud sound that ended in a snicker. "Oh, how wrong he was."

"He did learn quickly," she admitted with her first real smile. Tristan felt that smile as clearly as if she'd kissed him. "And from there respect bloomed. Because he respected me, trusted me, others did as well."

He'd have loved to have seen that. Savannah taking on Dem, who thought he ran the street. And perhaps he did, but Tristan knew Savannah. She never backed down.

"He protects you because of that regard." Tristan nodded as the carriage rolled to a stop. Pride warmed his chest. She always had so much to give, such desire to change the world. Here she was, doing just that. "And the women?"

"The gin runs more freely here than the rain." She waited while he exited before accepting his hand and following. Hers closed around his, a squeeze there and gone in a moment. "Dem sees the problem. But he also sees the profit. And in the rookery, money talks."

"It does in most places," Tristan agreed. He offered his arm, trying not to mourn the loss of her touch. After a moment, she accepted, and they walked toward the street, barely lit by any sort of lamppost.

"I'm hoping that here, it leads me to the men who are murdering my women."

IT SHOULD NOT HAVE BEEN SO easy to talk with Tristan. Not anymore. Yet as they walked from the corner where the hackney dropped them off toward the street where she'd spent most of the last three years, Savannah acknowledged just that. As if Tristan had never left, here she was, sharing her thoughts and secrets and desires with him.

It wasn't as if no one else understood. The reason she had decided on St. Giles was because her parents and extended family had instilled in her a need to help others. Not everyone was as fortunate as she, and Savannah used her wealth, and her understanding of the old remedies, to give back. Her whole family gave back in their own ways.

But if she closed her eyes and tilted her head into the slight breeze, she could envision her and Tristan walking along the square. Or through the woods at Nelda Hall. Just the two of them, off on their own, as they had been since Tristan learned how to walk.

She didn't close her eyes, of course. That would be far too dangerous here, and Savannah had no desire to continue on that path down memory lane. She'd spent the last three years avoiding memory lane.

Her mother's words followed her, however. Urging her to discover the truth so she could lay that part of her to rest. Did she really want to know why he'd left her all those years ago? Or was ignorance truly bliss?

Savannah had avoided any mention of Tristan, any hint of

why he'd left. With him now walking beside her, how could she avoid it any longer?

"What are we looking for?" His voice drifted over her, close enough that if she turned her head, Savannah knew she could kiss him.

She licked her lips as if she could taste the memory of his kisses. Longing welled up, closing her throat. It both paralyzed her and made her want to move closer.

"I don't know." Her voice cracked, and she hastily cleared her throat. "A group that doesn't belong. In the darkness, it'll be harder to spot them."

A missing piece nagged at her. About the stranger? About this morning and Nell? She had no idea; she couldn't piece it all together. Tristan distracted her from figuring it out.

If he had stayed, where would they be now? Married with at least one child, she thought with a longing she couldn't ignore. Working in the shipping business, perhaps. Or with him a well-respected lawyer.

Cursing her wandering mind, Savannah shook her head and focused on the street before her.

"There are a dozen taverns. All full," he added with a wry chuckle. "Should we start there, or would this group simply wander the street?" He paused, tugging her closer to the wall of the nearest building. "Do they confine themselves to this block?"

"I don't know," she admitted. "I have contacts here—the other streets are run by their own gangs."

"And Lyneé?" he asked. "She tends to those on another street?"

"No." Savannah looked around, but nothing seemed out of place. Still, unease slithered down her spine. "She accompanies me sometimes, as there are many in need of help. Ailene was attacked here. A few others before that, though I never saw the connection. I don't know if there is one."

"Women are attacked every day." His voice held barely

suppressed anger. She knew he hated that fact, that so many women were treated as less simply because they were women. But then, he'd been raised in a family of strong women.

"Yes, but this was different." Savannah couldn't explain it yet, not fully. "Then Nora and now Nell were killed here. There's something about this street, but I don't understand what."

"And that man no one knew." He made a humming sound. "For now, let's assume you're correct and he has nothing to do with this."

"All right." She could still envision the knife embedded in the building beside her. Whoever had thrown it had a strong arm. "The attacks happened at random times. No specific hour or schedule I could pinpoint."

"Possibly when they're kicked out of a tavern." He took her arm again, keeping her close. Savannah did not think about his hard warmth or the way he felt against her. How she'd missed the closeness of a male body so in tune with hers. Of Tristan's body. "Or when they lose at the gaming hells."

She frowned, pushing away the feel of his body so close. It wasn't as easy as she'd hoped. "This afternoon, that was different," she whispered, still trying to piece everything together. "At night, I can almost understand. No one could see anything."

"The daytime is different," Tristan agreed. "More dangerous." He grunted, that anger back in his tone. "More of a thrill."

"There are so many variables," she agreed, her voice hot and passionate. "I know this is a long shot, but these women matter. Their deaths shouldn't be dismissed, their bodies tossed into pauper's graves and forgotten."

It was why she'd paid for proper services. Why Mr. Christie had performed them.

"You're right." He squeezed her arm and slanted her a quick look. Tristan didn't take his gaze off the street, though many of the people crowding it now recognized her and moved aside. "We won't let them be forgotten."

"Thank you," she whispered. For all the troubles that lay between them, Savannah knew he meant it. Something in her softened; another piece of the castle wall she'd built around her heart chipped off.

"Don't thank me yet. We haven't done more than walk from one end to another." He paused at the opposite end of Denmark Street as if he stood on the dais at a ball. Or as captain on the deck of his ship.

Bile rose in her throat, and Savannah once more cursed her wandering mind. As if she needed the reminder.

"What do you see?" She didn't crane her neck no matter how she longed to. No sense drawing attention to them. Tristan's height did that enough.

"Nothing." He shook his head. "Well, people, taverns, the usual. But there's something missing."

"I know," she admitted. "Like something doesn't belong here." Frustrated with her lack of understanding, she gripped his arm tighter. No one approached them. The streets had cleared somewhat. Unusual, she thought. Though she'd never ventured here at night, except for the time Dem had sent word —a frantic message by one of his lieutenants—about Ailene.

"Or like someone is trying too hard to blend in."

A chill raced down her spine. "They know."

Tristan nodded. "This time of night, the streets should be more crowded."

"There's no music." Awareness slithered down her spine again, like a warning. Savannah turned, but no one stood behind her. That in itself sent a bolt of fear curling through her.

Tristan's voice lowered. "Have you seen Dem?"

"No, but this early, he might be with Ailene and the babe. Or planning with his lieutenants." Savannah looked behind them again, but nothing stood out as suspicious. Which made her more so, though she couldn't have said why. She also hadn't seen either Browne or Peters.

"We'll walk back the way we came," Tristan whispered. "Stay close."

Before she could answer, Savannah heard it. Not a scream, nothing so dramatic. A scuffle or commotion. Only enough noise to draw their attention. Tristan was already moving, not releasing her arm, and she lifted her skirts, thankful for her practical boots.

"We're too late," he said, though they'd only raced past a couple buildings.

"Find Dem," Savannah ordered the closest person, a man who looked pale in the darkness. "Now." He nodded and raced off. She didn't watch him leave. "Tristan?"

Oh, but it hurt, saying his name. She buried that, too, deep inside where she hid all her other hurts and pains.

"I'm sorry, Savannah." He looked up from where he knelt on the filthy street, which was clogged with filth and rubbish that was now blowing around him and the poor woman on the ground. "Find me a lantern," he barked into the night.

Savannah had no idea where the lantern came from, but Browne appeared next to her as if he'd always stood there. He handed her the lantern just as Dem raced to her side. As she held the light over the body, cold realization swept down her spine. She recognized the woman.

"Mary Kate," she whispered. "I'm so sorry."

"Robbie, fetch Mr. Christie. Take the boys, ensure his safety," Dem ordered, kneeling beside Savannah. "What are you doing here, Miss Savannah?" he hissed. "It's too dangerous out here now."

"Trying to stop this," she whispered back. "Is Ailene all right?"

"Aye." He sounded defeated. In the next breath, he stood, ignored Tristan, and squared his shoulders. "Who saw this?"

Leaving Dem to interrogate the crowd, none of whom

claimed to have seen anything, Savannah turned back to Tristan. He'd remained quiet during her exchange with Dem, and it made her suspicious. A quick glance showed her Browne and Peters had melted back into the crowd.

"What did you find?" she asked Tristan.

"What makes you think I found anything?" He glanced up at her, then over at the crowd Dem was addressing. "Nothing."

She didn't protest but stood, still holding the lantern. The night had chilled, the cold skittering over her skin, and Savannah wished she'd worn a warmer coat. It was of little matter now.

Tomorrow was soon enough to discover what little Dem would no doubt learn. And she wouldn't interrupt his interrogation. Not when her own safety relied on his influence. She glanced around the area but couldn't spot Browne or Peters again. Handing the lantern to one of Dem's lieutenants with a quick nod, she turned back to Tristan.

"I'd say we were out for an evening stroll, but I don't want to look suspicious." Tristan settled his hand on the small of her back and guided her back toward the church. "Let's hurry this along."

"I won't argue," she agreed. Ignoring his disbelieving snort, and the cold sweat gathering at the base of her back, Savannah focused on their end point. Whoever had killed Mary Kate had done so smoothly, quickly. There hadn't been time for a warning, a shout. Nothing.

It took only a few moments for Tristan to flag down a hackney, and soon they were on their way back to Grosvenor Square. Savannah didn't sit opposite him this time, but beside him on the hard bench as the cab made its slow way through the heavy traffic of the late season's activities.

For comfort? Maybe. For curiosity, yes.

"Well?" she finally asked.

"Mary Kate, was it?"

She nodded, and Tristan opened his hand. In the dark interior, Savannah saw a starched cloth, the creases still neat and visible despite the way it'd been crushed.

"Whatever struggle ensued, she grabbed onto him."

"Nice material." Savannah took the cravat and ran it through her fingers, her touch far lighter than her tone. "Very fine. Definitely not anything found around here. Mary Kate works—worked—at the same theater as Nell." The words caught in her throat. "They're both sweetmeat sellers and runners for the actresses. This could've come from there."

"You don't believe that." He tucked the linen into his pocket, and his voice sank into a boiling anger. "I don't think she took it from a patron as a gift. What would be the point? A cravat? Unlikely. Not with the way she crushed it in her hand. No, she ripped this from the man who killed her."

Cold fury replaced Savannah's fear. "Which means someone with money is stalking the street. For what?"

"A lark. A game." His voice held a restraint she found hers could not. Still, his simmering anger showed in the way he clenched his fist, the tension in his muscles. "Because they can."

"We're looking in the wrong places, then." She met his gaze. All thoughts of talking about the past had vanished. In their place lay only her desire for revenge. Justice. Her mind raced with ideas and plans, each more outrageous than the last. Finally, she settled on one that was at least somewhat conceivable.

Somewhat.

"I'll have one of my men ask around the tailors," he was saying. "Bond Street, Oxford Street, Pall Mall. Piccadilly, even, and the warehouses. I'll send someone who won't be connected to either of us."

"If these men are as wealthy as this cravat indicates, they'll travel in higher circles than St. Giles. There are still a few events this late in the season." She met his surprised gaze as the hackney rolled to a stop, determined to see this through. "I'm positive I can procure an invitation to at least one. See that you do as well."

CHAPTER 6

"You're doing *what*?"

The next morning, after rising far later than she normally did, Savannah breakfasted at the small table in her room. Her parents had already eaten and left for their morning activities, but Lyneé had stayed behind to enjoy a late breakfast with her.

Savannah had expected her sister's disbelief. She'd expected an argument or three.

She hadn't expected the laughter.

Once again, she hadn't slept well, her mind turning between her vague plan to find this rich man—or group of men—who enjoyed killing women and her all too easy reliance on Tristan. Savannah preferred not to dwell too much on that last part, but she'd come to a stop on the first.

Truthfully, other than investigating several society gatherings and dancing between the significant and subtle questions about what happened with Tristan, she hadn't a clue how they might find any hint about the perpetrators of these murders.

In the corner of the room, Jiesha watched her with wide, brown eyes as she happily munched on her walnut treat.

Savannah wondered if the rabbit might like a change in scenery. So far, she enjoyed eating and hiding beneath the bed. None of the servants said anything against her after Anna's rather dramatic introduction, but they were all wary nonetheless.

Still, Jiesha did enjoy scaring her in the middle of the night by hopping onto the bed and racing around it.

"I'm pretending to reconcile with Tristan so we can find the person or persons responsible for these murders." Savannah left the table for her seat by the windows as if that were the most normal response imaginable. "In this ruse, I plan on engaging in several societal activities that will, hopefully, bring us in proximity to the information I require."

Lyneé laughed harder. Savannah rolled her eyes and finished her coffee. Unlike Lyneé, who preferred tea, Savannah enjoyed the Egyptian coffee Tristan drank. One of the many things she tried not to think about when it came to him.

"Why not ask me or Mama along?" Lyneé asked, far too innocently for Savannah's comfort. "Papa, even, though I agree he has a tendency to overreact."

With his children's safety? In Hugh Shaw's mind, there was no such thing as too much safety. When it came to his family, "overreaction" didn't even enter his vocabulary. So far, Savannah had been lucky only Browne and Peters followed her. Though now that she thought about it, perhaps Tristan's presence had somehow eased Hugh's mind about Savannah's activities.

"Mama has her own life."

Lyneé snorted at that pathetically weak objection. "And me?"

"Two women entering the marriage mart this late in the season would cause far more talk. This isn't about me entering society; it's about me using my resources to discover a wealthy gentleman"—though "gentleman" was dubious given the circumstances—"who thinks murdering poor, working women is a game. This is about discretion."

Lyneé chortled again. Savannah seriously thought about throwing an egg at her sister's head. Or having Jiesha bite her. Did rabbits bite?

"Savannah…" Instead of finishing whatever she wanted to say, Lyneé merely shook her head again, still grinning.

"I need to be able to move in society without gossip." She huffed and waved her hand before Lyneé could laugh again. "Gossip about me is one thing. People already talk about the color of our skin and the means by which we earn our money. Focusing on me—rather, Tristan and me—will keep them off our true goal."

"You could simply investigate yourself." Lyneé sipped her tea, her eyes dancing mischievously over the hand-painted teacup. That factory, near Coventry, was of their many investments. "I'm sure many men would welcome the opportunity to court you, even at the end of the season, unorthodox as that is."

"I'm not looking for a courtship," Savannah snapped. She set her cup down with a decisive click.

Lyneé merely raised her eyebrows.

"I'm looking for a murderer. I only happen to be looking in a higher societal setting than I originally anticipated."

"That is concerning." Lyneé looked out the window, shaking her head. "It had never occurred to me that someone might wander St. Giles looking to murder just anyone. A grudge, yes, I could see, but this?" She shook her head again, all humor vanished.

"A whim, a bet, the thrill of it?" Savannah shrugged, privately agreeing with Tristan's assessment of the situation but unwilling to admit such a thing aloud. She already spoke too much of him, and *to* him, for her liking. No matter the pull still between them.

The harder she pushed him away, the nearer he drew.

Perhaps if she kept him close, she'd once more realize all the ways they did not suit. Abandonment, for one.

That was the only reason she could recall at the moment, however, and it vexed her to no end.

"Have you spoken to him about, well…" Lyneé waved a hand, the berry on her fork coming dangerously close to being flung off. "Things."

Savannah wondered if Jiesha liked berries. She meant to find a book or a pamphlet on the care of animals but forgot, what with everything. She'd ask Coyle, her lady's maid, to find something in the bookstore.

"No." Savannah sniffed and ensured the bricks that remained in the wall around her heart stayed intact. She was terrified that the more she strengthened that wall, the more cracks appeared. "There are no *things* we need to discuss."

"Savannah."

"Lyneé," she said in the same tone. "What discussion is there? 'Why did you leave?' *Because I wanted adventure.* 'Why didn't you ask me along?' *Because I didn't want you there.*" She swallowed hard against the pain closing her throat and stabbing her heart, but she kept her voice even. Savannah doubted she fooled her sister. "What more is there? There's no need to rehash that particular event, thank you."

"And this, ah…plan? Is a good one because you have no feelings for the man whatsoever?" Her sister did not sound convinced. Savannah didn't blame her.

"It's a good plan because it'll allow me to gain easy access into the last of the season's events." She ignored the obvious torture in this plan. It already cut through her. "It's simply a matter of convenience."

She had regrets, but there was no other way for her to investigate. Well, there might've been, but she couldn't think of one. Not without additional gossip. Plus, she didn't want any more of her women dying.

Lyneé snorted and finished her breakfast. She didn't state the obvious. She didn't need to. Lyneé was there when

Savannah discovered Tristan had left without a word. That he'd sneaked off on his ship, *without her*, with the barest of notes and the flimsiest of excuses. Lyneé had held her as she'd sobbed, her room a mess of anguish and rage and heartache so profound, she thought she'd wither away from it.

She hadn't, of course.

She'd moved bedrooms, redecorated in a lighter style than she'd previously enjoyed, and hadn't stepped foot in that room since. It didn't make the memory of Tristan's leaving any easier to handle. It barely made her feel better. But at least this room offered her a beautiful view of the rear gardens.

"What are your plans for the day? Another suffragist meeting?" Savannah asked, in a vain attempt to change the subject. Whatever they spoke of now, Tristan's presence hung in the air as if he stood beside Savannah.

"The offices with Papa." Lyneé stood. "Several ships put into port overnight, and the manifests need checking." She offered a sly smile. "And perhaps a talk with Mr. Fitzsimmons."

Laughing, which was always better than crying, Savannah finally looked through the mail Walters had delivered this morning. "I'm sure Mr. Fitzsimmons will welcome such an interaction." Had he told Tristan's man where she had been the other day? She glanced up from the stack of invitations with a faint, knowing smile. "He seems rather attentive."

"He's interesting," Lyneé admitted.

"What's interesting are these invitations," Savannah scoffed, waving one in the air. "Interesting isn't a man with whom you claim to enjoy spending time."

Lyneé waved away that observation with a huff. "Tell me about the invitations."

"I think," Savannah said slowly, holding up one from the pile, "we'll start with the Crichtons' afternoon picnic tomorrow. They've always been nice to Mama. And I enjoy spending time with Eliza."

"She might have an idea," Lyneé agreed. "She keeps abreast of all the gossip thanks to John's position."

How Eliza might have heard about murders in the rookery, Savannah had no idea. The knock interrupted her.

"Miss Savannah." Walters bowed, looking sour. "Mr. Conrad is waiting for you in the parlor. Shall I tell him you aren't at home? Perhaps gone to the country for the foreseeable future?"

Lyneé snickered, and Savannah swallowed a laugh. "I'll see him, Walters. Thank you."

"As you say, miss." Walters bowed again, but he didn't look happy.

Grateful for that small boost from the staff, Savannah finished her coffee and gathered the invitations. "Enjoy your meeting with Mr. Fitzsimmons," she called over her shoulder.

Savannah hesitated at the top of the steps. Her stomach jumped with nerves, but she couldn't decide if it was because of Tristan or finding this killer. Either way, she felt like she was stepping onto a new path.

A dark path in the middle of nowhere, and one that she had no idea where it led.

Annoyed with the direction of her thoughts, she hurried down the stairs and into the front parlor, where guests were received. Had Tristan ever spent more than a spare moment in that room? Another inconsequential thought she dismissed.

"You're out early," she said upon entering.

Dressed in a more fashionable waistcoat and jacket this morning, he looked as if he'd stepped off a fashion plate. Savannah frowned. She wore a plain morning gown since she'd planned to remain at home and brew tinctures. Where had he been? Or was he going somewhere?

"I brought cheese," he said in lieu of a greeting, gesturing to the table, where a small selection of cheeses lay next to what looked like fresh toast and a pitcher of carob juice.

"You did." Her steps faltered in time with her words.

Savannah hadn't expected this. She hadn't expected him at all this morning, perhaps a note sent round later with plans. Certainly not cheese and toast. "Why?"

He grinned, but his blue-green eyes remained guarded. It set her on guard as well. She had no idea what was happening. Savannah couldn't remember ever feeling so wrong-footed around him.

"This is a local cheese from the countryside around Antwerp. It's a hard cheese, slightly nutty, from one of the abbeys there."

Savannah cautiously crossed the room, as if he held a pistol aimed at her heart rather than an innocent piece of cheese. The invitations in her hand crumpled within her clenched fist, but she couldn't quite force her fingers to release them.

"Why?" she repeated.

Tristan silently thanked Arnault. His friend had been right about the cheese, but the look on Savannah's face told him she didn't waver as much as he hoped. Still, she enjoyed cheese, he'd always enjoyed spoiling her, and this seemed an opportune time to start again.

"I came with several errands," he admitted. She took another cautious step closer, as if he offered a poisoned apple instead of a delicious selection of cheeses. "I thought we could enjoy some cheese and toast while we discussed things. But let's start with Jiesha."

Another step, but she stopped just out of reach of the cheese. "Things?" Savannah shook her head. "Are you bribing me with cheese?"

Tristan offered a short laugh and grinned. She knew him too well for his own good. "Not bribing." He gestured for the settee and waited until she carefully sat on its edge. "Apologizing."

Her head whipped around, and her eyes watched him like he was a predator about to attack. He deserved that. Tristan set the toast and cheese on a plate; one he'd carried from Aunt Nadia's so he wouldn't have to ask Walters for one. He had a feeling he'd still be waiting if he'd done that.

"There's nothing to say," Savannah said, her cool voice chilling the air between them. She picked up the plate and nibbled the cheese. Humming appreciatively, she took another bite, then set the plate down.

"How is Jiesha? Is she settling in well enough?" He knew precious little about rabbits. One of the men had procured the hay when Tristan smuggled Jiesha from the offices, but that was as far as his rabbit knowledge extended.

He'd been careful to keep her in his cabin, allowing her the freedom to roam without getting lost—or stepped on—onboard the ship. No cages. Not after he'd liberated her from the too-small one in Van Zanten's office. Little Ricky, his cabin boy, had reluctantly watched that she didn't escape.

"Well enough," Savannah admitted cautiously. "Why a rabbit?" Her head tilted just the slightest, as if she didn't want to give away too much. "Of all the gifts you could've brought in your so-called apology, why her?"

Tristan caught her words. His *so-called* apology. While Tristan had planned on offering a full apology the moment he'd met her, circumstances had changed that plan. He didn't need to glance at the pocket doors to know they stood wide open, but, given the hour, her family was most likely not at home, off to their own errands. He was somewhat surprised she remained.

There was much he wished to discuss with her, and the apology sat at the top of the list. However, he had no desire to deliver it with a bevy of servants ready eavesdropped on their conversation. They most definitely did not trust him.

Another excuse.

"When I was in Antwerp, I planned on visiting Karl Van den Berg. You remember him?"

She nodded and picked up another piece of cheese. Van den Berg's sister had married an Englishman, a close friend of his eldest sister's husband, and Tristan had felt it necessary to at least pay the man a call.

"He was engaged in a tricky deal with Van Zanten…something about taking over part of Van Zanten's trade. I'm not sure why, but Karl was determined."

"All right." She sipped the carob juice and delicately wiped her lips.

"Van Zanten is not the nicest nor the most generous person I've ever met." Which might've been the largest understatement he'd ever uttered. "He collects things and displays them in his office, often in cages."

Savannah scowled and sat straighter. "He displayed Jiesha in a cage?"

"She was far too large for it," he admitted. The image of Jiesha inside that too-small cage still haunted him. "I've no idea where he found her. I'm not privy to the workings of rabbits as pets, but apparently, he bred them." His face darkened, and he glowered at the table of cheese and toast. "He abused his two office workers as well."

"Bastard," Savannah spat.

Tristan almost smiled. How had he forgotten that about her? She grew up on the docks, around sailors, so naturally she cursed like one. It was a point of consternation for her mother, but Savannah didn't let that stop her.

"Indeed." He held out the plate of cheese again, but she waved it off. "So, I took Jiesha, enticed the two office workers away with the promise of food and freedom, and found their families, who were also indebted to Van Zanten. Then I left with the man's cargo, the information Karl wanted, and no doubt a hefty bounty on my head if I ever return to Antwerp."

"Good." She laughed. A real, genuine sound that washed over him and made his heart pound faster. Oh, how he'd missed that sound, the echo of her laughter he'd dreamed about so often.

"I have a list of invitations for various events we can attend," she said, still grinning.

"I have some news on the cravat," he said at the same time.

She looked at her lap, where the small stack of now crumpled letters lay. Tristan struggled with his apology, the planned words heavy on his tongue. How did one even apologize to one's fiancée—former fiancée, he supposed—when one had literally abandoned her?

He didn't. She refused to hear him, and he supposed he deserved that, too. No matter how it cut his heart. He'd done this to himself.

"What have you chosen?" Tristan asked instead, torn between voicing his apology and letting her set the pace.

"The Crichtons' picnic tomorrow." She aimed her gaze at him, and he swore he saw indecision there. "And perhaps the theater tonight."

"Good choices." He smoothly switched from cheese to the cravat and pulled out the piece in question. "I had my first mate ask around about this. Arnault knows his fabrics and swears this is a special silk from China."

"Arnault?" Her hand hovered a piece of toast and cheese halfway to her mouth.

"Frederic Arnault," he said. "A good man and a better sailor." Tristan paused. He didn't want to go into how Arnault had handed over the captaincy of the ship to a man—Conrad or not—who had never captained a ship in his life. "A close friend."

Arnault was there when Tristan had second—and third—guessed himself over leaving without a word to Savannah, when he'd wondered what kind of stupid fool he'd been. When the weight of his actions had crashed down on him. He'd been young and stupid, but he'd still sailed forward, determined to find that elusive part of him he thought he'd been missing.

"He sailed with Karl during the wars."

Savannah finished her bite and hummed. "I see. You met—" She broke off, her back straight and her head high. She no longer looked at ease. "And does he think this cloth is sold here?"

"He said it's imported, so I have a list of several tailors I'll investigate." Tristan willed her to ask the question he knew she wanted to ask.

But with the parlor doors open and the distinct lack of privacy, he knew she wouldn't. Once again, this was not the place for apologies, discussions, or explanations. He knew part of him purposely put off such things; there'd never be a perfect time.

"All right." Savannah stood again and paced toward the window.

Tristan stood as well and watched her. The stiff set of her shoulders, the tilt of her chin. He didn't need to see her face to know she'd closed her eyes, pressed her lips tight together. Or that her hands were clenched in front of her, her way of keeping her emotions in check.

"Yes." He moved closer but stopped, not at all certain of his next step. Jaw clenched, he clasped his hands behind his back and rocked on his heels. "I'll make the arrangements for the theater tonight. The Royal Opera House? It's the closest to St Giles."

She nodded.

"Will *Tetya* Nadia do as chaperone?"

Her head jerked to the side, but she otherwise didn't move. "You don't trust my parents?"

"Your mother might toss me over the balcony," he admitted and swore her lips curved into the ghost of a smile.

Probably at the thought of his ignoble demise, but a smile was a smile.

"Be prompt." She turned around and faced him, that slight relaxation once again evident in her shoulders. "We have a lot to do."

"Are you returning to St. Giles today?"

"No, I—" She stopped, and her eyes narrowed. "Why?"

"I thought I'd escort you if you were," he said in as neutral a tone as possible.

"Why?" She grimaced at her repetitiveness. He knew she hated to repeat herself, but he didn't back down.

"Until we discover who is after these women, it's best you aren't alone." There, nice and simple. His temper boiled beneath those reasonable words; she always put everyone else ahead of herself.

Even him. Especially him.

"I won't have a guard," she shot back, her own temper boiling over. "Not you, not Browne, not the dock workers. Not even Papa."

Tristan didn't think Hugh Shaw would let his eldest child wander around unprotected, no matter her prowess with a dagger. Her father had apparently hired additional guards for her at one point, which only somewhat mollified Tristan.

"Someone tried to kill you, Savannah!" So much for reasonable. His temper boiled over.

"I fail to see how that affects you. Or why it matters so much when I was so easy to leave in the first place!" Jaw clenched, she glared daggers at him and turned for the door.

"You weren't."

In the quiet that followed that declaration, she stopped. Tristan didn't look away from her. Her arms were taut as she clenched her skirts, her body vibrating with anger and hurt and pain—all caused by him.

"You left," she whispered into the silence, her voice breaking.

"You kissed me goodbye that morning, lied about your plans, and left."

"I did." That was only part of the story, but he didn't press it. He moved silently across the room, but Tristan knew she could sense him doing so. She hadn't moved. "I'm sorry. No number of apologies will change what I did or the hurt I caused you."

"Why return?" He heard the tears in her voice, and it tore him in two. "You could've made port and never spoken to me. I would've heard about your return from Papa or *Tetya* Nadia, or maybe a simple rumor. We could've got on with our lives." She met his gaze, her eyes dry but he saw the heartbreak in them. "Our *separate* lives."

"That never occurred to me," he admitted. "All I thought about for three years was seeing you again."

"Yet it also took you three years to return." She stepped backward, chin tilted, and he reached for her. Savannah swatted his hand away and backed out of the room. "This is not a reconciliation. This is nothing more than a means to an end. It's convenient for us to pretend while we discover who owns that cravat. That's all this is, Tristan Conrad. Don't forget it."

At the doorway, she whirled from him and stalked across the foyer, leaving the cheese, and him, alone.

CHAPTER 7

"The second we step foot out of this carriage, there'll be talk." Tristan watched Savannah with a calmness she envied. Though she had a feeling it was all for show, the fact he exuded it with such confidence straightened her spine and wiped all emotion from her face.

"The longer we stay in this carriage, the more talk will spread." She glanced at Nadia and James, who both remained silent.

They had engaged in talk about the wars in India and the dissolution of Parliament. Not exactly small talk, but it occupied the ride and avoided personal matters. Now, swallowing around a dry throat, she forced a smile.

Without a word, her godmother rested her hand on Savannah's and waited. Her decision. Too late now; they'd specifically taken the carriage with the Shaw crest. While they weren't nobility or gentry, the Shaws were extremely wealthy shipping magnates. Consequently, they were highly sought after despite their so-called common ancestry.

Money talked louder than many things, including a freed slave as the matriarch of the family.

Savannah tilted her head and nodded as she watched Tristan tap on the roof of the carriage. The vehicle rocked as Browne jumped down and opened the door. Tristan exited and reached back to help her out. Automatically placing her hand in his, she didn't immediately register the crowd.

Tristan didn't care about her ancestry. That she was the great-granddaughter of a Jamaican house slave who'd been freed on the death of her mistress. That her great-grandmother never talked about the man who'd fathered her only child. Tristan didn't care about her money, either. Of course, the Conrads had plenty of wealth of their own.

He cared—or had cared—about *her*.

Her lips wouldn't quite form a smile, but she tried anyway. People were watching. The ripple that moved through the crowd echoed in her ears in time to the roaring of her blood. The evening was cool despite the warm day, but Savannah didn't know if the shiver that raced down her spine was a result of the temperature or this new adventure.

"Second thoughts?" Tristan asked as he leaned close, offering a gentlemanly arm as he scanned the crowd.

"No." She smiled wider and accepted the arm, all too aware of the role they were playing. "You?"

His low chuckle sent a different kind of shiver down her spine. One that pooled hot between her legs. That yearning returned. She mentally cursed him for that, though she'd never tell him she still wanted him. For three years, men had tried courting her. For three years, she had no interest in any of them.

None had made her blood race with yearning, or her heart turn over in her chest at the sight of his smile.

As they walked into the theater, she realized the truth of the matter: This was a terrible idea. It ranked first among any bad idea she'd ever had—number one of truly awful ideas. Whatever made her think she could go through with this fake engagement, Savannah had no idea.

THE LADY'S COURTSHIP

"Do you recognize any of the women?" Tristan leaned close and whispered the question so it floated between them. His warm breath felt like a caress along her skin.

Tamping down that ridiculous feeling, she reminded herself that his words were simply words—no more, no less. Once again hearing her mother's admonishment echo in her heart, Savannah turned. His eyes looked greener now as they darkened with his arousal.

Her heart skipped again, and she cursed her foolishness. Perhaps she did need to know why he'd left. Why he'd returned. And why he still seemingly cared. For her own sanity, since she didn't seem capable of turning away from him.

"No." She looked ahead, but she couldn't take in the people before her as they walked toward the St. Clairs' subscription box. They were a mass of faces and curious looks, nothing more, and she blinked away the image of Tristan's gaze solely on her. "I'll look again once we reach our seats."

They walked in silence, her hand quite properly on Tristan's arm, all eyes on them, and Savannah's heart conflicted. Aunt Nadia and Uncle James greeted several couples and waved her and Tristan along with concerned looks. They knew a great many people; it kept them in business. Savannah wouldn't take mingling from either of them, especially not for the simple fact that she didn't want to be alone with Tristan.

Which made no sense, as she'd proposed this venture. Oh, wrong word. Not *proposed*. Suggested. Yes, that sounded much better.

"What play are we seeing?"

He paused then laughed. "I don't know." He chuckled again, ruefully this time. "I suggested the Royal Opera House because of Nell and Mary Kate. This is where they worked. I wasn't thinking of the play."

Something in her relaxed. Not at the fact that he took this seriously—she knew he did. At the way he admitted to not knowing that small detail. Tristan looked at the bigger plan, not always the smaller details.

"Typical," she murmured with more affection than she meant, but she doubted he heard her over the crush.

The box sat empty since only Nadia and James accompanied them, and Savannah used the moment of seclusion to look around the theater. Women hawked fruits, sweetmeats, and marzipan to the crowd, while others slipped between the throng, no doubt carrying messages from male patrons to the actresses. Or perhaps some bolder female patrons to the male actors.

"I should've asked who was working tonight," she admitted as Tristan joined her at the balcony. "So many of the women make extra coin here."

"Did Ailene work here?" He didn't look below but at her. Necessary, she supposed, given their ruse. Heat flushed her cheeks and raced through her, reminding Savannah of happier times. "Before, I mean."

Savannah frowned. "No, she worked at Clarks." She met Tristan's gaze. A notorious gaming hell, though of course it wasn't called that. Merely Clarks. "Another victim did as well, but not all of them."

"No, too obvious."

"Yes. I would've realized Clarks was the key if all the women who'd been attacked worked there," she added, all too aware of Tristan's hard body close to hers, of his warmth and the way he watched her.

His gaze never wavered from her face, though Savannah kept hers on the crowd below. Her heart beat that much faster and, traitorous thing that it was, made her want to reach out and touch his hand.

Perhaps she ought to do just that, show those who were watching hungrily what they wanted to see. Calculated, determined, and not at all necessary. Because suddenly she very much wanted to touch Tristan's hand, feel his skin against hers.

Savannah curled her fingers into a tight fist. No matter how she longed to touch him, no matter how necessary she thought it might be for their ruse, she wouldn't. The walls around her heart cracked again, the pieces splintering but not yet shattering.

"I'll visit it," Tristan promised.

Her head swung around, and she met his gaze. Visit? Where? His own gaze held hers, dark and steady, as if he knew exactly where her own thoughts lay. Not on their plan, certainly, and she struggled to remember what they'd been talking about.

Just then, Aunt Nadia appeared, interrupting whatever moment she and Tristan had been having. "Ah. I think I see—" She waved behind her and disappeared once more.

Savannah didn't watch her leave. "Why?" She asked that so often, but she needed answers. "Why did you leave without a word?"

"THIS IS HARDLY the place for my apology," Tristan whispered just loud enough he knew she could hear him over the din. "Or explanations."

"Perhaps," she whispered back, her dark eyes unreadable. "Tell me anyway."

"I thought I was missing a part of myself," he admitted, the words harder to say now than when he'd thought them dozens of times over the years. "Philip and I had talked so much of adventure and seeing the world after the wars, that I wanted to do that."

"You always did." Her face remained a mask of curiosity. There was nothing untoward that the eavesdroppers might catch on to. "I would've gone with you."

"I know." Tristan took a breath full of hundreds of candles, a mass of people, and the scent of food. He wondered why he'd thought that would help and plunged onward. Or perhaps jumped overboard. "That's what scared me." She stiffened, which he'd expected, and he rushed on. "I wanted you with me. I always wanted you with me. But I thought I had to do this alone."

Her mouth twisted in a grimace, which she quickly smoothed over. Her chin lifted again, her back straight and eyes hard. People judged her enough, and Tristan knew she'd never allow them to see the real Savannah. He'd been granted that. Once. And he'd squandered it. "I see."

"Do you?" He shook his head. "I don't. Not anymore, not after the ship sailed and it was too late to turn around and return to port. I can't count the number of times I regretted thinking that if I left without a word, it might be easier."

"Did you find what you were looking for?" Her hands had curled onto the railing as the crowd took their seats.

Before he could answer—admit he still didn't know, wasn't certain, that yes he had and no he hadn't—Aunt Nadia and Uncle James arrived. Here, with so many watching them, wasn't the time or place to admit that what he needed was and always had been Savannah.

They took their seats, Savannah's gaze on the stage, Tristan's on her. Aunt Nadia sat behind Savannah and muttered very uncomplimentary things about both of them in Russian. Uncle James sat next to her and stifled his amusement.

Tristan couldn't have said what the play was about. The audience laughed, so he supposed it was enjoyable, but he didn't hear a single word. All too aware of Savannah's cold stiffness beside him, her face blanked of all emotion, he didn't move to touch her. As much as he wanted to feel the warmth of her even through their gloves, he kept still beside her.

He did, however, watch the crowd below.

"What are you searching for?" Savannah asked.

Startled, he jerked his gaze to hers and thought she could read his mind. She used to, before he made the biggest mistake of his life.

She turned just enough and tilted her head to the crowd below. "I'm sure many men here have cravats of the finest imported silk." Her lips turned up in the barest smile, for the crowd. Her eyes, however, remained cool as they studied him. "Even you."

"True," he admitted quietly, using their conversation as an excuse to lean closer. "I'm looking for movement." He kept his voice low, so it looked as if they held an intimate conversation. Tristan didn't miss the slightest of shivers that raced down Savannah's spine. "A group of men together. One of the runners returning to the same man multiple times."

"And have you found that?" Her gaze sharpened with her tone, and her fingers curled tightly on her lap.

The answer was still no. Tristan wanted to run a hand down his face, roll his shoulders. In this setting, with the weight of their ruse hanging over them and his very real desire to win her over, he simply shook his head. Burying his frustration and self-loathing only made his temper simmer hotter. "Not yet."

He had a vague sort of plan involving intermission and disappearing backstage, but he couldn't think straight. Not with Savannah so near and his apology so close.

Perhaps that provided the perfect reason for him to disappear.

"Do you recognize any of the women from up here?" He kept his gaze on her—certainly not a hardship. Tristan didn't care about the acting below or the crowd. He very much wanted to kiss her, location and crowd be damned.

Savannah lifted her opera glasses and scanned the area. Instead of following her gaze, he kept watching her.

"How is it that we never attended the theater?" He hadn't meant to voice those thoughts aloud.

Savannah tightened her grip around her viewing glasses, her only outward reaction. She paused in her scan of the crowd, but only for a moment.

"We had other interests," she said, so softly he almost missed it. Would have if he hadn't leaned closer. "Theater, opera, even picnics weren't how we wanted to spend our days." Slowly, she lowered her glasses and turned her head. "Or nights."

He reached out and placed his hand over hers. Let anyone watching them gossip. That was why they'd attended, for the notoriety, the attention. Beneath his touch, her fingers jerked.

"Did you want to attend?" he whispered as laughter echoed around them.

"I never thought about it," she admitted. "It wasn't something..." She shook her head.

He knew. It hadn't mattered then. They'd always made their own fun, enjoyed whatever lark or adventure they planned—or didn't plan, in most cases. They created their own entertainment; they'd had no need to watch it on a stage.

"It's almost intermission." She cleared her throat and slipped her hand from his. "Shall we find our way to the back staircase?"

"I'll slip away," he protested. "Less noticeable."

Savannah offered him the briefest of looks, one that told him exactly what she thought of that plan. Then she turned to Nadia and whispered something. Nadia, who didn't look at all surprised but somewhat smug, merely nodded. Even from this angle, he saw Uncle James roll his eyes. As the first half of the play concluded, Tristan stood and took Savannah's arm.

They slipped through the crowded hallways, past the footmen bearing drinks and the women selling sweets and fresh fruits. Ignoring the curious looks, they headed for the stairs.

"It occurs to me that we should've looked at the theater's

blueprints," Savannah said as Tristan led her across the lobby. "Unless you did?"

"I also had not thought of that," he admitted. "However, Uncle James is a sight more knowledgeable about the construction than any man ought to be. He's more than a pretty face, you know," he added, one of James's longstanding jokes.

"Naturally." Savannah offered a quiet giggle as he pushed open a side door partly concealed in the paneling. "He probably smuggled wine into the building."

"I've no doubt." He grinned and eased the door closed behind them.

In the darkness, Tristan wanted to pin her against the wall and kiss her senseless. Wanted to feel her skin beneath his fingertips. Wanted to hear her sigh his name. His cock stirred, his fingertips aching for her skin beneath his.

He did not pin her against the wall. Or kiss her, as tempted as he was. Instead, he took her hand in one of his and felt his way down the pitch-black hall with the other.

"I expected more lighting," she admitted, her voice pitched low. "Someone uses these tunnels; they'd have to find their way."

"Is it suspicious?" He shrugged and turned slightly right, keeping along the wall. "I think everything is."

Ahead, a lone candle lit the way, and he slowed their pace even further. Squeezing her hand in a no doubt unnecessary warning, he pulled her closer against the wall.

Tristan didn't hear anything and peeked carefully around the corner. Empty. He squeezed Savannah's hand again, and they continued onward. At the next corner, which was far more brightly lit than the previous one, the corridor turned in two directions. One, if his sense of this building was correct, lead backstage. The other onto the street.

"If my sense of the building is correct, that way leads backstage." Tristan gestured with his free hand. "The other leads to the street."

"The stage," Savannah ordered.

Halfway toward the clearly marked doors, they opened. A brief crescendo of shouting rolled out as a plainly dressed woman exited, her hands in the pockets of her apron.

"Moll." Savannah's quiet voice stopped the woman.

"Miss Savannah?" Moll smiled and offered a quick curtsy. She eyed Tristan curiously but didn't greet him. "What are you doing here? Begging your pardon."

"We're looking for information," Tristan said.

"About the murders." Moll shivered and looked over her shoulder at the now closed doors. "I don't know nothing."

"I know," Savannah soothed, taking the woman's hand in reassurance. "Are you running notes for any of the gentlemen?"

"Aye. One of them is sweet on Miss Cornelia, has been all season." Moll looked behind her again. "I have to go; the second half is about to begin."

"We won't keep you," Tristan said, stepping aside. "Have you seen anything out of place?"

Moll shook her head and skirted around them. Tristan stepped closer to Savannah, trying not to grin.

"If you see anything," Savannah said, "let Dem know. He knows how to contact me."

"Yes, Miss Savannah." Moll hurried down the hall.

"A season-long affair," Tristan said, watching her leave. "But I've seen numerous women carrying notes back and forth. Where are the others?"

Just then, male laughter drifted from the opposite end of the corridor. Taking Savannah's hand again, Tristan dragged her to the intersection, away from the stage doors. They barely made it before a pair of finely dressed men appeared.

Savannah pulled him against her, her eyes unreadable as they locked with his. Then she was kissing him, or he was kissing her, and nothing else mattered. Only the feel of her lips pressed against his, the slow sweep of her tongue, her almost imperceptible sigh. Tristan braced his hands on the wall and pressed close against her.

He knew she was kissing him so that the two men walking past didn't stop and converse or grow suspicious. Knew she'd done it for concealment as much as misdirection. He knew all that and did not care.

Cupping the back of her neck, he kissed her harder. The memory of their last kiss paled in comparison to this one. It burned through him, a wildfire he could never tame. He'd once thought he wanted to, but now all he cared about was letting it engulf him.

He cursed his gloves, that barrier between his fingers and her skin, but he didn't want to take the time and remove them. Didn't want to pull away, stop this passion burning between them.

"Tristan." The word, as soft as a caress, pulled him back to the present.

He ran his fingers over her jaw, her cheek, his gaze locked with hers. He knew he should step back, wait for Moll's return, and ask about the other women. He doubted the gentleman she was passing notes for was their culprit, but he couldn't rule that out.

Instead, he cupped Savannah's cheek and pressed his mouth against hers again.

"You were all I thought of for three years. No one else ever mattered. I'm sorry I left. I'm sorry I thought I needed to find adventure. I didn't."

She watched him, her eyes softening. Eventually she straightened and dropped her hands from his waistcoat. She pushed against him slightly and he obliged, stepping back. Head tilted, Savannah cleared her throat and licked her lips.

"Find Moll. She'll know who else is working tonight." She

looked down the hall. "I'll find Aunt Nadia and meet you back in the box."

Tristan grabbed her hand. "Be careful, Savannah."

She nodded slowly. "You, too. I don't want anything happening to you before you tell me everything." Then she turned and left, the only sound the faint swish of her gown.

CHAPTER 8

*S*tupid.

Savannah licked her lips, tasting Tristan there, and hurried through the foyer looking straight ahead. Stupid, stupid, stupid. What had she been thinking, kissing Tristan like that? She hadn't been thinking—that was the problem. She'd heard the men's laughter, didn't want to be caught, and reacted.

Because of course kissing Tristan was her reaction.

He kissed the same as ever. Tasted the same. The press of his body against hers reminded her of the many times they'd stood in that same position. Only the touch of his hand on her cheek felt different, the barrier of his glove unusual in their long acquaintance.

Acquaintance.

She snorted as she found their box and slipped inside. Acquaintance—what a thin, fragile, threadlike word for their life together. The first time Savannah met Tristan, when he was two and she four, they'd connected. They'd just drifted toward each other like a ship putting to tide. Inexorable. Inseparable.

Several patrons eyed her suspiciously as she took her seat, head high and very much alone. She ignored them all.

Returning alone was, no doubt, the most scandalous thing she could've done in their eyes. Aunt Nadia and Uncle James waited in their box, as if they hadn't moved. James's eyebrows shot upward, but Nadia merely tilted her head, face placid, and gestured for their seats.

"You seem to have lost someone," she whispered in Russian.

Savannah gave her godmother a slight nod as the curtain rose for the second half. "He's making a nuisance of himself with the staff," she answered in kind. Nadia had taught her own children, Savannah and her siblings, and the Conrad siblings her native language, a private game amongst them when they were young.

When she was a girl, it'd been exciting to learn a language almost no one else in London understood. She'd envisioned traveling Europe, blending into the Russian countryside, finding spies.

She hadn't taken it as seriously as Tristan had, of course.

"I'll find him," James said with a beleaguered sigh.

"And your breathlessness?" Nadia turned just enough so it looked as if she watched the play, as if they were discussing some tidbit about it. But Savannah knew her godmother's entire attention rested on her. "From your run back here, no doubt."

"No doubt," she agreed. She knew they both understood it was lie.

But she couldn't admit what had truly happened. How even now, her lips tingled with the feel of his against hers. How her heart raced, her blood hot, arousal pooling between her legs. Shifting in her seat did nothing to assuage that burning need. It only brought attention to her.

Damn Tristan! Or damn her—she'd instigated the kiss. She'd proposed—again with the terrible choice in words—this charade. This farce. This…heartbreak.

Savannah looked below but saw only a colorful blur of

people facing the stage. She tried to focus on the play, but nothing made sense.

"When I suggested this," she told her godmother, "I thought it would be easier."

"Because you no longer have feelings for him?" Nadia fully turned from the stage and watched her. Her voice gave away nothing about her feelings on the matter. Her face remained a mask of polite concern. No *I told you so* or mocking smirk.

"I don't know what I feel," Savannah admitted. The first time she'd done so since Tristan's return. Since his leaving, for that matter. Perhaps talking with him wasn't the most terrible idea ever. No, the most terrible was this idea, pretending they were engaged. Engaged again.

Perhaps she should've taken Lyneé up on her offer, but Savannah hadn't wanted any of the scandal that tainted her to touch her sister. There must've been a half-dozen other options, but even now she couldn't think of one.

Nausea made her lightheaded. She closed her eyes, willing her stomach to settle, her heart to stop pounding quite so hard.

"Sorry I'm late." Tristan slipped into the seat beside her and offered a charming, easy smile, as if they hadn't just kissed in the staff corridor. As if she hadn't sunk into that kiss. As if the last half hour—the last three years—hadn't happened.

James resumed his seat beside Nadia without a word. Only a few sconces lit the box, casting shadows over them.

"Discover anything?" she asked, the words making her chest ache with the effort it took to push them out. Savannah tilted her head to show off the diamonds and pearls sparkling in her hair and forced a polite, teasing smile, one designed to show their renewed relationship.

He leaned closer to her, his face toward the stage once more, as if he enjoyed the play as much as the rest of the crowd. Laughter at whatever just happened on stage filled the theater.

She curled her hands around each other and stared ahead, all too aware of those who were watching them.

"Many things," he said enigmatically. It took everything in her not to swing her head around and stare at him. "But, for tonight's purposes, I discovered that all the women are scared. Not only those who live in and around St. Giles. Even the actresses who live well in their own townhouses."

"Women talk. They share information. I know you look at things differently, Tristan, but not many men care about the fears women carry. They dismiss such things." Savannah kept her face blank, though her stomach clenched at the news. "But I'm certain it's not enough to stop the attacks. Especially since they're occurring in daylight as well."

She slanted a frown in his direction and quickly smoothed the expression off her face. Theirs might be a private box, but people watched and listened. They were supposed to have reconciled—any hint otherwise would ruin that perception.

"I will stop them." His words carried a weight, a promise, a vow. "I swear, Savannah, I won't let this continue." He covered her hand with his and squeezed it. "*We* won't."

She believed him. Not because of his words, which would've sounded like a boast coming from anyone else, but because she knew him. He *had* been raised differently. To him, women were not property but companions. Equals. He'd always treated her as such.

"I know." She licked her lips, and his gaze dropped to her mouth.

Unable to stop her lips from parting, she all too vividly recalled their kiss from earlier. She wanted to kiss him again. Not to see if he tasted the same—clearly, he did. But because she simply wished to kiss him again. And again.

It hadn't mattered before, when she had the freedom to kiss him. Now it felt scandalous. A forbidden fruit she strained for, ignoring the fire she played with. Annoyed at her mixed metaphors, Savannah returned her attention to the play.

"I'm not ready," she heard herself say, just low enough her words reached her own ears. "I owe you nothing, not an explanation nor my continued presence."

Closing her eyes, she pictured Aunt Nadia and Uncle James behind her. Whether their attention was on the stage or a conversation in the next box or an internal monologue, she had no idea. But her godmother's presence kept her sane in this tumultuous swirl of emotions when the past had reared up and clenched her throat.

"You do not," he agreed in that same quiet tone. "I'm the one who should offer you everything on my knees."

Startled by his admission, she watched him from the corner of her eye. "Yet you still left."

"I made many mistakes," he admitted.

Once again, she wondered if another woman was one of them.

"I have no right to ask, but I will anyway. Will you grant me the chance to explain?"

"I have no idea what you can confess that will make anything better. It won't fix the last three years, or, I don't know, whatever you hope to accomplish." *Talk to him.* Her mother's words echoed in her heart, and Savannah nodded. "But I think, for my future, it is in my best interest that I listen to you so I may put the past aside."

His hand covered hers again as the audience laughed and applauded. "That's all I ask."

It sounded so simple. An easy conversation—not even that on her part. All she need do was listen. If she didn't wish to speak, she wouldn't. This was all on his shoulders.

Savannah stared unseeing at the stage. She didn't really believe it would be simple. Because talking with Tristan meant telling him of her pain of these last years, and she didn't think she'd keep quiet about that.

TRISTAN STOOD outside the theater and watched the Shaw carriage disappear down the street. He'd deposited Aunt Nadia, who watched him with an unreadable expression, Uncle James, who grumbled about fools beneath his breath, and Savannah, who didn't watch him at all, into the carriage with their footmen and promised to be safe.

Uncle James had offered to accompany him, but Tristan refused, claiming he needed time alone.

He hadn't disclosed his hastily constructed plan, he suspected they knew where he was headed. He turned toward St. Giles, a fashionably dressed gentleman out for a walk after the theater. His khanjar, a specially made Egyptian dagger his mother had taught him how to use, lay strapped to his hip beneath his evening jacket.

The warmth of the summer evening pressed around him, and he briefly lamented not strolling along with Savannah. Hand in hand, her wide smile brightening his night, her soft whispers wrapping around him. The promise of them. The one he'd rejected.

Walking with her here wasn't safe—last night had proved that. And he'd never endanger her because he wanted her by his side.

He wanted many things, but right then he wanted his head on straight. It still swam with her kiss, the hot spice of her lips pressed against his. The memory of the thousand other kisses they'd shared. The promise he'd walked away from.

Denmark Street bustled with after-theater activity. In the darkness, the rundown buildings loomed awkward and menacing at the same time. They closed in on the street like a heavy fist. People lingered in the streets, watching the foot traffic or screaming up three stories to their neighbors.

He sensed the man before he saw him, but didn't alter his step or his posture. His dagger lay within easy reach should he need it, and he'd learned how to smoothly unsheathe it long before he knew how to use it. Best be prepared.

If that wasn't the family motto, it ought to be.

"Ah, the used-to-be fiancé." Dem's voice echoed softly along the darkened street from two doors ahead.

"Dem." Dem nodded, and the man who had been acting as Tristan's shadow melted into the crowd. Tristan raised an eyebrow and tilted his head back slightly. "Impressive."

"This is my street, fiancé." Dem said it with a straightforward reasonableness. He didn't seem surprised that Tristan knew he was being followed. "What are you doing here?"

"Taking a walk." Tristan stretched out his hands in show. "It's a nice night."

Dem snorted, and Tristan grinned wider. Behind him, life went on as normal, except no one bothered him. Not even the suspicious brush of a pickpocket. Dem held the power here, Tristan granted him that.

"Thought you was at the theater with Miss Savannah."

"I was. She's safely home now." Tristan didn't know why he felt the need to say that, to tell Dem that Savannah had left with no threats against her life. To show he cared? That was hardly Dem's business. It came as a shock when Tristan realized he meant to reassure Dem about Savannah's safety. "I came to see about the other women."

Even in the darkness, Tristan saw the flash of incredulousness on Dem's face.

"Other women," he repeated flatly in clear disbelief. "Why?"

"Not everyone has Savannah's way with a dagger, or the protection of her name and money." Tristan waited, watching

Dem. He saw the struggle on the man's face. He didn't blame him his disbelief. "What other murders have there been?"

"You ask a lot of questions for a used-to-be fiancé."

"I always ask a lot of questions." Tristan grinned, a quick one, there and gone. "I'm a question-asking gentleman."

Dem grunted then stepped back. "Come inside. There's too many ears here."

Surprised, Tristan followed Dem down the street and through the door Savannah had stood before the other day. This must be where Dem and his sister, Ailene, lived.

Inside the small dwelling, a pair of candles stood sentinel against the darkness of the windowless room. A young woman, dark haired and tired eyed, held a sleeping baby. She did not look surprised to find him in her house.

"Ailene," Dem said softly, the harsh demeanor of the gang leader replaced by the worried tone of a brother. Tristan understood that all too well. "This is Miss Savannah's former fiancé."

Ailene's soft blue eyes, haunted and sunken, met his. She nodded. "I've heard of you, Mr. Fiancé."

Tristan smiled his most charming smile and bowed low. "Please, call me Tristan."

Dem grunted again, but Tristan thought he detected a hint of amusement in it. "He thinks he can stop the attacks."

"I will." The words escaped Tristan before he could temper them. "I don't boast." He paused. "All right, yes, I can sometimes boast. But I mean this." He leaned forward and met Ailene's gaze. "Do you think Miss Savannah would have anything to do with me if I wasn't honorable?"

"You left," Dem reminded him. "As I recall, you're the used-to-be fiancé. Not the current fiancé."

Ooph. Dem knew how to twist the knife, didn't he? Good on him. "That is between Miss Savannah and me only, and it's not why I'm here."

"You can stop this?" Ailene met his gaze, hers harder now. She looked at her sleeping child and shuddered. "The attacks."

"Yes. Savannah and I will." He paused again. "I know it doesn't seem like it's possible. Attacks such as these happen all the time. But I promise you. Together we can stop them."

"What do you need to know?" Ailene whispered. She looked from Tristan to Dem and held her brother's gaze.

Dem nodded at her. Tristan would bet his ship that, given the closeness of the siblings, Dem would help because of his sister. His continued power over the street aside, he clearly cared for Ailene.

"When the attacks started," he said, loathe to interrupt the moment between siblings. "Savannah told me some. What more do either of you know?"

"Rich lords think they can take whatever they want." Dem snorted angrily as he hovered behind Ailene. "They walk our streets after the theater, looking down on us."

"For how long? When did the attacks begin?" Tristan asked. He wondered if Dem had ever thought of holding office. He had no idea what was involved in that, he'd never looked into it himself, but Dem had a passion for change.

"A year ago." Dem's gaze flicked down to the baby. "At first, we didn't think it was anything more than, well…"

"Attacks on women?" Tristan couldn't keep his own anger under wraps. It coated his words, making them harder than he'd intended.

"We don't have the safety your money affords you," Dem shot back.

Swallowing a retort, Tristan nodded. "Unfortunately, money doesn't buy many women safety."

He couldn't count the number of times Savannah had been harassed as they'd walked the wharves or from the Conrad Shipping offices to the Shaw ones. Because of her sex and her skin color. Tristan had fought countless men over it.

"It buys us less," Ailene said. She looked at the babe and shuddered again. "I wasn't the first. There were at least four before me."

Tristan slowly nodded, unwilling to ask any more hurtful questions. He'd make a list: who, where, when. See if anyone remembered anything. Savannah had said Ailene was the last one violated. There had to be a reason for that.

"My first mate might've found where the cravat came from. Mary Kate tore it off her attacker."

"And you think that'll help?" Dem grunted again. "You have big dreams, used-to-be fiancé."

"I have promises to keep," Tristan corrected. "And mistakes to remedy."

Ailene held his gaze, her own fathomless in the scant candlelight. When the babe fussed, she startled, as if she'd forgotten she held him. Or held her? Tristan had no idea.

"I promise." He stood and held Dem's gaze. "If you need anything, send word to Conrad Shipping. Tell them Tristan sent you."

"We don't need nothing from you."

"Not for you," Tristan corrected. "For the child."

"Shaw?" Ailene looked down at the crying child.

Taken aback by the name, Tristan swallowed his questions. She'd named the baby after Savannah? It tugged deep inside him, but he only wordlessly nodded and left.

Outside, on the mostly deserted street, he turned for the wharves and his ship. Tristan didn't know what additional questions he had for Arnault, if any, but he didn't want to return to the Grosvenor Square house yet. Aunt Nadia would have questions—or at least knowing looks—and he didn't want to answer anything yet.

Those answers belonged to Savannah alone.

CHAPTER 9

The next morning, Savannah was quite unsurprised to find Tristan waiting for her after breakfast.

Her father scowled, looking as angry as he had when she'd managed to utter the words around a closed throat and shattered heart that Tristan had set sail. Without her. "I can remove him," he threatened, his voice low and hard.

"No, Papa," she assured her father. "It's all right." Probably.

"Talk with him, Savannah," her mother told her once more, though she didn't scold Hugh for threatening Tristan.

Lyneé looked far more sympathetic toward Tristan than Savannah liked. She didn't ask why; she barely understood her own feelings on the matter. Lyneé's sympathy took Savannah off guard, made her feel even more wrong-footed than she already did.

"At least he'll keep you safe," Lyneé said as she nodded at her own footman and headed off to wherever her plans took her today.

But physical safety seemed secondary compared to keeping her heart safe.

Walters scowled at Tristan, and Browne ignored him,

staying in the foyer. It was far too early for this sort of headache.

"May I introduce Mr. Frederic Arnault." Tristan gestured to a tall man with curly blond hair and sparkling blue eyes. "Frederic, Miss Savannah Shaw."

Mr. Arnault bowed, an extravagant show that brought his tall frame low and graceful. He would not disappear into the background no matter where they were. Savannah eyed him with curiosity and a thousand questions racing through her mind.

"Mr. Arnault." She nodded in return and offered a slight curtsy. His lips tilted upward, and his bright blue eyes danced with mirth. "I understand you're responsible for tracking down the silk from the cravat."

"A few well-placed questions," he agreed with a small wave of his hand. "Tristan tells me you're familiar with Karl Van den Berg."

"My family has done business with him," she agreed cautiously. Why the caution, Savannah had no idea. The war was over, and Karl had returned to his legitimate cargo as far as she knew. Even if he continued his smuggling operation, what did it matter to her?

"We imported many fabrics," Arnault said smoothly, as if "imported" wasn't code for "smuggled." Savannah suppressed a grin. "It wasn't difficult to learn the difference between the better quality and the cheap counterfeits."

"I appreciate you looking into this," she said sincerely. Against her better judgment, Savannah found herself liking Frederic Arnault. Though she was still not certain why he stood in her front parlor.

Tristan took her arm and led her away from the doors. As if he'd read her mind, he said, "Arnault won't be accompanying us to the Crichtons' picnic. He's here to speak with your father."

Her eyebrows shot upward. "About the silk?"

"About imports, yes." His hand was warm on her bare arm, and Savannah couldn't decide whether she wanted more of his touch or if she should shake it off. The constant struggle between her two selves exhausted her. "I thought it better for them to talk here, away from the prying eyes of the wharves."

"And you think Papa might know something about it?" Savannah shook her head and took a half-step back. "I already asked, of course."

Tristan dropped his hand and nodded, his blue-green eyes sharp on hers. "It's a step, to see who's importing what. Hugh always keeps track of the competition."

"All right." She agreed with that; her father would know, of course. He kept up with most of the other shipping companies, their cargo, their destinations, their merchant contacts in other countries. Who to do business with and who to avoid.

She stood there for another moment, watching Tristan and trying to discern what her own next step might be.

"Let me introduce Frederic to your father. I'll be right back." Tristan watched her as if she might run from her own house, but Savannah only nodded, taking this moment to breathe freely. Arnault offered another gracious, low bow and disappeared into Papa's offices in the rear of the house.

Savannah thought she should follow. Make the introductions herself, given the complicated relationship she now shared with Tristan. Whatever that relationship was, she had no idea. At one time, it wouldn't have mattered. Now…

She did not take the men to her father's study, did not perform those introductions though she ought. Rather, she stood by the windows and watched the street.

Perhaps after all this, after they discovered the murderer, after she and Tristan went their separate ways once more, she'd visit Christiane, her oldest and closest friend. Savannah frowned. She couldn't remember where Christiane lived.

Dover with her family there? Had Christiane traveled to

Nelda Hall? Savannah frowned harder. She genuinely had no idea. Despite the St. Clairs' living a mere five houses from hers, Savannah had truly cut off all contact with anyone who knew Tristan. She hadn't spoken to any family outside her immediate one since emerging from her grief.

She'd write to Christiane, ask Aunt Nadia where she lived now, perhaps actually visit her godmother and family instead of pretending they all didn't live down the street. For now, all she could see was Tristan.

With her eyes closed, no matter what she thought of, it all revolved around Tristan. Ships and cargo and St. Giles Rookery, picnics and theater and carriages. There stood Tristan, watching her with those penetrating eyes. Savannah wished she could blink him away, force him back into the locked trunk in her mind where she'd stuffed her memories of him three years ago.

"Are you ready?"

His voice startled her, and she whirled from the window. Words flew from her lips before she could stop them. "Why are you here?"

His head tilted, but he didn't pretend to misunderstand. "Is this the best place for such a conversation?"

"Here, in the carriage, on a walk through the square?" She waved it off but didn't look away. "Does it matter?"

"Let's walk the square," he offered. "It's still a little early to leave for the picnic."

The Crichtons' picnic was a ninety-minute drive from town and wouldn't begin until two o'clock at the earliest. Eliza Crichton was a lovely woman, warm and caring, but never on time. Not even, as Savannah recalled, for her own wedding breakfast.

"Let me find Coyle," she said, not entirely certain if she spoke the words or if they forced themselves out.

Her lady's maid didn't say a word when Savannah told her about the walk with Tristan. She merely nodded, kept her comments—and facial expressions—to herself, and went off to find her cloak. For a breath, Savannah debated asking her mother, but Sophia had her own plans for the day. She and Aunt Nadia were off somewhere.

Again, she paused. Savannah had no idea what plans her mother had with Aunt Nadia. In fact, today had been the first time she could remember in three years that Sophia had even mentioned Aunt Nadia specifically.

Savannah shook that off, though it lingered. Nagging at the back of her mind, asking her what else she'd cut out so completely.

It hadn't even occurred to Savannah to ask her mother to chaperone her at Eliza's picnic, as scandalous as that sounded. Even when she and Tristan had been inseparable, she rarely had a chaperone and these days, she was accustomed to making her own way.

Savannah pinched the bridge of her nose. Honestly, everything about their life from before had been scandalous.

The late morning sun shone brightly , and Savannah took a moment to enjoy it as Walters disapprovingly closed the door behind them, with Coyle and Browne walking two steps behind. She tilted her face upward and let the combination of warmth and sunlight seep into her. Coyle did her duty, chaperoning Savannah as if she and Tristan couldn't run off—as if they hadn't numerous times before.

The silence stretched between them for entirely too long considering Tristan had been the one to suggest this walk. That awkwardness weighed down on her, but Savannah kept her head high. People were watching. They always watched her, and now, with word of her supposed reconciliation with Tristan spreading, they'd watch her with even more scrutiny.

"I'm listening," she offered, though her voice snapped more than she'd have liked. She tried to clear her throat, but bitterness lodged there, choking her.

"I don't know where to begin," he admitted. He clasped his hands behind his back, tilting his head just enough that it looked to the outside world like they spoke of the weather. Not of deeply personal matters. "I thought I did, but now it all sounds trivial."

Hot anger singed her skin. Savannah clenched her jaw and kept her gaze straight ahead. She would not shove him into the street or slap him again. In fact, she curled her hands around her reticule to keep from doing so.

"Trivial," she repeated. "The last three years are *trivial*. Your leaving is *trivial*."

"No." The word blasted between them like a pistol shot. "Not like that," he admitted in a softer tone.

She felt his gaze on her but couldn't look at him. If she turned her head, she might break. Instead, Savannah put one foot in front of the other and focused on the square ahead of them.

"What I meant is that every reason I thought I had is worthless now."

"They had to have been important." Her temper boiled again, making reasonableness a thing of the past. "You left without a word, disappeared onto your ship with a five-line letter that explained nothing, and vanished for three years. And all that is worthless now."

"Do you know what it's like to run from yourself?"

They entered the square, with its towering trees and manicured paths. If others walked through here, Savannah didn't see them. She focused on keeping herself straight, head high, tears deep in her heart where no one could see them.

In the distance, a dog barked, horses neighed, and carriages clattered by. Savannah kept her attention on Tristan. The soft crunch of his steps beside her, the tempting warmth of his body.

The kiss from last night.

"I know what it's like to stay," she said, those damnable

words flowing once more. "I know what it's like to think you had everything, only to find out you have only yourself."

"You always knew yourself, who you were, what you wanted. I admired that about you—envied even. I thought I knew myself," he admitted softly beneath the canopy, a slight breeze drifting between them. "I thought I had everything, but I kept hearing voices."

She stopped them and eyed him sharply. His lips twitched. "Not like that."

Rolling her eyes, she continued walking. "All right." He meant the voices of his youth. The stories he used to weave about great adventures and fantastical voyages. "You mean Philip's voice." She didn't sigh but wanted to. "The stories the two of you made up, about spies and excitement."

"I wanted that adventure, the one with spies and pirates and winning against all odds."

He paused, but Savannah couldn't stop moving. Afraid if she did, she might never start again.

"Philip left for his own adventure. Esme, Grayson, and Yara had had theirs, and I—"

"Only had me." She wanted to vomit. Her breakfast churned unpleasantly in her stomach, and she swallowed hard, her palms sweaty.

"No." The word shot between them again and roared in Savannah's ears. "I had everything. *Everything*. But I—I thought I needed more." The words rushed from him now, and Savannah did stop moving then. She turned and watched him, her entire being focused on his next words. Nothing else mattered. "I thought a little adventure, sailing across the North Sea and the Baltic, the cargo and the open sea and the—I thought it was all I needed."

He met her gaze, his eyes full of regret. He was no longer the laughing, charming man she'd once known, nor even the one who had showed up in St. Giles mere days ago. Now he looked broken, as shattered as her heart had been when he left.

"I was wrong. All I needed was you."

TRISTAN HAD MORE he wanted to say. Words and apologies and reasons. He felt them all bubble up in his throat, wanting to break free. He held Savannah's gaze and watched her struggle to keep her emotions in check. No matter how expressionless her face remained, her dark eyes told him all he needed to know.

"I'm sorry," he whispered. "I wanted the adventure I dreamed about as a boy, but it never mattered. The only thing that mattered as a man was you."

Savannah opened her mouth only to instantly snap it closed. Lips pressed tight, hands wrapped around themselves, she turned around. "Let's walk back to the carriage." She closed her eyes and didn't look at the passersby who stared. "I'm tired of being talked about."

They walked in silence, poor Coyle and Browne behind them. At the head of the square, he saw their driver waiting beside the carriage.

"Why didn't you return?"

A strange combination of longing and adventure. Tristan didn't know how to voice that mixture. He'd already left, had boarded the ship, sailed away, and left that note. It had been too late.

"I'd already hurt you. If I stayed away three days or three years, it remained the same."

She nodded, the barest movement of her head. "And your return now?" She swallowed hard. "You clearly planned that. Found me in St. Giles, brought a present."

"How is Jiesha?" He smiled, hoping Van Zanten had gathered all the bad luck possible after Tristan took the rabbit and the man's two indentured servants, as well as their families, who Van Zanten had kept locked away.

"Terrifying the upstairs staff." Savannah sighed, and her shoulders relaxed slightly. "She sits there, chewing on her hay and walnuts, and occasionally running in circles, but the staff is very wary of her." Again she paused, and her fingers loosened just the slightest. "I'm glad you found her."

"I didn't have a plan when I left," he admitted. "It might seem like I did, but in truth, I did not."

She looked at him askance. "You'll forgive me if I don't believe that. You always have a plan. You take after Yara."

"In some ways." He nodded. "Perhaps I should say yes, I did once." Tristan pushed away all the plans he'd made and broken. All but one, even though they moved closer to the street and the carriage that'd take them to the picnic. "When I decided to leave, it wasn't planned. I'm sure you won't believe me, but I promise you, I didn't plan it for weeks. Or even days."

"I see." She nodded, and he wondered what she did or did not see in his confession.

Tristan snorted. "I didn't even pack a bag. I literally found one of my family's ships and prepared to leave."

"Don't lie," she snapped, all the relaxation of her shoulders gone. "You forget, I grew up on the wharves. I know ships and crew manifests and tides."

"I know." He stopped them just before they left the square and faced her. "It truly was that quick. Arnault, he was captain of the ship. All of a sudden, I thought—this was it. I could board and live out all those stories. So I boarded. I don't know what it was about me, the youngest Conrad, who had never captained a ship in his life, but Arnault let me have that title. I changed the crew manifest, sent a note round to the offices so they could inform my parents, and—" He stopped.

"And that note to me."

"And the note to you," he repeated. "It was not planned or

thought out. It was—it was the only thing I'd never truly thought through before."

"Do you regret it?" Her voice held no inflection, and her gaze watched something eminently fascinating over his shoulder. Her fingers twisted around her reticule again, the only outward sign of her feelings. With her shoulders straight and her head held high, no one could tell anything was amiss by looking at her.

"I regret not asking you to join me."

Her gaze flew to his. "Why didn't you?"

He sighed. "I don't know."

Savannah huffed and crossed the street, uncaring of carriages, pedestrians, and pickpockets. Tristan hurried after her, cursing as he skirted a coach's wheels.

"Savannah—"

"Let's leave." She didn't look at him as Browne helped her into the carriage.

Muttering several inventive curses, Tristan followed her. "I thought about it," he admitted as they waited for Coyle. "I did. But something in me thought I needed to do this alone."

"I see." She still didn't look at him.

"I don't think you do," he countered, keeping his voice low. He didn't think anyone could hear them over the racket of hooves and wheels on the street, but this conversation was solely between them. "I didn't think things through; I didn't plan this out. I literally decided one moment and left the next."

Her gaze met his. "I would've joined you."

"I should've asked," he agreed.

"And this return? Why now?"

"I missed you." His voice cracked. "I missed you from the moment the ship sailed. Hours into the voyage, I knew it had been a mistake. But by then it was too late."

She nodded and pulled aside the curtain. The breeze cooled the interior as Coyle entered the cab and they jolted forward.

They maneuvered along the streets toward the outside of town, where the Crichtons held their annual end-of-season picnic.

Tristan let the silence stretch, but he had one more piece of the last three years' puzzle to solve before they arrived. He didn't want to spring it on Savannah, but she'd made it clear she was done listening. For the moment.

Instead, he thought back to what he knew of Eliza and John Crichton. As the carriage bounced harder than a ship in a storm, all he remembered was that Eliza's mother and Sophia Shaw were good friends, and that Eliza accepted Savannah, no matter that society considered her so-called merchant class. Or that her family had descended from slaves.

Tristan had once been friendly with John Crichton and now recalled the man's interest in the shipping business. Perhaps today was the day to start rebuilding some connections.

CHAPTER 10

The moment Savannah stepped from the carriage, Tristan at her side, Coyle behind her, she knew this was a mistake. Not the picnic itself; it was a lovely day. Not even the promise of seeing old friends whom she'd lost touch with after her broken engagement.

It was the fact that Tristan did indeed stand beside her.

She reminded herself she'd wanted this, the stares, the talk, the fact that people would flock to them both—separately and together—for all the gossip they could glean. Even the servants would surround Coyle for any salacious tidbit.

Savannah looked at her lady's maid, who nodded and stepped beside her. "Don't worry, miss. This isn't my first match."

Savannah's lips twitched at Coyle's confident assertion, and she watched the woman disappear to the side, where the staff stood. For as late as they were, after that...that *conversation* in the square, a line of carriages still headed in their direction.

"Savannah!" Eliza held open her arms in an enthusiastic and genuine greeting. She did not look at Tristan. "Oh, I'm so glad you're here." Quickly embracing her with a light kiss to each cheek, Eliza stepped back. Her smile faltered and she reluctantly looked at Tristan. "And Tristan Conrad."

Tristan, ever the consummate gentleman, smiled and bowed. "Mrs. Crichton, a true pleasure."

"Hmm." The edges of Eliza's smile froze, and her gaze cooled. "Savannah, dear, come meet my sister-in-law. She's in her second season and more interested in travel than in securing a husband."

Savannah nodded at Tristan, trusting him to discover whatever he could. He knew why they were here, why they showed the world, or at least the upper crust of British society, they had reunited. The moment they discovered the perpetrators of the attacks, the faster they could resume their separate lives.

The stab in her heart was simply a residual ache from the long, bumpy carriage ride. Nothing more.

"You've forgiven him?" Eliza hissed the moment they'd left Tristan behind. "I'm sorry, Savannah." She squeezed her arm, and Savannah wondered if she might ever relax again. "I didn't mean to spring that on you."

"It's been a rush of…change," Savannah admitted. "I wasn't expecting, well…" She trailed off, unsure how she'd finish that sentence. Drat, she should've planned her answers better. Or at all, for that matter.

"Are you certain about this?" Eliza asked, plastering on a bright smile as they approached a group of people Savannah recalled being friendly. At that moment, she couldn't remember a single name from any group of people, even those she used to enjoy spending time with.

"Eliza, I'm not certain about anything," she admitted. Savannah half turned and looked for Tristan.

She easily spotted him despite the distance and the crowd. As if he knew she was watching him, Tristan turned and met her gaze across the field.

"He still loves you." Eliza sounded almost surprised. Almost. "I guess that kind of love never really dies."

Her gaze shot back to Eliza's. "What do you mean?"

Savannah didn't know if Eliza's comment sickened her, bolstered her, or something else. Something in between.

"Savannah, darling, you two have been in love with each other since you could walk." Eliza shot her a knowing look, one only slightly tinged with jealousy. "I always envied that. The way he looked at you, the way you two knew each other so completely you needn't speak."

It stabbed her, that memory of how easy things used to be. The warm confidence that had once wrapped around her, knowing that she and Tristan were simply Savannah and Tristan. Always. Eliza's words echoed her earlier thoughts. Savannah hadn't realized how deeply she'd held that perception. How cold and isolated she'd become in the years since his leaving.

"We're working through things," she admitted. "He's only been back a few days, but..." Savannah looked at Tristan again, unsurprised that he easily met her gaze.

"Don't rush anything, darling." Eliza squeezed her arm again as they joined the group. "But if it's what you want, I'm so happy for you."

What she wanted? Savannah had no idea. Tristan's explanation this morning had done something inside her.

"Ah, Miss Shaw."

Startled, she blinked up at the man who addressed her and dug through her memory for a name. "Lord Shilby." She offered a curtsy and smiled up at the aged Baron of Shilby. "I had no idea you'd be in attendance today."

"I rely on the weather, my dear." He lifted her hand to his lips and offered a smiling kiss to the back of it. "Today is a good day to venture out and enjoy. I'm never sure how many more I'll enjoy, so I take advantage of what I can."

"I'd forgotten how much I enjoy your company, Lord Shilby." Yes, her shoulders relaxed, and she felt the beginnings of a companionship she hadn't had in three years. Perhaps her mother and sister were right, and she needed to mingle with those she'd once considered close acquaintances, if not outright friends. "It's been too long."

"Walk with me, Miss Savannah." Unable to resist his invitation, she nodded at Eliza and threaded her hand around Shilby's arm, not sure if it was more for propriety or his own security. They moved slowly, his walking stick surprisingly firm on the uneven ground as he led her to a refreshment tent.

A slight breeze cooled the afternoon and rippled along the tents, carrying with it the scent of wildflowers and lemon balm. Savannah looked out over the meadow and wanted to run through it as she had when she was younger. For once, not a cloud marred the sky, and the day proved as beautiful as the morning had promised.

"How are you faring, my dear?" Shilby asked before she could form a question about his son, whose name she couldn't remember.

No, his grandson. She'd been so out of touch; her memories of those she used to know had vanished. Shilby's son had died in the wars. It was only him and his grandson now.

"I'm quite well," she answered almost truthfully.

He shot her a concerned look, his sharp blue eyes seeing more than she'd have liked. "I see young Conrad has returned." Shilby snorted. "I'd heard rumors, but I also heard you slapped him hard enough to send him back to his ship."

Savannah laughed. She couldn't remember the last time she'd laughed so freely, and oh, it felt marvelous. She wanted to know where Shilby gathered his information. As far as she knew, he'd never even heard of Denmark Street, but his wry, almost sour delivery of that line sent her into gales of laughter she hadn't emitted in far too long.

"He's strong enough that it only set him back a couple of steps," she joked in return, still laughing. "Hardly enough to keep him away." Savannah grinned, another sliver of weight off her shoulders, easing from around her heart. "Wherever do you hear such rumors?"

"Bah, you know better than most the necessity of holding on to information." He eyed her as a footman poured a glass of wine for Shilby. She waved it off and accepted the weak lemonade instead.

"I do," she agreed, sipping the beverage and covering her grimace. "But why St. Giles? What could possibly interest you there?"

Shilby's gaze swept the tent, and he turned for the field, where several groups enjoyed shuttlecock and bowls. "Come, my dear." He held out his arm again. "No sense giving the gossips anymore fodder."

"My intent here was just that," she admitted as they strolled the meadow. Best take charge of the conversation. This wasn't the only one she'd have over her and Tristan's supposed reunion. "I'm weary of the rumors and gossipmongers, of the stares and whispers."

"Bah," he snorted again. "People will talk." He slowed his pace, and they meandered toward a large oak, where several tables and chairs had been set up, but, as yet, no one had utilized them. "You know that better than anyone else."

She did, but she preferred not to dwell on the hateful whispers about her ancestry or skin color. The parts about her merchant-class parents she could deal with well enough. Her money might be new, and her father might work for it, but their wealth far outstripped most of the nobility. At least the Shaws also took care of their workers and helped the poor.

Proud of her family and her heritage, Savannah lifted her chin and met Shilby's gaze. "As you say," she agreed.

THE LADY'S COURTSHIP

"What do you know of the troubles in St. Giles?" Shilby settled into his chair and set his glass on the table.

Surprised at the rapid change of subject, Savannah sat opposite him. How on earth did he know about the murders? "I know a lot about the area, Lord Shilby."

He waved that off with an impatient flick of his wrist. "How many times have I told you to call me George?"

"As many times as I reminded you I wasn't going to marry your grandson."

Shilby sighed mournfully, but his eyes sparkled. "A true tragedy, that. The two of you would have made a brilliant couple. You're too smart by half, Miss Savannah." He raised his glass in salute. "I debated matching him with Crichton's sister, but she's more interested in seeing Italy and Greece than marriage."

Smart woman, in Savannah's opinion. "Regarding your curious interest in St. Giles, what information do you have about what's been happening?"

"I don't have many friends," Shilby said instead of answering her question. "Not many I trust, at least." She nodded in understanding and sipped her lemonade. "I consider you a friend."

Touched, she set her glass on the table and placed her hand over his. "That means a lot. George."

Shilby guffawed and downed his whisky in a single swallow. "That's what it takes to have you call me George?" He shook his head and in the next breath turned serious. "Word is there are murders there in broad daylight."

"Yes," she agreed, not seeing any reason not to. She had questions about his sources and why he cared, but she swallowed them down. "With no pattern to them, other than the victims are women who work the theaters. They're all killed the same way." Her voice lowered, though only the trees bore witness to their conversation. "A quick slash across the belly, deep enough they bleed out almost immediately."

Deep enough there was nothing she could do to stop it, to help them or ease their suffering. Nothing save hold their hands as they died. And swear she'd find the culprit.

Shilby nodded. "I've heard that." He held up a hand to forestall her obvious question. "I know many people, my dear." He shook his head. "A beautiful partnership," he added mournfully. "You won't find those criminals here. Eliza and John aren't the sort to cavort with such unsavory types."

She watched the old baron intently and only then realized how savvily he held his thoughts. Shilby used his age as an advantage, and she applauded that. "Do you know where I might discover such unsavory types?"

"Have you ever been to Vauxhall Gardens?"

"No," she said, surprised. "I always wanted to visit, only never did. Why?"

"The fireworks are a sight to see. And it's a fair bit safer than the rookery. A far better place for Conrad to take you, now that he's returned." He stood, and she took his arm again. "Are you and young Conrad truly engaged once again?" He eyed her as they slowly crossed to the tents, the breeze cooler now than she'd expected. Or perhaps it was the chill of Shilby's oblique warning. "Or is it a ruse?"

"I think you know the answer to that, George." Savannah didn't know herself.

"I can't figure it," he admitted. "You always made a handsome couple, and of course your families are well connected to each other." He mournfully shook his head. "Damn shame. Still, keeping power and money intertwined is always smart."

"Perhaps I'll see you tomorrow night in Vauxhall Gardens?" She stepped back, just as conflicted as before over whatever relationship she and Tristan did or did not share. At least she had a new point of focus for the murders.

"I'll make it a point, my dear." He kissed her hand and winked.

Shaking her head and smiling, Savannah turned for Eliza and her sister-in-law—Angela, she thought. Savannah wanted to find Tristan, knew he'd watched her walk across the meadow with Shilby. Instead, she walked purposefully toward Eliza, determined to remember the joy she'd once enjoyed with her friend.

A quick look showed Tristan with the same group, still watching her. It shivered down her spine and out to her fingertips, as if his hand had wrapped around hers and tugged her close.

"Eliza." She smiled brightly, but her friend slightly narrowed her eyes at the brittleness of that smile. "Would you introduce me to Miss Angela?"

IF HE HAD to listen to any more banal conversation about Parliament, taxation, or the amount of money they were forced to spend on the poor for another moment, Tristan might find himself in the gaol for murder. At least his parents would be proud of the reason; it'd be justified.

Once upon a time, Savannah would've been right beside him. Tristan looked across the field to where she stood and wondered how she'd feel now. Indignant over the conversation to be sure, but what of his actions?

He had purposely decided on this group of men. He knew many of them; they'd often tried to invest in Conrad Shipping cargo, then turned around and talked down about his family. Needless to say, they were never invited into any sort of investment, though at the moment they didn't seem to care as he regaled them with stories of Antwerp, Riga, and Rostock.

John Crichton was an exception. He didn't care about social standing, despite being the cousin to a duke. He took people at their worth, not their so-called status, which made him a rare man in Tristan's acquaintance.

"Conrad. I didn't know you'd returned." Crichton's gaze slid toward the other tents, where Savannah stood with Eliza and John's sister. His voice remained as bland as the others in this group, though his quiet, penetrating gaze spoke otherwise. Most of the men here underestimated Crichton, who used it to his advantage. Tristan knew better.

"Only just," he said easily, only part of his attention on the conversation around him. As the youngest Conrad, he'd learned early that splitting his attention kept him out of trouble.

"Walk with me; I'm eager to hear of your adventures." Crichton nodded to several of the men who were watching him with various looks of mockery.

"Still playing the fool, I see." Tristan tilted his head in salute since he didn't have a glass to raise. He never drank; his father had an addiction to alcohol, so they were all mindful not to consume it, even in passing. "Though clearly those men are the more foolish, as they've yet to catch on."

"People see what they want to see. You know that." Crichton gestured for the drinks table, but Tristan waved it off. "Eliza tells me you and Savannah have reunited. Mere days after your return."

"You don't sound convinced." Tristan kept his voice low though he trusted, or used to trust, Crichton, and there were no eavesdroppers nearby.

"Your departure was rather…abrupt, shall we say?" He shrugged, but his gaze didn't waver. "I trust your voyage was a profitable one?"

"Immensely." Tristan had yet to write to his parents about his return, though he suspected Aunt Nadia had sent a trusted messenger round the moment he arrived. They'd discover his return soon enough, when one of the company's secretaries delivered the manifests to Grayson, who now ran the company.

"Trade is booming now that all the embargoes have been lifted. Karl Van den Berg has set up his own offices in Amsterdam and transports goods throughout the Low Countries."

"And that's why you've returned?" Crichton raised disbelieving eyebrows. "You finished your voyages, made your money, and came home?"

Tristan paused before he could deliver a flippant answer. He and Crichton had been friends before he left, not merely friendly enough. They'd run around Harrow together, where Crichton had attended after something happened at Eton, Tristan never did learn what. Harrow, where Tristan ignored all other women and carried on a robust correspondence with Savannah and Savannah only. Not even his mother received as many letters.

"The last three years have taught me much about myself, John." His gaze returned to Savannah, who was laughing with Eliza and a couple other women. She looked relaxed. "And the mistakes I made."

"Hmm." Crichton didn't sound convinced. "Eliza and I were surprised when Savannah accepted today's invitation." He paused, and the weight of what he didn't say—that Savannah hadn't accepted any invitations since he left—lay heavy between them. "Even more so when she wrote you would be accompanying her." Another significant pause, though Crichton was far too polite to say anything negative about the situation outright. "As her fiancé."

"I've learned," Tristan said honestly, "that talking with one's fiancée helps a great many things." He waited, but Crichton only watched him. Definitely time to change the subject. "Have you heard anything about murders in the rookery?"

Crichton snorted and shook his head. "Is that why you're here?"

"I'm here because Savannah wanted to attend." Tristan watched her again, his heart aching, his mind racing with questions about the last years, what she'd done besides healing and midwifery in St. Giles. Why she apparently hadn't socialized.

"Lord Shilby is concerned," Crichton admitted. "He'd never admit it aloud, but he's been asking questions about the area, and I doubt it's for redevelopment."

"Shilby?" Tristan shook his head and eyed the group they'd just left. "You mix with an odd group, John. Always did."

"They're useful." Crichton smirked, there and gone in a moment, before the bland smile he normally wore reappeared. "You should know that, Tristan."

CHAPTER 11

"Well?"

Savannah looked up from the pile of correspondence she only pretended to read. Instead of the words written before her, her mind raced over yesterday's events. Her and Tristan's conversation, of which she'd only scratched the surface. She still had questions, and she knew they'd only started down the path of what happened.

She was still trying to sort through Lord Shilby's comments and her and Tristan's ride back to the square. And their incredibly awkward goodbye.

"Well what?" She met Lyneé's gaze with as innocent a look as she could muster.

She'd enjoyed yet another wonderful sleepless night in which her memories of Tristan's kiss overlapped with his confession about leaving her.

"Don't give me that look, Savannah." Lyneé huffed and sat across from her, pouring a cup of tea. She settled Jiesha, contentedly chewing a piece of hay, on her lap. She did not elaborate.

"Eliza's picnics are always entertaining." Savannah sipped

her own coffee, not in the mood to rehash all that had happened yesterday. Or the last few days. "I understand John's youngest sister is determined to travel rather than marry. And Lord Shilby attended."

"Still trying to marry you off to his worthless grandson?" Lyneé tilted her head and stared into her teacup. "Perhaps not a terrible idea. They're wealthy, the title is older than many, and they possess a great deal of land. Definitely someone who'd stay at home."

Boredom, tediousness, bland dinner table conversation for the rest of her life. Not a man she'd ever imagined kissing, let alone making love with. Yet something George Shilby had said yesterday nagged at her. What had he said about his grandson? Whose name Savannah couldn't even remember.

Something about a brilliant couple. George Shilby didn't suffer fools and never, ever talked down about his grandson— perhaps also named George? She truly couldn't remember. Despite their familial ties, Savannah doubted George would've let that keep him from disparaging the man if he thought it warranted. Perhaps it had been the grandson who reported the murders?

"He suggested Vauxhall," Savannah admitted, too exhausted to sort out the tangle of thoughts racing through her sleep-deprived brain.

Instead, she reached around the table and plucked Jiesha from Lyneé's lap. Stroking the white-and-black rabbit's soft fur, Savannah seriously considered returning to bed. Or at least the chaise lounge, where she might close her eyes for a few moments.

"Are you going?"

Back to bed? Yes, she'd very much like that. "No, I have—oh. Tonight?" Savannah shook her head, but all that did was make it spin and remind her that she needed the sumptuous breakfast before her. She set Jiesha on the floor, where the rabbit promptly hopped off under the bed, then piled her plate with eggs, toast, fresh yogurt, and berries.

"When else?" Lyneé frowned at her. Then, as if she'd read Savannah's mind, she said, "Perhaps a nap would not be out of order. You look exhausted. Are you sleeping at all?"

Of course she wasn't, but admitting it only meant that Lyneé would force her to admit more. Such as her conversation yesterday, which she didn't wish to repeat.

"As I'm sure you understand, the last few days have been busy."

Lyneé snorted as Savannah forced herself to eat the yogurt and berries. "Busy. Is that what it's called these days? Finish your eggs, Savannah."

Sipping her coffee instead, she tried to remember where their conversation had originally headed. Right. "We'll visit Vauxhall tonight." She paused. "Though the place is much larger than either of us can safely watch, I believe we can at least observe the right crowd."

Had Lord Shilby known more? Was he going to tell her something about the murders at Vauxhall? That seemed wrong —why not tell her yesterday afternoon at the picnic? She couldn't make the connection this morning. Still Vauxhall felt wrong, a misdirection though she doubted Shilby would do so purposely.

Savannah dutifully finished her meal and willed her stomach to settle. Then she stared blindly at the invitations on the tray beside her, the ones Walters had silently delivered with a concerned look, and tried to form a plan.

So far, the one she had devised included pretending to be engaged to Tristan and kissing him in the staff hallways of the theater. Her brilliance at planning had lost considerable shine.

"I don't think this fake engagement was at all wise," she admitted to her sister.

"He didn't say anything during your stroll yesterday?"

Lyneé's voice softened, and she quietly set down her teacup. "Nothing about why he so abruptly disappeared? Or reappeared?"

"He did," Savannah admitted slowly. "He said he had no plan, that it was something he felt he needed to do." Savannah stopped, the last berry sticking in her throat. "I don't think we're finished with that conversation." She paused and smiled ruefully. "I'm certainly not."

All her anger, the spewing hot rage she wanted to rain down on him, was still bottled up inside her. Now, however, Savannah didn't know if those words of loss and anger meant anything. Perhaps her lack of sleep had tempered her anger and sense of betrayal.

"And after?" Lyneé asked the same question she had days ago, but Savannah still hadn't an answer. Lyneé finished her own toast, setting her napkin beside her plate. Her dark eyes watched Savannah seriously, without that hint of anticipation from earlier.

"After?" Savannah repeated less in question because she had no idea.

"Please," Lyneé scoffed. "Don't tell me you haven't thought about after."

She had. Mostly that Tristan would leave her again, since it seemed she was so easy to leave. "I've thought about it," she said softly.

"Truly?" Lyneé watched her carefully, voice softer now. "About the scandal that will follow you? Two broken engagements to the same man isn't something society overlooks."

Savannah knew but waved it away with a shrug. "I'm not interested in marriage." It tasted like a lie, but she didn't want to think about it just then. First, she needed to sort through her feelings for Tristan. "Right now, my focus is on the murdered women, on giving them the justice they deserve."

"And after?" Lyneé asked again. "What happens then?"

"I don't know," Savannah admitted.

They'd go their separate ways, with perhaps less hurt and anger and recrimination. Perhaps she'd seriously consider Lord Shilby's grandson. Though, with the scandal of two broken engagements to the same man, he probably wouldn't consider her, no matter what George claimed. Maybe she'd live out her life helping in St. Giles, without a husband.

"I need to get through today first." And tonight, and tomorrow night.

And she needed more than a walk through the square to speak with Tristan. Before her heart forgot its hurt and only remembered his kisses.

TRISTAN HAD WANDERED the house since before dawn. He'd finally written his parents, letting them know of his safe arrival. He'd also written Esme, his eldest sister, and let her know he'd been staying in London, though she probably already knew that. Aunt Nadia would have told her, of course.

He'd already met with a suspiciously wide-eyed and far-too-innocent Arnault about where they planned to sail next. Arnault was more interested in his and Savannah's rendezvous in Vauxhall this evening than in port destinations. Finally, Tristan agreed to a meeting with John Crichton.

Tristan hadn't an answer for Arnault, no burning desire to sail or see new lands. Once upon a time, he'd thought about sailing toward China, but now he thought closer to home. He wasn't running away until he and Savannah had sorted through the last three years.

Now he stood before the Shaws' door, no closer to any answers.

Walters opened the door, his gaze trained somewhere over Tristan's shoulder, and offered a monotone greeting.

"Miss Savannah is just finishing breakfast. You can wait in the front parlor."

Tristan didn't protest. Once upon a time, he'd have joined her without question. Now he stood by the window overlooking the just-waking street and accepted his outsider status.

The day had dawned overcast, the wind cooler as it blew along the street, picking up small bits of rubbish and leaves. Tristan clasped his hands behind his back and watched it, thoughts swirling with the leaves and discarded broadsheets.

He felt her presence before she'd said a word. A lifetime of staying near her, always the two of them, hadn't deserted him as he'd once thought. "When I left," he began, still looking at the street, "I thought I'd return a different person."

Savannah closed the doors behind her and stepped further into the room. "Do you feel like a different person?"

"Yes and no." He tilted his head from side to side and turned from the windows. "I saw lands I always dreamed about. I met people I never would've met here. Arnault, for one." His lips twitched. "I found Jiesha."

"You don't sound…I don't know, happy. Changed. Pleased with your choices." She sounded cautious herself.

In the silence between them, Tristan watched her move across the floor, her steps quiet, the only sound the faintest swish of her gown. She stole his breath, that ache for her unrelenting.

"I can't remember all I said yesterday," he admitted. "Words weren't adequate to explain my feelings. I missed you every day. Every minute of the day, no matter what went on around me." Tristan met her guarded gaze. "I'm sure that sounds trite and unoriginal, as if I hadn't left of my own free will."

"I—" She swallowed but didn't look away. She eased another step into the room, around the settee, her fingers clasped gently in front of her. "I understand that," she finally admitted. "That contrast of fury and heartbreak and of missing you desperately."

She closed her eyes for the briefest of heartbeats, only to open them and watch him as if she expected him to leave once more.

"I wrote you daily," he admitted. "Like when I was at Harrow." Tristan's lips quirked, and he shook his head. "It's not enough; I don't know that anything ever will be."

"Why did you find me in St. Giles?"

"I followed my heart," he admitted. "We docked, and while I spoke with one of the secretaries, Arnault visited your offices. The secretary knew where you were and, I think before he thought better of it, told Arnault. So I put Arnault in charge of the unloading, and I went to find you."

"Will you leave again?" Her fingers briefly tightened around each other, but her face remained still. "After all this, with the murders, will you leave again?"

Not without her. Never again. Tristan didn't know if she wanted him, if she could ever forgive him, but he'd fight. For no other reason than he hadn't before.

"That depends on you," he admitted. "I want to make things better, see if we can work anything through, but I know I have a lot to atone for. Since I'm being honest, I do have another confession."

Her back stiffened, but she nodded warily.

"You're the only woman I ever loved. The only one I ever touched. I never wanted another, and I don't foresee a time when I ever would."

The mask covering her face cracked, and she looked honestly surprised. Her lips parted, and she seemed to struggle for words. Tristan crossed the room, skirting tables and chairs, and took her hands.

They gripped his, cold and shaking slightly.

"You don't?" Her voice barely carried between them. "I thought…I thought you wanted other women, that's why you left so abruptly. That you wanted to explore without me because you didn't want me—"

"No." He squeezed her fingers. "Savannah, no. Never. You were the first woman I ever kissed and the only one I ever wanted to."

She blinked and nodded ever so slightly. "And now that you've had your grand adventure? Now that you saw those places? What happens now?"

"That's still up to you." Which wasn't exactly what he wanted to say, but he was no fool.

Deep in his heart, he was terrified that he'd push too hard and lose her forever. He'd fight all of Denmark Steet for her. Dredge up every mistake he'd ever made. All for another chance.

"All right." She nodded, and for the first time since he saw her on that street in the rookery, Tristan thought she looked relaxed around him. Not so guarded, not so tense. Not as if she were about to break. Her fingers were still wrapped around his, looser now, as if she didn't grasp him with everything in her, afraid he'd vanish once more.

Progress, he thought. Hoped.

After another silent moment, Savannah dropped his hands and stepped back. "Have we a plan for tonight?"

"Plan?"

"Yes," she said dryly, with a look that clearly called his brain into question. "A strategy, an organizational idea, an understanding about what we're walking into and what needs doing."

He didn't roll his eyes, but it was a close thing. "I know what a plan is, Savannah," he muttered.

"You used to. Things change." She sat primly on the settee and tilted her head up to look at him. But her mouth had lost that tense look of the previous days, and her gaze softened.

He did roll his eyes then and sat beside her. "I'm uncertain if attending Vauxhall tonight, or any night, is worth our time."

"I can agree with that. However, I also trust Lord Shilby."

"You would," he muttered before he could think better of it.

Savannah glared, and Tristan met her gaze with an innocent look of his own. "Is he still trying to marry you off to his doormat of a grandson?"

"He knew of the murders, brought them up himself," she reminded him rather than answer the question.

Which meant, as far as Tristan was concerned, that yes, Shilby had indeed tried to match them. Again. He let it go, or tried to. It wasn't as easy as the words made it sound.

Before his departure—which sounded rather tame compared to what it truly was—Tristan hadn't cared. Savannah was anyone's idea of a perfect match. However, back then, she'd been his. Now, jealousy wormed through him, a hot, sickly feeling.

"I am curious how he knew," Tristan finally said. He swallowed against his jealousy, the part that made him want to find Shilby, and his grandson, and have it out, one way or another. Instead, he shoved it aside. "Whatever happened in the rookery isn't likely to make it to the floor of the House of Lords." He paused and tried to remember his conversation with Crichton. That memory was slightly jumbled with their other conversation, about him and Savannah, but Crichton had mentioned Shilby's interest in the murders.

"John said he knew something. Not he himself, I don't think," Tristan amended. "But that Shilby was concerned with it."

"The fact that both men knew of it, had spoke of it with us, tells me there's more to this than the women of St. Giles being murdered." Savannah paused again, and he wondered what she was thinking.

He used to simply know. But then, in all their time together, they'd never tried to solve a murder. Or murders. Still, he agreed with her.

"What?" He shook his head. "A roving band of young bucks out for sport? Why would either Shilby or Crichton care? They have more morals than most, I agree, but I'm still not seeing the connection."

"If you were carousing with friends," she said slowly, "where would you start?" Savannah turned and met his gaze. "I don't necessarily mean you. I mean a young buck."

"One of the gaming hells, I'd think." He let the part about not him slide. She knew he didn't gamble or drink. She knew all his secrets, those he didn't think even his parents or closest friends knew.

"And from there?" She frowned. "More drinking and gambling, so you'd move on to another hell?"

"Most likely. There are dozens of brothels, and even more gaming hells." Tristan paused. "I think we're starting in the wrong place."

She met his gaze, already nodding. "We're looking at the afterward, not the beforehand. What happens in the very end, when they stumble their way here." She frowned again. "Why would Lord Shilby direct me to Vauxhall? It's nearly three miles from Denmark Street, on the opposite side of the Thames."

Tristan ticked off his ideas on his fingers. "He either knows something we don't, or he wants something from you." Like marriage to his grandson for one.

Savannah was a diamond of the first water, and he'd fight—and had—any man who said otherwise. But no man of the *ton* would consider marrying her. They'd made that abundantly clear.

"Or he's misdirecting us," Savannah finished. She frowned and shook her head. "I doubt it's that. He need never bring up the subject at all, but he made it a point to. So why Vauxhall? He seemed keen on meeting us there."

Tristan stood, pulling her up with him. "We'll speak with Dem and see what the women know about the brothels."

She watched him curiously. "You'll visit the local brothels?"

How many times in a single conversation could they use that

word? If Tristan were a betting man, he'd have placed money on her father calling him out for introducing it. Then again, Hugh hadn't so far, even with more than enough reason to do so.

"You are not accompanying me," he insisted flatly.

She opened her mouth, then shook her head. "All right. I can agree with that." That went smoother than he thought. But if Savannah agreed, she'd keep her word.

"I'll pick you up after supper." He still held her hand and squeezed gently. "I'll check in with Arnault, see if he's found anything more. I have my cabin boy eavesdropping on several of the stores Arnault is looking into."

"I need to visit a couple women first, and Eliza has invited me to tea. And I'll send Lord Shilby a note about us not attending Vauxhall tonight." She watched him carefully but didn't pull away. "Will you join me for an early supper? Before we make our way to Denmark Street?"

He smiled, feeling a piece of his heart slotting back into place. "I'd be delighted."

CHAPTER 12

"Do you know how tediously exhausting it is to wander Bond Street in search of the exact maker of a very specific black silk cravat?" Tristan sighed dramatically as he walked up behind Savannah on the crowded street.

She turned, unsurprised to see him, since they'd already made plans for dinner. That gave him pause. Not because Savannah wasn't constantly aware of her surroundings—one had to be in the rookery, especially a woman. No, for a heartbeat, he hoped it was because she knew he'd followed her. That she knew it was him, as she had once always known where he stood.

Now, standing with her in the most unlikely of places, he swore Savannah's lips twitched. Whether in annoyance or humor, he couldn't tell, but at least it was a reaction. She walked along the street quite alone, which made the skin between his shoulders itch. He knew she carried her dagger in her specially made pocket, but it would take her precious seconds to reach for it.

Even if she wore it on her hip, it'd take too long as far as he was concerned. Then again, she'd assured him that Dem and his gang would protect her. They might, but at that moment, he didn't see anyone else following her.

"Where's Browne?" He looked behind her but didn't see her footman or Peters. Not even one of Dem's lieutenants.

"Waiting at the carriage," she said, pausing near an abandoned doorway and turning to face him. "Why? Miss him already?"

Tristan ignored that, though part of him was grateful for the joking manner in which she said it. He asked seriously, "Why isn't he protecting you?"

She sighed but didn't roll her eyes or snap at him.

Definite progress, he thought.

"He was, for a long time. Still would be, if I let him." She stepped closer, and her voice lowered. "Part of it is that the women weren't comfortable, and if he stood behind me, they wouldn't share what was truly the problem. He helps deliver food baskets to the houses that will accept them, then waits beside the carriage. An added protection for any would-be thieves."

"All right." He still didn't like it, but at least it was a valid point. "And the other reason?"

"Dem controls the street. If it looks as if he can't protect me, then he loses power, and I lose protection. No one wins."

Tristan scowled. "No one is protecting you now." He waved a hand around them, where people milled through the filthy streets, some in threadbare shoes, most of the children barefoot. Not one looked like her protector.

"As I'm sure you remember," she said condescendingly, "I can take care of myself." Savannah paused and frowned. The relaxation in her shoulders stiffened now, and her eyes grew wary. "Though I admit, it's odd no one is here. Not even Robbie, who usually follows me everywhere."

He remembered Robbie. The lad had raced to do Savannah's

bidding, finding the vicar and reporting sharply to Dem. Had that been for show? To show Tristan, the newcomer, just how much power Dem had over this little street?

Having spoken to both Dem and Ailene, Tristan doubted it. They cared about Savannah. Indeed, many of the people here did. Even at the theater, Moll had shown worry about Savannah's questioning so dangerous a topic.

"Why are you here?" Savannah asked, her hand on his arm. Probably to draw his attention back to her and away from the street. Still, her touch was warm and soft. "I'm sure it's not for the sights, as captivating as they are."

He snorted and steered her forward once again. Not Dem's house, he noted. "Who are you here to see?"

"I see many women. Several have had babies in the last month and need care." She stopped again, hugging the house, heading away from the street and its river of filth. "Browne and I delivered food to several mothers earlier. No one here has enough, especially not the new mothers. I bring enough food for the family for a couple of days, but it's best I do so with an armed guard."

That made sense. Food was the costliest commodity. If Savannah delivered baskets every few days, she'd need more than one guard, though Tristan knew Browne could hold his own better than most. He'd fought in the Peninsular Wars, part of the Rifle Corps. Knowing that didn't lessen Tristan's unease. He wanted to say more, but he knew her all too well. He'd fight with her about her safety later—and it'd be a fight, no doubt about that.

One thing at a time.

"What did you find out?" she asked, nodding at his pocket, as if he carried the cravat with him.

"Do you know how many kinds of silks there are?" he asked easily. Glancing around as if he hadn't a care in the world, he noted several men watching her from across the street and down three houses. She didn't seem concerned, and Tristan didn't recognize any of them from his time here. Not part of Dem's gang, then. "Who are they?"

Savannah slid her gaze to the side and sighed. "People who don't approve of my being here. Those who don't want their wives or daughters accepting the help of a woman of my color."

Tristan scowled. He didn't know if his next step involved thrashing the lot of them for that insult or something else, but Savannah's hand stopped him. This time, she hadn't placed a staying grip on his arm, but took his hand.

"They aren't worth it. Dem controls them, for the most part. Those who don't accept my help aren't forced into it, but that doesn't stop a small number of people from trying to run me off the street." She paused, holding his gaze. "The cravat?" she asked again, softer this time. She also, he noted, hadn't released his hand.

"Right." He memorized the faces of the small group—four men who looked as filthy and malnourished as the rest of the street—just in case they made a move he didn't like. "Silks. There are far too many for me to keep track of them all."

She offered a small laugh and tilted her head, looking up at him with a slight smirk. "You are many things, Tristan. Fashionable isn't one of them."

"Not fashionable!" He glowered, but his lips lifted slightly. He looked down and met her gaze. When he looked up again, the men had drifted away, into one of the houses. "I would have you know I'm quite fashionable. The height, even, I'd say."

"My apologies." Her lips twitched again, and he swore she fought back a laugh. "Perhaps I should've said you aren't cognizant of the *latest* fashions."

"Hmm," he mumbled disbelievingly.

"Silks?" she prompted innocently.

"I spent the morning wandering Bond Street with Arnault.

He knows more about fabrics than anyone has a right to," Tristan grumbled.

Arnault had lectured him on silks, satin silks, imported Chinese silks, and the method for discerning quality based on how much…something was in the silk bundles. Twigs? Debris? Arnault had specified, but Tristan couldn't remember the term now.

He'd also spent the morning ignoring Arnault's none-too-subtle hints that perhaps Miss Savannah would like this silk or that as they passed the dressmakers and milliners. That maybe he should think about gifts for the lovely woman rather than murders and assailants.

"Tristan," Savannah cut in disbelievingly. "You once quoted to me an entire treatise on newfound animals on the penal colony of Australia. If anyone has more knowledge about anything than they should, it's you."

"I like animals," he muttered. "I'm not that fond of silk production."

She rolled her eyes, which sparkled in the hazy overhead light. Thin clouds covered the sky, making the day seem to shimmer rather than shine. He'd forgotten that particular quirk of London, that it could rain one minute and be sunny and cloudless the next.

"And this imported silk. You found a seller?"

"Arnault is still working on that," he promised. "My cabin boy is still eavesdropping around various sellers."

"Then why are you here?"

I missed you. I'm sorry. Please forgive me for being an idiot. I love you.

He had a list, but, somehow, they were never in the perfect place to talk. Or maybe there was no such thing and he put it off because her answer, and a future without her, terrified him.

Savannah waited, but he didn't immediately answer.

"Please." She sighed, annoyed with both herself for wanting more from him and with him for not being able to offer it. "I have several more families to visit before my tea with Eliza."

"It's—" He reached out and stopped her, holding her hand tightly in both of his. "It's not that. I'm here because I need to keep you safe. That has never changed. I'm here because I realize I talked a lot about what I wanted and not about you."

"About me?" Savannah took a startled step back. "What about me?"

"What you did in the last three years." His voice remained quiet. Not soft, but…sorrowful, she thought. "How you changed."

"I didn't chan—" She cut herself off. Of course she'd changed.

She'd hidden away, cut off contact with friends and family and anyone who had known Tristan. Christiane, her oldest and dearest friend. Aunt Nadia, her beloved godmother. Every single one of the Conrads, though she'd always regarded them as close as her own family. Her grandmother, whom she hadn't seen in years because she refused to travel to Nelda Hall.

"I didn't…at first," she admitted, the words coming haltingly from her as if pulled out. "I didn't know what to do."

Then, because it was important to her to say and for him to know, she swallowed and dived in.

"I cut off all contact," she admitted, skipping over the pain of his sudden departure. No need to rehash the crying and anger and heartache. "Your parents wrote, arrived within days. I'm sure Aunt Nadia told them, or perhaps Esme. She visited, too. I couldn't speak to any of them, though they were all understanding of why." Her lips twisted, and the pain she'd buried for so long finally began to diminish. "I think they wanted to skewer you as badly as I did."

Tristan grunted and nodded. "I'm sure. I deserved it, too."

She held his gaze and wanted to agree, but finally found it within herself to release that pain and anger. She'd held onto it for so long that she truly had changed.

"Then I picked myself up. I didn't know what else to do, so I gathered Browne and found Denmark Street." She nodded around, at the street as familiar to her as her own, even with its ever-changing residents, its crumbling façade and stench. "I help here. I'm useful here."

"You thought you weren't useful before?" He couldn't mask his surprise. His hand tightened around hers, pulling her closer both physically and metaphorically.

"I don't know," she admitted. "I had to move on after you left. Become more independent, I suppose you could say. Or as independent as a woman can be."

"What do you want now?" he asked, his fingers soft over the inside of her wrist.

Savannah didn't think that stroking made her forgive him, but it felt as if with every stroke of his fingers on her bare skin, a piece of her anger evaporated.

She shrugged. "I don't know."

"Savannah. What do you want?"

"I don't know how to say it any more plainly," she snapped, tired of arguing, of the weight of her anger, of not knowing what she wanted.

Mostly that. She'd wanted Tristan for so long, wanted the life they'd planned together. Then he left, and she'd been forced to pick up whatever pieces of her life remained, to build them into a wall surrounding her heart. One that protected her from hurt, from the searing agony of having been left behind.

"I don't know how to forgive you, Tristan." She hadn't meant to say his name. Doing so hurt, though of course he stood before her watching her with guarded eyes that looked like he'd break at any moment. "I don't know what you expect of me."

"I don't either," he admitted. "I know I hurt you, that 'hurt' is not an adequate word to describe it. I—I was a fool, thinking my leaving wouldn't change anything."

Savannah thought she should stay angry at him. He left; he had no right to look so worn down and exhausted. Yet she couldn't, not when he stood before her looking broken. When she had changed also, and there, she realized, lay the crux of the matter.

Forgiving him wasn't the hardest thing she'd ever had to do.

"I've always been the planner of the family. You're right; I take more after Yara than anyone else." His lips twisted into a rueful grin. "I planned everything out, planned out a life with you." He gingerly squeezed her hand.

"I know. I was there," she added in jest, but it came out quieter than she'd wished.

"I planned everything from my career to our future, but suddenly there it was. This opportunity." He shook his head again, and his words tumbled out faster. "I didn't run from you, though I know it might look like that. It was more, here's a ship. Here's a ship that's sailing out right now, and you can go with her."

"So you said." She eyed him skeptically. "I find that hard to believe. It's not at all like the Tristan I know." Knew.

"I didn't say it was wise." He didn't smile or joke it away, but held her gaze, serious and steady. "It simply was. That's what I chose, and I chose wrong." He shook his head, eyes closed for a brief moment. When he met her gaze again, the weight of that choice sat heavy in his eyes. "I don't know if Arnault thought I was running from something or what, but I eventually told him about you."

His fingers brushed the inside of her wrist in long, slow movements. Savannah shivered, her fingers flexing against his at the forgotten touch. She struggled for a comment, anything, but could only manage, "He must have been very confident in his role if he let you captain the ship."

Tristan tilted his head and frowned. Slowly, he nodded, his fingers still doing delicious things against her skin. She wanted to pull away. She wanted him to never stop.

"I hadn't thought of that, but you're right. He knew what he was about, saw me, a green Conrad out for adventure or risk or whatever, and offered me that chance."

"Why tell me this now?"

"Because telling you my feelings is important. I should have told you before I left, but I didn't fully realize them then. Things would've been different if I had."

She pulled back, too tempted by his touch, his heartfelt confession. She needed space. She couldn't breathe and doubted it was because of the closed-in feel of Denmark Street and the houses literally falling down around them. Her hand dropped from his, and she took another step back. She didn't know how to respond. "Thank you" seemed trite.

"I don't know how I feel," she admitted honestly, taking another step backward. "I—when you left, it felt as if my heart had been cut out and stomped on."

"I'm sorry." His anguished whisper floated over the growing distance between them. "It's so inadequate, but I am. Deeply."

Savannah nodded and turned, at a loss about their next steps. Or hers, for that matter. She gripped her basket, tears blurring her vision, her only thought that she needed to leave.

"Savannah!"

Tristan's shout, the cold fear in it, made her whirl back toward him. She instinctively reached for her dagger, her heart pounding in fear.

She didn't see what happened. One minute, tears blurred her vision and her throat ached with too many emotions to properly sort through. The next, Tristan's face filled her view, his eyes wide with fear and anger and something else.

Then he tackled her off her feet, and the world spun.

CHAPTER 13

The problem with people trying to murder you, Savannah thought as Tristan's body slammed into hers, knocking her to the ground, *is that it's always unexpected.* She supposed, as she gasped for breath and absently wondered if it was because of the impact or Tristan's body pressed tight against hers, that was the nature of such things.

Better to lie in wait for the chance than let someone prepare.

Blinking up at Tristan, the overwhelming odor of rubbish and sewage wafting around her and something she never wished to identify seeping through her gown, Savannah opened her mouth, wished she hadn't, coughed, and tried again. She pushed against his chest—also a mistake. His solid muscles tempted her far more than she wanted.

Oh, but she wanted. It burned through her, a wildfire of need she'd suppressed for three years. She must've made a sound, because he looked down at her, his blue-green gaze blazing with worry and fear and, yes, desire.

"Savannah."

The way he said her name rushed through her, curling her own desire hotter and tighter until she thought she'd forget everything that had happened between them. She wasn't proud that it took her more than a moment to tamp down that desire, but she did. Eventually. Somewhat.

"What happened?" To her own ears, her voice sounded calm. A definite point in her favor despite the way her heart raced and her body yearned for his touch.

Damn traitorous thing.

Tristan stood in one smooth, graceful move and offered a hand. As unwilling as she was to take it, she was equally unwilling to touch any more of the street than she already had. Accepting his help, she allowed him to pull her off the street, all too aware of the wetness against the hood of her cloak. Grateful for the barrier, she gingerly removed the hood and let it drop against her back.

It did so with a wet plop.

Savannah grimaced. That was never coming clean.

"Someone tried to kill you," Tristan said, as if she hadn't been there.

"I am aware," she said testily. When Tristan had shouted her name, the fear in that single word had frozen her blood. A shiver raced down her spine and her heart refused to calm. Other than the breath knocked from her, and the stench on her cloak and gown, she wasn't harmed. "Did you see who?"

"No, he was in a greatcoat." Tristan frowned and looked around the street. "I don't know which direction he went, either."

Savannah nodded, only belatedly realizing what a foolish move that was. The incident had rattled her more than she'd have liked. "How do you know he tried to kill me?"

She met his gaze, somewhat steadier now. Tristan gripped her elbow, uncaring about the grime, and she took a deep breath for the first time since seeing him. Perhaps for the first time in three years. But she didn't shake off his hand or step back.

Not yet. She needed that comfort, even as the buzzing in her head quieted.

"I saw the glint of the blade." He frowned. "I don't know where the man came from, he appeared off the street. I only saw his knife. Nothing else made sense, only the blade aimed at you."

She blinked up at him as the street returned to its normal activities—drinking, gambling, and ignoring everyone else. Savannah heard what he hadn't said. That he'd focused on the blade, on her, not on the person wielding it.

"You could've tackled *him* instead," she offered, rolling her shoulders against the pain that crashing to the street had caused.

She looked around for her basket and stooped to lift it, wincing at the sharp stab of pain when she did so. Savannah ignored it and picked up the basket, which was also soaked through with grimy rainwater and rubbish and unmentionable slime. There was a dent where someone had kicked it. Holding it away from her skirts, though she didn't know why she bothered, Savannah met Tristan's gaze.

He blinked at her. Then he grinned and laughed, steering her back down the street toward St. Giles in the Fields and her carriage. "I hadn't even thought about that."

"Of course you hadn't." She almost laughed, but her stomach was twisted into knots, and her heart continued to race. "I am grateful," she said softly, holding his gaze and offering a small smile. It was the most her lips could move, no matter how she tried. "Thank you."

"This is the second time someone's tried to kill you." His voice lost its humor, its edge now harsh.

"First," she corrected. "That man had nothing to do with me. He was clearly the target." She paused and remembered that day, though it blurred now with what just happened.

"Savannah." He snapped her name, but she held up a hand.

"I'm tired, filthy, and hungry. I need to apologize to Browne for the mess I'm about to create in the carriage, I should find Dem and tell him what happened so he can assert his authority, and I'll need a bath."

Desperately.

"I can agree with all that." He sighed, turning her to face him. "I don't care how you feel about it, or about me."

"Tristan," she warned, already knowing where this conversation was headed.

"Savannah, someone tried to kill you!" He tempered his voice, but his fear and anger shook through her. "I don't care if you think it was the second time or the first. I'm accompanying you every time you visit St. Giles from now on."

"I can take care of myself, I don't need—" She stopped.

She'd had that argument a hundred times over the last few days. And that was when no one knew for certain what had happened. Now, there was no getting around it. Someone had clearly tried to kill her, slice her open as they had the other women.

Savannah wasn't invincible, no one was no matter their wealth. Standing on the street, aching from Tristan's tackle, and more determined than ever to discover who murdered her women, she nodded. She was finished closing herself off, making her own way when she had resources and people willing to help.

"All right." She almost told Tristan he couldn't tell her family, but that would've been pointless. "I'll inform Papa he needn't hire any of the dockworkers." That was something, at least. "But I warn you, I won't stop my work here. And I won't hide myself away."

Not anymore. Never again.

Tristan nodded. A curt agreement, but an agreement, nonetheless. "I know you won't." His voice softened, and his hand caressed the inside of her wrist where her glove stopped.

Arousal danced over her arm, shivering across her shoulders

and down her spine. Once more, she wanted to jerk her hand away from his all too tempting touch. Once more, she did not. Savannah told herself it was because she didn't want to show weakness.

But it'd been so long since he'd caressed her, since she felt anyone's soft touch on her skin. She hadn't wanted anyone else. Ever, not since the first time they met.

"I'll find Dem and let him know what happened." He looked behind her, scanning the area as if he might see the man who attacked her. They both knew he was long gone. "There's little he can do now, but if he has as much power on the street as you say, then you're right. He ought to know."

Tristan turned, and they resumed their walk for the carriage. When Browne spotted her, his eyes widened, and his face paled.

"Miss Savannah!" He raced across the street, ignoring people, hackneys, and horses alike.

"I'm quite all right, Browne." She offered a small smile, but her body ached, and her nerves hadn't quite settled.

"Someone tried to kill her," Tristan said, his voice commanding. "From now on, I'll be accompanying her every time she visits here."

Browne, who had up until now eyed Tristan as if he were the filth on the bottom of his shoe, offered a curt nod and grunt of agreement. "I'll inform the servants, miss. We won't allow you to come here alone."

"I will talk to my father," Savannah said as Tristan helped her into the carriage. That ought to be about as much fun as having half the company's dockworkers follow her around.

She'd managed to convince her father that Browne needn't follow her everywhere. After her initial encounter with Dem, and her own prowess with her dagger, Dem had ensured her safety. That had changed now, and Savannah wasn't fool enough to brush this off. Someone had, indeed, tried to kill her. It left her shaken and vulnerable.

"Be careful." Tristan leaned in, his eyes blazing. She had a feeling it wasn't only anger and fear there. It drew her in, and though she scolded herself for the move, Savannah leaned toward him. "I'm not ready—"

To lose her. He didn't say the words; he didn't need to. Savannah understood. Another brick in the wall around her heart crumbled and fell away.

"You be careful," she warned. "You promised me dinner tonight."

His hand brushed her cheek, and he leaned in, pressing his lips against her forehead. Savannah most definitely did not melt at the touch.

"For you, always."

"Ah, the used-to-be fiancé." Dem walked casually up to Tristan, who was in no mood for pleasantries.

The glint of the knife still blinded him, even now. Tristan didn't know how he'd even seen it. It wasn't as if the man had brandished it like in a play, all wide arcs and sloppiness. No, he'd used it well enough. Small, controlled movements, Tristan realized now. Precise. He'd been lucky the shimmering London light had illuminated the blade before the attack.

"Someone tried to kill Savannah."

Dem stopped dead in his tracks, as if Tristan had said the king himself walked down the street. "Miss Savannah?" he asked, as if either of them knew another woman named Savannah who helped in the rookery.

Tristan held tight to his temper. He knew Dem watched over these streets, but no one had complete control over everything. Not even the small length of Denmark Street. "Do you know another Savannah?"

So much for holding tight to his temper.

Dem scowled, his face darkening. "Who?"

"I didn't see a face. I can only assume it was the same man who's been terrorizing the street." Tristan closed his eyes. As much as he didn't want to admit it, he agreed that if Dem remained in power, Savannah would be safer. That was all that mattered. "She's home now. Safe."

Dem let loose a list of inventive curses that took even Tristan aback. His hands balled into fists, and he looked as if he might take out his anger on the nearest building. Given the shoddy workmanship, he'd no doubt take it down.

"I don't want to discuss this on the street." Dem turned sharply on his heel and stalked back the way he came, toward his own house.

It was only then that Tristan realized Dem, Ailene, and baby Shaw were the only ones occupying their house. Given the overcrowding on the street, and the poverty that suffocated the area, that struck him as off. Still, he kept quiet as Dem pushed open the door into the darkened interior.

There were no windows. Those that had once faced the street had been boarded over with even, precise boards. What sort of scheme did Dem run that afforded him enough money for resources such as good, solid wood and the nails to hammer them in?

"Ailene, someone attacked Miss Savannah." Dem's voice had gentled, but he spoke plainly. He immediately sat in the chair beside her and took her hand, his own touch as soft as his voice.

Ailene's gaze swung from Dem's to his. "Who was guarding her?"

"No one." Tristan tried keeping his temper under wraps. It wasn't Ailene's fault, or her hand that had wielded the blade. "She was alone on the street."

Dem's gaze narrowed on him. "Where was Robbie?"

"I didn't see him. None of your men." Tristan eased into the seat opposite them. The chair creaked ominously. "I did, however, see a group of men Savannah said didn't like her helping here."

Dem spat another round of inventive curses. "They think they can overthrow me."

"It wasn't them," Tristan said, watching both siblings. "This was a single man. He wore a greatcoat and carried a knife. Savannah is unharmed. I saw the blade and pushed her out of the way."

Even now, despite his fury and fear, Tristan felt her body beneath his. His trousers tightened at the memory. At the memory of a dozen other times they spent together, her body pressed close against his.

"Did you see who?" Ailene's voice shook, but her shoulders straightened.

"No." Tristan shook his head. He'd been too busy saving her, tackling her to the ground and out of harm's way. He was too scared to do anything else, and his fear had clouded his thoughts, controlled his actions.

"Miss Savannah should've been protected," Ailene scolded Dem. Or perhaps both Tristan and Dem, since she glared at him, too.

"Which means someone on the street saw it and didn't report back." Dem drummed his fingers on the table, and Tristan was struck by the dynamic. Far different from what he'd witnessed last night.

Or perhaps not. Perhaps Tristan had seen what they wished him to see. Or seen what he expected to see. Dem controlled the street. It was what Savannah believed, what everyone believed. As he sat at the table with the pair of them, Tristan thought perhaps that very carefully crafted façade had fooled everyone as it was meant to.

Clever.

"It also means whoever is behind these killings specifically targeted Savannah." Tristan voiced the words that sent ice through his veins. He hadn't told her; he hadn't wanted to admit it himself. Anyone could see she wasn't a resident here.

"Then they want her gone." Dem narrowed his eyes at the table. "Why? No one cares about this place." He paused and lifted his head, his gaze meeting Tristan's. "Except her."

The ice in Tristan's veins turned into cold rage. "You think they deliberately tried to kill her so no one else would bother with Denmark Street?"

It made sense. In a twisted sort of way, one based on hatred and anger. If no one cared about the street, if no one bothered to support the people here, the killers could continue on, without interference. But Savannah cared. She advocated for them. Her forgotten women.

Ailene rested her hand on Dem's curled fist and watched him.

He met her gaze, then stood. "Someone saw something."

"Find Robbie," Ailene added, voice harsh.

"And see who those men are," Tristan added. "They're trouble."

Dem snorted at that, and left without another word, but Tristan remained. He watched Ailene as she lifted the fussing baby from the bassinet. "We're used to being forgotten here," she whispered as Shaw settled down. "Miss Savannah and Miss Lyneé changed that. A lot of folks, they don't want anything to do with either woman."

Tristan stiffened. Far too many people commented on the color of Savannah's skin, thinking it made her less than. He didn't want to argue with Ailene, but he'd never let a slight against Savannah pass.

"Do you know how Dem came to control the street?" She dipped a rag, no doubt left by Savannah, into a small bowl of something and let Shaw suckle on it.

"No." Tristan stood and turned his back, giving her the

privacy she needed to take care of her child. This wasn't the place for him, but he wanted to hear the story anyway.

"Our parents died when Dem was young. Gin." Ailene grunted that last word but didn't elaborate. So many died from gin. It flowed everywhere, especially here. "I raised him, but we hadn't anywhere to live, anything to eat. Do you know what it's like to be so hungry you imagine you're eating air, and it fills you?"

He didn't, but he didn't interrupt. Tristan doubted she wanted an answer. She already knew he'd never gone without.

"I worked at one of the gaming hells, started in the kitchens, worked my way up to serving wench for the most high-class customers. Every penny I earned went to feeding us, clothing us." She stopped, and he heard her voice break. "Kept me and Dem from the drink."

"Is that why you two live here alone?"

She laughed, a small sound. "Some of Dem's gang stay upstairs. They pay us rent. But I promised him we'd never again go hungry. No matter what we had to do."

"So he took control." Tristan's head tilted. "Who ran the street before him?"

"Smarter than you look, used-to-be fiancé." She offered another small laugh. "The one before was a bully. Slapped people around, hurt his women. A mean drunk."

Tristan's hands curled into fists. "Did Savannah know him?"

"Miss Savannah wouldn't have any dealings with him, but no. Dem had already taken over by the time she came to us."

Which meant Dem had held the power here for years. Impressive. "I promised you I'd discover who was responsible. I'll keep that promise." He stepped for the doorway. "But know this—Savannah is my priority, my only priority. If I have to burn the place down to keep Savannah safe, I will."

"That is not the way to win her affections. You need to court her, show her you still love her." Ailene's voice held a note of amusement now. "Have you tried poetry?"

Tristan laughed and opened the door. "Not yet."

But it did remind him of the trunk of letters locked in his cabin onboard his ship. Letters he wrote every day, telling of his travels, of his heartbreak, even though he'd been the one who left.

CHAPTER 14

Walters took one look at her and shouted—the poor man *shouted*—for the maids to carry the water upstairs. The household sprang into action. As grateful as Savannah was for such things, all the fuss made her roll her eyes.

Still, at least she wouldn't wait too long for her bath. Walters's gaze flicked to Browne, who carried her basket in, and his eyes narrowed. He didn't say a word, merely waited.

"Mr. Tristan was with her," Browne said before Savannah could get a word in edgewise. He sounded contrite, embarrassed even. "Stopped the man and saved Miss Savannah."

Walters harumphed. Savannah suppressed a smile.

"I'm all right, Walters," Savannah promised. Her shoulders ached, and she smelled as if she'd taken the entirety of Denmark Street with her when she left, but she was otherwise unharmed. "However, a bath does sound lovely. Is Mama home?"

"No, miss, she and Mrs. St. Clair haven't yet returned. I'll send a footman out with a message."

Walters held up a hand before Savannah could protest. She swallowed her words and nodded.

"However," he continued, "Miss Lyneé has just arrived."

Best get this over with, she supposed. "Hold off, Walters, please." The butler made a disgruntled sound deep in his throat, but Savannah plowed on. "I'll need to send a message to Mrs. Crichton. We had plans this afternoon, and I'm afraid I shan't be able to keep them." She added that last with a rueful smile. "I'll send Coyle down with the note momentarily."

And, she realized, one to George Shilby about Vauxhall this evening. Even if she'd been up to so social an outing, she and Tristan had already nixed the idea.

Walters bowed and stepped back, eyeing the hem of Savannah's cloak and gown with growing horror. Savannah, for her part, hefted the material as high as possible and tried not to let anything drop on the stairs. She'd owe the maids an apology for that, too.

Once in her room, a wide-eyed Coyle stepped from the bath where the footmen were even now filling it with buckets of warm water. "Miss?" Coyle squeaked.

Lyneé burst in, looking frantic. "Savannah!" She crossed the room, clearly intent on embracing her, but stopped short. Wrinkling her nose she made a revolted face. "What is that *smell?*"

"The street." Savannah sighed and only barely waited for the footmen to clear out before moving onto the hardwood floor and letting her cloak drop with a disgusting plop. "Someone tried to kill me," she admitted. "Tristan saw the knife and pushed me out of the way. Unfortunately, that involved tackling me onto the street."

Coyle struggled with the ties along the back of her gown. Part of that might've been because she stood as far from Savannah as possible. "They're wet clear through," she muttered.

"Cut them." Savannah grimaced. "Please. The faster I'm out of this thing, the better."

"There's no saving that," Lyneé agreed.

"Can you do me a favor?" Savannah looked over her shoulder, but that pulled on sore muscles. "Write a quick note to Eliza. We were supposed to enjoy tea together this afternoon."

Lyneé gave one final look at the gown and sat at the writing desk. Savannah turned back around, swallowing a gasp of pain. Not even the servants would let her leave the house if they knew she'd hurt herself. She'd be lucky if she could convince her parents she was safe in Tristan's company.

Savannah closed her eyes, and clearly envisioned his frantic gaze on hers in those moments after he'd shoved her to the ground. If she ignored the stench and the pain, she could also clearly remember the solid weight of his body pressed against hers, too. That was worth focusing on, she decided.

No matter how she did or did not feel about him, Savannah wanted him. Even now, as Coyle sliced away the ties of her gown, she wanted him. For three years, Savannah hadn't allowed anything past the wall surrounding her heart.

Tristan, damn man, worked his way through. She didn't know if it was because he was the only man she'd ever loved, ever wanted, or if she was simply tired. She spent three years' worth of energy keeping that wall upright and secure. She let go of those few bricks that had crumpled and oh, it felt freeing.

"I'll find Walters," Lyneé said, already at the door. "Then I want to hear everything."

Savannah sighed.

"I'm going to give Browne a right talking to," Coyle muttered as she worked the knife through the last of the ties. "Do you want me to cut away your chemise?"

Though she felt terrible about it, Savannah nodded. "I'm afraid everything is ruined, and I don't fancy getting any of that muck on me."

Coyle huffed in agreement. "Letting you wander around that street alone," she continued on about poor Browne.

"He only did what I asked," Savannah protested as the gown

fell away in a puff of stench. "Oh, there's no saving that at all is there."

"No miss." Coyle lifted her foot to kick it out of the way, then thought better of it. "Can you step over it?"

Savannah did, then turned back around so Coyle could slice through her remaining undergarments. "Browne guards me when I deliver the food baskets," she reminded Coyle. "Otherwise, he stays with the carriage. You know I can't see to the women, the new mothers, with him standing behind me."

Coyle gave a snort worthy of a sailor and remained quiet. Savannah had a feeling that no matter what she said, it wouldn't stop her lady's maid from giving Browne a good talking to. Poor Browne. Savannah had a feeling he'd be accompanying her everywhere, no matter what she insisted, from now on.

Then again, she'd be lucky if only he, and perhaps Peters, followed her. If her father had his way, she'd have an entire army of guards.

"Now then." Lyneé reentered with a pair of maids, one bearing a tea tray, the other carrying a tray full of the poultices Savannah had made just the other day. "Let's start at the beginning, shall we?"

That was the last thing Savannah wanted. Gingerly stepping over the pool of clothing around her ankles, she ignored her nakedness and headed for the tub. Really, all she wanted was a bath, a hot, cleansing bath to wash the filth from her and help her muscles relax. She'd have liked something to cleanse the inside of her nostrils, too, but didn't think anything had yet been invented. Perhaps a smear of peppermint oil along her upper lip might help.

"I'll find a pair of old gloves. Perhaps the gardener has a pair." Coyle frowned at the pile of clothing. "Aye, I'm afraid none of them can be salvaged."

"Please don't overwork yourself for a pile of cloth." Savannah eased herself into the bath with a grateful sigh.

Coyle hummed again and disappeared. Savannah closed her eyes against the expectation in Lyneé's gaze.

"Pour me a cup of tea," she said. Savannah rarely drank tea, but after everything that happened today, she needed it. "I'm in the mood for something soothing."

As Lyneé poured the tea, a delicious pu'er from one of their direct merchants in China, Savannah told her the story. All of it, though she didn't want to admit how she felt about Tristan. Didn't want anyone to know she still cared for him. Or perhaps did again.

"You're getting close," Lyneé said after Savannah had finished. She started into her tea, a frown marring her wide mouth. "They're directing their attack at you, rather than the poor of the street."

"Do you think it's because I'm in the way? Asking questions?" Savannah paused, but forced the next words past the lump in her throat. "Or because they want me gone for other reasons?"

Lyneé waved that off. "Whatever the reason, it doesn't matter. They're after you, Savannah."

Before Savannah had the chance to reply, Eliza burst in, Walters hot on her trail.

"I'm sorry, miss," Walters began, staying a respectful distance from the open door of her sitting room.

"It's all right." Savannah froze in the tub, suddenly and desperately wishing she'd placed the screen in front of it before anything. That hadn't been high on her list of requirements for her afternoon. An oversight, she now realized.

"What happened?" Eliza demanded, ignoring Walters as she slammed the door closed. "Lyneé's note said you'd been hurt."

Savannah glared at her sister.

"You're finally coming out of your shell," Lyneé protested and poured another cup of tea. It was only then that Savannah realized there were three cups on the tray. Sneaky. "I thought having a close friend, as well as your favorite sister—" she winked here— "could only help."

Eliza hauled over a chair, unclasped her cloak, and gratefully took the teacup. "Thank you. Phew," she added with a dramatic sigh as she sat in the chair.

"Did you race over here on foot?" Savannah demanded, finally lifting the linen cloth and scrubbing her skin. The bath water had cooled enough that she debated calling for more heated water. However, she still had plans for the rest of the day and very little time for lollygagging in the tub.

"Don't be ridiculous." Eliza grinned, smoothing a hand down her morning gown. "I hired a hackney. Far quicker."

Lyneé snickered. Before anyone could say more, Jiesha hopped from under the bed, her preferred nesting place, and into the middle of the floor.

"You have a rabbit?" Eliza paused and eyed Jiesha, clearly fascinated. "Where did you find one so beautiful?"

"Tristan." Savannah turned to her sister. "Lyneé, grab her, please?"

Lyneé did as she asked and set Jiesha onto her vacated chair.

"He, ah, liberated her from a merchant in Antwerp," Savannah said.

"Savannah was just telling me how Tristan saved her life," Lyneé interrupted, no doubt before the conversation deviated further.

Eliza's eyebrows shot upward, and she leaned over. "Start at the beginning. And then perhaps you can be honest and tell me the truth about your reunion."

Savannah absolutely did not want to—she'd only have to repeat the story again for her parents—but she obliged. Talking settled her, she realized, as Lyneé began working oils through her hair. Sharing with Lyneé and Eliza boosted her in ways she didn't know she needed.

She had isolated herself too much, and though opening up

like this hurt, it also felt necessary. It was a relief to tell people close to her all she truly felt, as if doing so shared the burden, though Savannah knew only she could make any decisions about her future.

"Hmm," Eliza said, chewing on a fairy cake. "I do applaud your ruse. However, I'm hurt you chose not to include me in it."

"I apologize," Savannah said, now enclosed before the fire, wrapped in her dressing gown and several layers of blankets Coyle insisted upon as she and Lyneé fixed her hair for her dinner tonight. "I thought it for the best."

"Ha," Lyneé interrupted. "What she means is that she thought this pretense would last only a couple days, and she could go on with her life as if Tristan had never returned."

Savannah pulled back, scowling, but Lyneé tugged sharply on her hair. "That isn't true." Then, because she'd already admitted so much and something in her didn't wish to stop there, added, "I didn't want to admit to anyone anything. Not how broken I was when he left, nor the maelstrom of emotions I felt at his return."

Eliza's soft hand squeezed her shoulder. "I'm so sorry you went through all of that alone. I should've pushed harder when he left. Insisted on seeing you."

Savannah placed her hand over her friend's. "It wouldn't have mattered. I didn't talk with anyone. The servants had strict instructions. They'd have only seen you out."

"Does your dinner with Tristan tonight mean you've truly reconciled?" Lyneé asked.

"I don't know," Savannah admitted, but she smiled. "But I think I wish to try."

TRISTAN HADN'T EXPECTED the rest of day to crawl by as it had.

He wanted to see Savannah again, ensure she remained safe.

He'd stepped onto their street, but had resisted knocking on her door. She was locked in her house, with a bevy of guards, and no doubt a nice bath. She was safe. He repeated that to himself as he'd walked from Grosvenor Square toward the wharves.

He repeated it while he met with John, talking over cargo and destinations. As he stood on the deck of his ship, he knew Savannah was safe in her home, but those few minutes of terror refused to dissipate.

Given what happened earlier, and his interesting but less than satisfying talk with Dem and Ailene, perhaps he ought to have. Below the surface, he buzzed with anticipation for this evening. Well, the part with Savannah.

She'd told him some about her life, but he wanted to know more. How she'd spent the last years, what she'd done. Other than healing.

He also wanted to figure out why these murders occurred in daylight when the streets were far more congested in the evening. Granted, he'd never planned a murder before, but he'd have thought that doing so when fewer people might notice would be important.

Every time he closed his eyes, he saw the glint of that knife. Felt his muscles freeze. A heartbeat later, and it would've been too late. No matter how he let that moment play through his mind's eye, Tristan saw nothing more. Not the man's face, no distinguishing marks, nothing. Only that knife. Only as it aimed for his Savannah.

"Tristan, you still with us?" Arnault's voice snapped him from his thoughts.

Squinting into the hazy glare over the Thames, he turned and met his friend's gaze. "Something happen?"

"Something always happens," Arnault joked, but his gaze remained serious. "That's the nature of life. But since that Crichton fellow left, you haven't been with us all day."

"If you were visiting a brothel, what time would you arrive?"

Arnault's gaze narrowed. "You want to visit one?"

"No. Well, yes. But only in hopes of discovering who's killing these women."

"And you're taking Miss Savannah?" Arnault rolled his eyes upward and shook his head.

"I am not," he protested. Arnault didn't seem to hear him.

"No, no, Tristan. That is not the way to win her over. I taught you better. Cheese, flowers, yes. Brothels? You're a fool."

No denying that. "She'd rather have a dagger than cut flowers. She prefers we walk in fields of them. Of flowers," he clarified, though he thought it obvious. "Not daggers. The cheese she enjoyed." And they'd talked. A brilliant step, he thought.

"A dagger?" Arnault eyed him curiously, a gleam in his gaze that set Tristan's teeth on edge. "I knew I liked her. Now, what about these brothels you aren't taking her to? Where did you want to begin? By the wharves, the theaters?"

Shaking his head, Tristan looked over the wharves and toward the large corner building where his family's offices sat. Further up, Shaw Shipping, and what was now St. Clair Shipping, had their offices. They used to operate under one banner, but with the wars, the three families decided to separate—the better to secure government contracts, ensure private investors, and mitigate the threat of piracy and loss.

After this afternoon, brothels were the last thing on Tristan's mind. He didn't want to leave Savannah, even with her guards. Even in her own house. She'd been attacked, singled out. Not because she lived in the rookery or worked at the theaters or gaming hells.

Because of their questions? Because she enjoyed Dem's protection? Because she helped? He had no idea, and that bothered him.

"There are too many brothels in London," he said aloud, working through the problem. "Even by the theaters." There were dozens, and that wasn't even counting the poorer establishments. He had no idea where to even begin.

"Perhaps brothels aren't the place for you," Arnault said after a moment, echoing what Tristan had been thinking. "How does Miss Savannah feel about your visiting one of those establishments?"

"It's not as if I'm visiting for pleasure," Tristan muttered.

"You are courting her, are you not?" Arnault eyed him but didn't wait for an answer. "No matter your reasons, I don't think a brothel is the way to regain her affections."

"I'm trying," Tristan muttered. "But I destroyed her trust when I left."

"Trust is fragile, like a mast in a storm." Arnault leaned against the railing and watched him with eyes far older than his age. Tristan wondered what he'd seen, and who he'd lost. "Strong on the surface, but delicate under pressure."

"I always looked at it like a castle wall. Brick by brick." Tristan stopped. "And just as easily breached," he supposed. "A well-placed cannonball—or an act of betrayal—and its stability disappears."

"You are rebuilding your trust with Miss Savannah." Arnault clasped his hands in front of him. "You need it. She is a beautiful and wise woman."

He paused, and Tristan knew what he was going to say next. To brace for it, he gripped the ship's railing harder.

"Why did you leave? You spoke much about her, about the plans you two made. But never that."

"A misguided attempt to find what I thought I lacked."

"You found me," Arnault chortled, and Tristan smiled at his friend, chuckling along with him. "You're a fool, Tristan Conrad."

"I know." He clasped Arnault on the shoulder and headed below deck. He needed a shave, and he wanted to hear the latest gossip Little Ricky, his cabin boy, had for him. "But at least I have you in my life!"

Arnault's laughter echoed after him.

Crichton's visit had been all business, Tristan hadn't shared the attempt on Savannah's life. It had rattled him too deeply to speak of even to Arnault. Still, Tristan thought he sensed a thaw in Crichton's demeanor. Not as many suspicious looks and a return of the camaraderie they once shared at school. Tristan hadn't planned on repairing his broken friendships— he hadn't even thought about it. His entire being had focused on winning Savannah back. Now he saw how naïve that had been. When he'd left so abruptly, he'd burned far too many bridges.

Today's meeting had begun to repair at least one of them. Even if Tristan didn't captain this ship, Crichton had several good ideas for investments.

In Tristan's cabin, Little Ricky was waiting with a steaming bowl of water and the shaving instruments laid out in a neat row.

"Is it true?" Little Ricky all but vibrated with energy as he eyed Tristan.

"Depends on what it is," Tristan said casually as he sat in his chair. His leg bounced and his hands gripped the chair, unable to relax.

Still, he knew what Little Ricky meant, even if the boy's energy caused him to bounce around the room rather than ask directly. Maybe he'd wait a moment or two before the shave, just in case that energy caused the boy's hands to shake.

"Are you not sailing with us anymore?" The words came out in a stage whisper, Little Ricky's dark eyes wide and curious. "Meneer Arnault said you have a sweetheart."

Tristan couldn't fathom reducing Savannah to a mere sweetheart, but he let that slide. Little Ricky was still young. Tristan's gaze slid to his trunk, still locked securely against the wall. The

THE LADY'S COURTSHIP

trunk with the letters he'd written to Savannah, all neatly tied together.

"I haven't made any plans for the future," he told Little Ricky.

As he said the words, however, he knew he'd stay and fight for Savannah. He wouldn't run again—never again. He'd stay and do whatever he could to regain her trust until she told him definitively that she did not want him.

His heart hurt at the thought, but any heartache was his own fault. That fact wasn't easy to remember, but it was the truth.

"But who will captain us if you don't?" Little Ricky lathered shaving cream on Tristan's face as he spoke.

"Meneer Arnault, if he wants." Tristan hadn't thought about it. For all his planning and brains, when it came to winning over Savannah, she became his sole focus. "Either way, you'll have a place on this ship, or any other in the Conrad fleet, until you no longer want one."

Little Ricky didn't answer, but then, he was shaving Tristan, and the conversation passed. While he wanted to hear the ship's gossip, what happened on the wharves, Tristan could only think of Savannah.

"Is it true your lady is from a rival shipping company?" Little Ricky asked as he wiped off the straight razor.

"Rival?" Tristan laughed. "Not exactly. She's the eldest daughter of Hugh Shaw of Shaw Shipping. They're close friends of the family."

"Hmm."

"What else has the ship said?"

Tristan closed his eyes. That knife still glinted sharply in his memory. Forcing his mind from that image, he listened as Little Ricky rattled off the latest news from the wharves—the usual—what the crew had ferreted out about the murders—nothing—and bets on one of the other shipping company's cargo.

"And your other job?" Tristan's gaze slid back to the trunk, but he needed to hear what Little Ricky had learned about the silks, first. "What have you learned about the cravat?"

"I've been to every shop Meneer Arnault told me to go to," Little Ricky said, rattling them off in quick succession. "I bribed a couple of the shop boys, some looked half starved. And I did what you always said, Captain."

The boy stood proudly now, a satisfied grin on his face.

"What did you do?" Tristan asked, amused. He did not grin, not in the face of Little Ricky's pleased look.

"I told them, the ones that looked half starved or who was beaten by their masters, to find the ship. We'd take care of them."

Tristan reached out and placed a hand on the boy's shoulder. "I'm proud of you, Little Ricky. That is exactly what I'd expect of a sailor with Conrad Shipping."

Little Ricky's thin chest stuck out so far that Tristan wondered he didn't pop. He did grin then, pleased that the lessons he tried to instill in the lad had taken.

"You'll return this afternoon?"

"Aye, Captain. I won't let you down."

"I know you won't."

Little Ricky finished his shave and Tristan returned his attention to the letters in his trunk. "I'll need a messenger," he said, unable to tear his gaze from it. "I need to send a package around to Miss Savannah."

"I'll see to it," Little Ricky said proudly. "You can trust me, Captain."

Tristan smiled at his cabin boy. "I know I can."

CHAPTER 15

"*You're* certain?" Savannah's mother eyed her carefully as Coyle finished pinning her hair. "I'm unharmed. The bath did wonders." Savannah smiled confidently.

By the time her parents and Aunt Nadia had burst into the house, frantic with worry, she, Lyneé, and Eliza had moved from her private sitting room and reconvened in the salon. As much as she hated to admit it, Lyneé had been correct to invite Eliza. Her friend's presence had helped ease Savannah's tension in the aftermath of the attempt on her life.

Anger had replaced fear by the time she recounted what had happened to her parents. It'd taken quite a bit to talk her father out of storming Denmark Street and finding the perpetrator. Or locking her in her room for the rest of her life. In the end, Savannah had agreed, and willingly, that Browne and Peters would accompany her every time she left the house.

No more leaving Browne at the carriage, no more relying solely on Dem for protection.

Savannah didn't say it aloud, but knew Tristan wouldn't leave her alone, either. That knowledge warmed her, and more of the wall that once surrounded her heart crumbled. For the first time since his return, she didn't mind.

Now, in her rooms, she met her mother's worried gaze in the looking glass and smile.

"I'm also certain you have your own plans."

"Hmm." Sophia pressed her lips together and narrowed her eyes. Fear and worry still bracketed her mouth, and she hadn't stopped touching Savannah since she'd arrived, frantic and ready to storm Denmark Street with Hugh. "I said you should talk to Tristan."

"And I am." Savannah held up a hand. "I know, I know. Talking and solving a murder aren't the same, but I'm listening."

Her heart listened a little too much, but she kept that to herself. Her gaze drifted to the small chest that had arrived shortly after her parents. The messenger, who proudly declared himself Captain Tristan's most trusted cabin boy, had delivered it with a flourish worthy of the highest courtiers.

Savannah opened it but hadn't yet read the letters. As tempting as they were, she wanted to hear about his life from Tristan.

Tonight was for them. And their next step in discovering the murderer.

Mostly for them, she thought as she reached for her mother's hand and squeezed it. "I know you worry, and I don't blame you. What happened today was—not at all what I expected." She'd never anticipated whoever was behind these murders to go after her. A tactical error, one she wouldn't make again. "However, Tristan will be with me."

"Hmm." Sophia eyed her with the same sly humor Lyneé did whenever he was brought into the conversation. "I do trust him to take care of you," she admitted. "Will he break your heart again?" Her mouth relaxed into a small smile, and she added in a lighter tone, "I suppose, if you must move rooms again, we can always move you to Morgana's room. Your sister seems quite content in the country with your gran. Though," Sophia said seriously, "I might hunt him down this time."

She'd have to stand behind Savannah. Still, she didn't believe Tristan would hurt her, not again. Of course, Savannah had thought that before, would've sworn in church in front of the Bishop of Canterbury himself, that Tristan wouldn't have ever hurt her.

She'd been wrong then. Now?

"I don't think he would've left me had we married," Savannah heard herself say. "I don't believe he'd have boarded that ship and sailed off then. Was he scared of that commitment?" She shook her head, confident in this. "No, it wasn't that. From what he's said, and I believe him, I think it was a matter of *if I don't go now, I'll never know.*"

Had it hurt? Dreadfully. Would she have been happy, knowing he'd married her anyway but always longed for the sea? No. Never.

"I'll still skewer him if he hurts you again," her mother promised.

Savannah laughed, a wave of love moving through her. It cracked those last bricks around her heart. Standing, she kissed her mother's cheek. "I know. But I think it's different now."

Tristan found himself, she saw it in the way he moved, the way he acted. She'd never have known the difference, three years ago, but now it shone plain as day. Perhaps they'd both needed these years. Though she could've done without the soul-wrenching heartbreak.

"All right." Sophia kissed her cheek. "Be careful, Savannah." She squeezed her shoulder. "Please. I never want to feel that fear again."

"I know. Browne and Peters will be with me. And I won't needlessly venture onto the street, at least not until we find who —" She swallowed hard and gripped her hands tighter around each other. It wasn't every day someone tried to kill her.

"Your father and I are headed to Lady Hamilton's dinner. We can cancel."

Savannah hid her surprise. Her parents often attended dinners and soirees, mostly for business. Very few of London's society accepted them given their heritage. Lady Annis Hamilton was an exception, but Savannah couldn't remember the last time she knew of such an event.

One more aspect of her family's lives she knew nothing about. Part of Savannah was gratified that they continued on with their lives. She hadn't, but it was foolish of her to think everyone else would so utterly change. The other part of Savannah berated herself for pulling away so thoroughly that she hadn't known of such things until this week. Never again, she vowed.

"I'm surprised you convinced Papa to attend, given what happened."

"Savannah, darling." Sophia ran her finger down Savannah's cheek, mindful of Coyle and her work. "If you weren't having supper with Tristan, and we didn't trust him to keep you safe, nothing short of the four horsemen could stop your father." She sighed. "As it was, he reminded me that this was your choice."

Oh. Savannah hadn't expected that. Her mother was the more level-headed one in the family. Her father being the voice of reason? It set her world askew. "I won't leave the house without Browne or Peters," she promised again.

"We always allowed you more freedom than we perhaps should have." Sophia shook her head. "But all four of you are strong, capable people, and your father and I are so proud of all of you." Her gaze softened. "We don't regret giving you that freedom, even if most of the world might consider it scandalous. I think you're stronger for it."

"Thank you, Mama." Then, because she was heartily tired of talking about herself, she asked, "Anyone in particular in attendance tonight?"

"Besides the countess's unmarried son?" Sophia winked and laughed. It held a strained, tired quality. "He's quite handsome." With another squeeze to Savannah's shoulder and a kiss on her cheek, her mother walked for the door. "Lord Shilby will be there with his grandson. Apparently, they're interested in some cargo."

Shilby had said something about that, at Eliza's, after their talk about St. Giles. Savannah had thought he was tossing it out as a hook, but perhaps she was wrong. With the wars over and the seas relatively safe once more, perhaps he truly did have an interest in shipping. Had he planned to attend this dinner when he'd invited her to Vauxhall? Or after she'd sent round that note about not attending tonight?

Savannah rubbed her eyes. Her thoughts raced round and round, and she had no answers.

"There you are, miss." Coyle stepped back and eyed her handiwork. "Though I think it's a bit fancy for a night chasing a murderer." She shuddered at that last.

"It's perfect. Thank you, Coyle." Savannah had determined she'd look her best no matter what. Unfortunately, she couldn't decide whether it was for her own confidence or to impress Tristan, and she hated that. "No need to wait up. I'll be fine."

Coyle didn't look convinced, either over her fancy hair with its carefully placed combs decorated with butterflies, her blue evening dress, or the fact that she planned to dine with Tristan.

Even after her bath, a faint ache still throbbed along her bruised shoulders.

However, Coyle nodded. "Be safe, miss. And good night."

Coyle tidied up the room while Savannah sat on her bench. She needed a moment. Just one, so she could gather her thoughts and feel what lay in her heart about Tristan. The Tristan of today, not the one she knew from three years ago.

Her afternoon with Lyneé and Eliza had helped. Savannah

wanted to move forward, see where this new path took her and Tristan.

Standing, she took one final look at herself in the tall looking glass and nodded at her lady's maid. Poor Coyle did not look convinced that this was at all a good idea. Savannah wanted to protest that it was only dinner but doubted that would appease her.

With a final smile, Savannah headed downstairs, toward the front parlor, and only then realized she had no idea if she should wait for Tristan in her rooms or elsewhere. They'd never stood on ceremony; they hadn't the need. Now that she thought of it, this entire supper was scandalous. True, they dined with a household of servants, but her parents were attending another event, Lyneé was off someplace, and she certainly hadn't a chaperone.

Pinching the bridge of her nose, she continued down the stairs, past portraits of her great-grandmother, Raeni, and her grandmother, Cedella. It hadn't occurred to her until that moment that this dinner might look unseemly from the outside.

Clearly her parents trusted her, though they'd been more concerned with Savannah's wellbeing than propriety.

They trusted her, despite the threat of scandal, and that bolstered Savannah considerably.

"Mr. Conrad is waiting for you in the parlor, miss." Walters bowed slightly, his voice without any inflection whatsoever.

"Thank you, Walters." She paused for only a heartbeat. "I trust you'll ensure the staff is aware that this is a perfectly proper supper."

"Of course, miss." Walters paused. "We want you happy, Miss Savannah," he admitted, the second biggest breach of etiquette she'd ever witnessed from the usually proper butler. The first, of course, being earlier when he'd bellowed for the maids. "If he breaks your heart again, you've only to say the word."

Her lips twitched, and emotion closed her throat. For one

moment, tears blurred her vision. "Thank you, Walters. I—That means a great deal."

Walters bowed and disappeared. Savannah didn't watch him leave but walked for the parlor where Tristan waited. He had dressed for the occasion in a richly tailored green waistcoat and coat with hints of silver threading.

Savannah hoped he'd dressed for her and not the brothel later tonight. Shame they'd canceled Vauxhall. They'd have looked stunning together.

"Will anyone be joining us?" He held out his arm and escorted her toward the informal dining room, his gaze trained only on her.

"No," she admitted. "I hadn't thought of a chaperone. It took half the afternoon to convince Mama and Papa that I was unharmed." She paused. "They're at Lady Hamilton's, if you feel the need—"

"No." He offered his most charming grin, the one that made her knees weak. "I promise I'll be on my best behavior."

Something in her relaxed. Only the two of them, as it had always been. No need for pretense or talking around the subject she desperately did and did not wish to speak about. "My understanding is that the staff has made a pact, one they'll enact if they suspect you've been improper."

He snorted but nodded solemnly. "Please just send my parents a note about my fate and where my body might be discovered."

"I'm sure it won't come to that." She grinned and felt a bit lighter than she had a week ago. Or even a day ago.

"I noticed more guards." He sat beside her at the small table the family used. "All heavily armed."

"I managed to convince Papa that stationing half the shipping crew around the house wasn't a good idea." She offered a wry smile, but her statement hadn't been that much of an exaggeration. "His other option was locking me in the house for the next five years."

Tristan only nodded at that statement, which was, unfortunately, also not an entire exaggeration. Annoyed, Savannah huffed and glared at him.

"I'm not saying being locked in the house is a good idea," he said swiftly, holding up a hand to ward off her response. "I'm merely saying—"

"Careful," she warned.

"I applaud the additional guards," he finished with a charming grin.

Tristan's closeness shivered over her arms and down her back. The arousal she had only ever felt around him burned through her, heating her blood and making her want things she had no right wanting.

This was the path she'd chosen, however. Savannah took a moment, trying to gather her thoughts, but the memories of their time together rushed through her.

"I didn't have any interest in another man," she heard herself admit. Cursing her tongue, she focused on the soup in front of her. It didn't help. The words flowed out of her like a river, and she was helpless to dam it up. "After you left," she whispered, "I devoted myself to the women of the rookery, those society forgot."

"Grandmother Raeni would be proud," he said quietly, a hint of his own pride in his voice.

Her great-grandmother, the woman who began the tradition of healing, of helping those who needed it, would have been proud, indeed. She was a freed slave who inherited her former mistress's fortune upon her death and decided neither society, her skin color, nor her lack of formal education was going to stop her.

"Not everyone wants my help," Savannah admitted ruefully. "Because they don't want charity or because of my skin color."

She brushed a fingertip over the back of her dark hand and sighed. She met Tristan's gaze and the spark of anger in his blue-green eyes. She knew he'd fight anyone who so much as thought of slighting her. "Then I met Dem, and things changed."

"Why did he accept you? Other than he tried to bribe you into paying for protection." Tristan's grin flashed over his face. "Not that he shouldn't have—everyone should—but I know his sort."

"He thought he could intimidate me."

Tristan laughed so hard he nearly choked on his soup. "He didn't strike me as a fool," he finally said.

Savannah grinned. This, this right here, was what the innumerable meals they'd shared had been like. How they'd spent their time together for so many years. Just the two of them, eating together, being together—utterly inseparable. She waited while the soup was removed and the fish served, those memories weighing heavily on her.

"He is not." She paused for a dramatic beat. "Not after I threatened him." Tristan snorted again. "He's a fair hand with a knife, but it's a small thing compared to my dagger."

Tristan shook his head, still grinning. "He clearly knows better now." Then, more softly, he added, "I'm sorry I missed that."

She stared blindly down at her fish. "I wouldn't have met him if you hadn't left. Nor Ailene. It's a different world there, one I never imagined being a part of."

Her grandmother was also a healer and a midwife, but she chose to practice her profession in the openness of country, living in her own suite of rooms at Nelda Hall. Gran and Tristan's mother were the closest of friends, and they strongly believed in helping others no matter their circumstances.

"I wanted to walk in Gran's footsteps," she admitted, the words almost too quiet in the silent room. "When you left, I saw two paths before me. I could cry over you—" And the abject despair nearly undid her. It'd taken months for her to claw her way out of that black pit. "Or I could help. I chose to help."

"And if I had stayed?" Tristan asked, equally quiet. "Would you have chosen that same path?"

She slowly blinked and met his gaze. "I thought to follow in Mama's footsteps, entertaining for the business and helping the ladies of the ton with their ailments, as a way to garner support and money for our causes."

"I loved the woman you were," Tristan admitted.

Her heart cracked open once again at his mournful tone and his use of past tense. *Loved.* Which was ridiculous, as he clearly wanted her—he'd made that clear enough.

Then he smiled. "The woman sitting beside me now steals my breath."

"I'm the same woman." Her words caught in her throat. His admission stole her breath and made her heart sing.

Damn traitorous thing that it was.

"You are, but you're stronger." He shook his head. "You were always strong, of course, but it's different now. I can't explain it in words." He placed a hand over his heart. "I can feel it."

"If this is a roundabout way of justifying your—"

"No." He took her hand. "I don't know the people we might've been if I'd stayed. But I do know I want to try again. Do you?"

She held his gaze, felt the heat of his touch, longed for it on her skin. For the feel of his hands cupping her breasts, his mouth tasting along her inner thighs. She missed the warm, solid weight of him against her, the feel of his powerful thighs beneath her as she took him deep inside her body.

"I want to never hurt like that again," she said. "I want you to never shatter my trust."

"I know." His hand firmly held hers, his gaze steady. "I can never make up for the past. I could blame Philip and the stories we wove about adventures, but ultimately the decision to leave rests squarely on my shoulders."

He paused again, and her throat closed with a hope she dared not name.

"I do promise you this: I'll never leave you again, Savannah. Not unless you want me to."

"Perhaps, maybe, we might try. I don't guarantee anything," she rushed to add, though he hadn't done more than squeeze her hand.

She wanted to kiss him again. Wanted to make love to him. A future? A small part of her heart tugged at her. Another try? Savannah wanted to see where this led. With the new Tristan, because he was right about that much.

He'd changed as well, now stood more confidently at her side. His head wasn't so far in the clouds, something she hadn't even noticed when they were younger.

"Let's see where this takes us." She removed her hand and stabbed a bite of fish perhaps a little too determinedly. "One step at a time."

CHAPTER 16

"I know you sent a note round to Shilby," Tristan said as the footmen removed the final plates. "However, I believe we should return to Denmark Street tonight."

"I thought you were searching the brothels?" Savannah asked in surprise.

"There's too many." He shook his head, but she had a feeling it was more than the number of them. "And I'm not convinced we'll find answers there."

"You think they're still on the street?" She tilted her head. "You think there'll be another attack. Why tonight? There's been no real pattern."

"I know." Tristan shrugged and stood, moving around the table and offering his hand. "I still believe they'll attack during the day. But I feel there are answers on Denmark Street that we haven't uncovered."

"Are you certain about this?" Savannah asked as they stood from dinner, ready for whatever the night had in store for them. She was definitely not dressed for a visit to Denmark Street, but wouldn't take the time to change.

Browne and Peters would accompany them, of course, no

questions asked. They were both determined not only to see her safe, but to bring the culprit or culprits to justice. Despite her gratitude for the additional protection they'd provide, Savannah couldn't shake a faint thrum of unease.

"I'm certain I could have the entirety of Conrad and Shaw Shipping accompany us. I'm debating whether I should bring Arnault and some of the more rambunctious members of my crew. I'm not sure at all." He rolled his shoulders, looking tense. The candlelight glinted off his hair, making his frown look harsher. "Am I certain these men will be at the brothels and not the gaming hells? No. Am I even sure where to begin looking?" Again, Tristan shook his head. "Not at all."

"I still don't understand the change from evening to daylight." She tapped her fingers on the table, trying to sort everything out but coming up blank.

"It's almost as if they upped the stakes." He paused, and a chill ran down her spine despite the pleasantness of the dining room and the comfortable meal they'd just shared. She met his gaze across the table and suddenly knew what he was going to say next. "Like they placed bets with each other to commit these murders in daylight because the chances of being caught were higher."

"They started with the attacks on women. They stopped— why?" Savannah closed her eyes and cursed herself. "Because the season ended. Oh, stupid, Savannah." She met Tristan's gaze. "I never connected it until now. The violations, they stopped with Ailene because the season ended."

"The season is almost finished now," he pointed out. "Why not start again after the opening ball? Why wait until two weeks ago?"

"I don't know." She shrugged. "I never said murder made sense."

"No, only that we're right. The man or men who are doing

this are part of the *ton*." He ran a hand down his face. "There are too many places to search."

She shuddered and curled her fingers around her skirts. It did not steady her in the least. She'd carry her dagger out in the open tonight. But she still didn't think it would be enough. "It wasn't the *thrill*"—she spat the word with distaste—"they sought. They wanted more."

Tristan rounded the table in a quick stride and took her hands. They'd touched so often over the years, but barely at all since his return. Once more, the feel of his skin on hers raced hot in her veins, making her long for more. For one dizzying moment, Savannah wanted to toss caution, propriety, and sensibility to the winds and kiss him here, in front of the servants. Escort him upstairs and see if they fit together as they always had.

Suddenly, and somewhat unreasonably, she wished she'd worn gloves with her stylish blue dinner gown. But then, she'd felt an unreasonable need to impress him tonight. A nighttime stroll along the rookery didn't seem like the makings of a courtship.

Courtship? Her head rejected that word. Whatever had she been thinking? Her heart, however, embraced it.

"I don't like this. None of it makes any sense." Tristan shook his head and tugged her from the dining room toward the small parlor, where the ladies usually retired after more formal dinners.

"Tristan, I won't sit idly by."

He was already shaking his head. "I'd never ask you to. But you said yourself that Shilby brought up the murders and Crichton even mentioned Shilby talking about them. Why? What does Shilby know, or suspect, that he'd even care? What do either of them have to do with St. Giles Rookery? Why would two highly connected men, who never set foot in in a rookery and couldn't point out Denmark Street on a map, be so informed?"

It raced over her skin, chasing away all her desire. Well, perhaps not *all* her desire. That always simmered beneath the surface, even when he was gone. Savannah dropped his hands and stepped back, not so much to clear her head, but so she could pace, follow his line of thinking.

"This isn't about the women." She nodded, turning in a small circle, her gaze trained upward on the plaster crown molding. "Though it infuriates me to admit it, the women are secondary to whatever Shilby and Crichton know." Her hands curled into fists and then uncurled. "But why bring it up at all?"

"I don't see a connection," Tristan stood off to one side as she walked, but Savannah knew he tried to work through this problem. None of it made sense. "Perhaps there's a bill on the floor about crime…I've no idea. I haven't followed British politics recently." He met her gaze, but all she saw there was his determination. "I think it's about time I do."

"Let's start with Dem. I doubt there's anything he hasn't told us. But after this afternoon's, ah, *incident*, he might have more information." Savannah didn't necessarily want to return to Denmark Street.

"Incident?" Tristan repeated, watching her with a skeptical expression.

"I don't have another word," she muttered. She'd racked up far too many "incidences" in the last week. "'Attempted murder' sounds so…harsh."

He rolled his eyes. "Two *incidences* are two too many, Savannah."

She couldn't argue with him there. "I still don't think that first one was deliberately aimed at me." Savannah paused again. "Looking back, I'm not sure if that was a misdirection or not."

"You think someone killed a man beside you and threw a dagger at you, all for misdirection?"

Put like that, it sounded daft. "Perhaps not," she conceded. Tapping her fingers against her waist, she wondered if smoothing her fingers along the frown bracketing his mouth might send the wrong message. "However, the stranger's murder doesn't fit the pattern we're working with."

"That I can agree with. Rifle shot rather than a knife, man instead of a woman." Tristan tilted his head, eyes looking past her as he worked out that part. "Those men who were watching you in the rookery earlier…do you think it was one of them who threw the knife? Used the commotion of the shot to try to remove you from Denmark Street?"

"They'd have to have known about the rifle shot," she protested. A chill danced over her arms, but Savannah dismissed it. Unfortunately, for all the people she helped, there were a greater number who didn't want her help. Who spat at her feet or moved to the other side of the street.

"Not necessarily, but I agree, it's a stretch. It could've been a coincidence, the timing of it all." His gaze cleared and watched her, somber now. "I haven't spent as much time there as you." He took her hand again, and another shiver raced over her, this one far more pleasurable. "I'd like to change that. If you agree."

Savannah held Tristan's gaze, wondering if that might be the next step in their relationship. "Thank you for the letters."

He blinked, surprised by the change in subject. "Did you look at them?"

"My afternoon was a tad overcrowded," she said wryly. He didn't grin or laugh it off but watched her seriously.

Reading them so wouldn't change anything. Still, a small part of her thought perhaps it might add context to her three years without him. Reading about his years on the sea, visiting various ports, might erase the gulf between them.

She stepped forward and took his arm. Perhaps these last days had already erased that gulf.

"I'd rather hear about the last three years from you." Saying the words aloud solidified her choice. Her path.

"I'm sure you didn't write me," he said, somewhat ruefully. "I don't blame you. But I'd like to hear what else you've done while I was away."

Savannah smiled and her heart skipped a beat at his interest. "Mostly what I've told you," she said slowly as they stopped just outside the foyer. "Finding out who I am, I suppose you could say."

Savannah paused. Finding out who she was. She thought she knew. When he'd left, she'd drifted for a bit, then settled into her new life, one she'd chosen. One she was proud of but wouldn't have ever known if he hadn't left.

Because she insisted on honesty, demanded it since his return, she admitted what she hadn't realized until just then. "I would've been happy if you hadn't left," she said slowly. "Content, even. Would I be the woman I am now? No. And I like the woman I've become very much."

Tristan lifted her hand to his lips and kissed her palm. "I love the woman you've become. I loved who you were," he repeated what he'd said over dinner. "But the you right now takes my breath away."

For one more moment, Savannah wondered what their life would've been like. Then she let it go, dissolving as easily as a leaf carried away by the current. Holding his gaze, she felt freer than she had since Tristan's return. Turning for the foyer, where Walters waited for them, she stepped onto another new path.

"A small change in plans, Walters," she told the butler. "We'll be heading for Denmark Street with Browne and Peters."

"In a hackney, miss?" Walters did not look at Tristan.

She met Tristan's gaze, who nodded. We, she'd always liked the sound of that. She and Tristan, together. "I think so," she agreed. "No need to announce our arrival."

"I'll inform them, miss."

Walters left while Savannah buttoned her pelisse and tugged on her gloves. The nights had grown cooler despite the warmer days. In the silence of the foyer, anticipation thrummed along her nerves.

"When you left," Savannah whispered, "I didn't understand. I cut off all contact with my friends. Eliza, Christiane. Until tonight, I hadn't realized how insulated I'd become."

"I'm sorry." Tristan took her hand and pulled her closer. "I broke your trust."

"You did," she agreed. "But I chose that path." She didn't want to admit she hid away from society, from those who knew her. "Not because of the scandal, though that was…loud."

Tristan looked stricken. "I hadn't even thought of that." He closed his eyes, and for a heartbeat, he looked broken. "I'm so sorry, Savannah. I was so focused on me, on seeing—I hadn't even considered that."

"I know. I didn't care what anyone whispered about me. I'm used to the talk, but it seemed—I don't know. At the time, it felt right that I just turn onto a new path." She sighed and remembered tonight's conversation with her mother. "Mama told me that she and Papa were headed for Lady Hamilton's. I cut myself off so thoroughly that I hadn't even realized they still socialized with the countess."

It sounded strange now, admitting such a thing. Of course, her parents still socialized with their friends. But the scandal of their eldest daughter's broken engagement had touched everyone, which had made her hide away even more.

Perhaps that scandal hadn't affected them quite as much as she once feared.

"That's why you immersed yourself in St. Giles. Why you spend your days there."

"Not solely to escape the scandal," she corrected him. "I'm sure I could've disparaged you, spread rumors about you up and down the social strata, but until this moment it never occurred to me." Savannah nearly laughed as Walters's careful, precise footsteps echoed down the hall. "I grieved, pulled myself up, and did what I felt was right. Helping those women felt right."

It had settled something inside her she hadn't realized was missing. Marrying Tristan had been all she'd ever wanted. She'd planned on following her mother's footsteps in society.

Sophia Shaw held court on her own terms. She knew the shipping business as well as any of them, but had chosen, instead, to use her own knowledge of various female ailments to help society's women. She was trusted by those women and their families and held their secrets close. Though that had also been Savannah's plan, now she saw a different way to help, one all her own.

"The hackney has arrived, miss. Browne and Peters are waiting for you." Walters bowed, flicked a glance at Tristan that didn't hold any of his previous acrimony, and held open the door.

Outside, the streets sat in an interesting glow of clouds, mist, and the barest hint of hazy, setting sun. The days were longer now, and Savannah suddenly wished for those days where she and Tristan wandered the grounds of Nelda Hall until the sun fully disappeared. The breeze cooled the streets, bringing with it the hint of rain that had threatened all day.

"Miss." Browne nodded as he held open the door with a short bow and a glare at the hackney's driver. "You won't be alone, Miss Savannah."

"Thank you, Browne." She smiled at him, not at all sure this was a good idea, returning to the scene of her attack. Still, she felt it necessary.

Tristan climbed into the hackney and sat beside her as Browne closed the door. At least she wouldn't be alone.

"Will you continue to help at St. Giles?" Tristan asked once the hackney started to move.

"I don't know." She had no idea what the future might hold.

Not anymore. "Once, I had mapped it all out. Now, my priority is finding these murderers, discovering why Lord Shilby—and his grandson—have such an interest, and ensuring Ailene and her babe are healthy."

Tristan nodded, a small, proud smile playing around his lips. She wondered what he thought, saddened she no longer simply knew. "Do you know what Ailene named the child?"

Surprised, Savannah shook her head. "No, she hasn't said."

"Shaw."

Her own smile blossoming over her lips, she laughed. She held Tristan's gaze and relaxed against the hackney wall. "I like the sound of that."

The rest of the ride they enjoyed in silence. And for the first time since Tristan's surprising arrival, Savannah considered the silence comfortable. Easy. Almost, *almost*, like old times. Things between them wouldn't ever be like that again, but perhaps, they could be better.

Before she had the chance to work through that, they'd arrived.

"I've rarely been here at this hour," she admitted softly as Browne and Peters descended from the hackney. Much, it seemed, to the driver's delight. "The second time was with you." She glanced at him, but they both remembered their visit only the other day. "The first time was when Ailene was attacked. Dem sent Robbie."

The poor lieutenant had been frantic, nearly incomprehensible. But she'd gone, despite the danger.

"Really?" Tristan took her hand, which surprised Savannah. She'd grown used to his formal manners, but her gloved hand wrapped in his made her feel more settled. Steady. "Never seen the street with the sun barely lighting it?"

It was an odd look. Like the street was caught between waking and sleeping, she'd have said in a fit of poetic whimsy. The moment they stepped onto Denmark Street, three men followed them. That didn't surprise Savannah, since every one of Dem's people knew her.

"It is beautiful," she whispered, all too aware of Peters and Browne following her and Dem's men following them.

"Even with our entourage?" Tristan grinned down at her. He vibrated beside her, ready for a fight. "All of them?" he added, but she wasn't surprised he noticed the others, too.

"Miss Savannah, why are you out so late?" Dem's voice carried from one of the doorways—not his and Ailene's. The men following them melted into the shadows. "Used-to-be fiancé, I thought you knew better."

"Have you ever tried talking a woman out of something she wants?" Tristan asked, still ready beside her, prepared to fight anyone who looked at her wrong. It warmed her, reminded her of their time before.

Some things, she realized, hadn't changed.

"Is Ailene well?" Savannah asked, all too aware of her fancy attire. She'd dressed for a quiet dinner with Tristan, not a walk down Denmark Street.

"Aye," Dem said cautiously.

She waited before he finally nodded and led them a few houses down to where they lived. He knocked once, a short rap on the door that was clearly a signal, then unlocked it. Ailene looked healthier than even this afternoon when Savannah had seen her last.

"Miss Savannah, I'm so happy you're here." She nodded cautiously at Tristan and lowered her voice. "Have you found the man who attacked you? Are they the same as who attacked me?" She swallowed but her voice didn't waver. "All of us?"

"Not yet," Savannah soothed, holding Ailene's hand tightly with her own. "That's why we're here. Is the babe well?"

"Aye, as healthy as can be. Thank you for the food."

"Have you learned anything else?" Tristan asked Dem as Ailene handed over the child to Savannah.

"Oh, there's talk," Dem agreed. "Nothing about your attack this morning, Miss Savannah, and I'm sorry for that." His voice hardened. "Someone saw something, and I'll find out who."

"Anything else?" Tristan asked as she checked over the baby.

Dem snorted. "Whispers of horrors stalking the street, of demons stealing the souls of our women down to hell."

"Is that new?" Savannah paused as Tristan snorted.

Dem merely grunted.

"You don't believe that, do you?" she asked, looking between the siblings.

"No," Dem spat, and Ailene shook her head mutely.

"They're men," she whispered, the terror of her attack still clinging heavily to her. "The one—he was a man. Not a demon or devil. Only a man."

"That doesn't make it better," Tristan said quietly. "Only more real. I promised you we'd stop them. That's why we're here."

Carefully setting the child in the small bassinet she'd given Ailene, Savannah turned. "They'll never stop. Whether the same person attacked me this morning or not, these attacks won't stop."

"True," Tristan agreed, that anger simmering in his tone once more.

"These men? No. I think they're waiting." Dem sighed and looked upward, his muscles taut, hands fisted.

"Did any of the victims work the brothels around here?"

"If this is how you speak in front of the ladies, no wonder you're the used-to-be fiancé." Dem shook his head and glared. "No. None."

"Do you know of a Baron Shilby?" Savannah asked, still not sure how he was connected.

"A baron?" Dem laughed but quickly lowered his voice so as not to wake the child. "You have the wrong street, Miss Savannah."

"He seems interested," she stated. "I want to know why."

"Has anyone other than us asked questions?" Tristan tilted his head and silently moved toward the door.

For all the ramshackle shabbiness of the street, the door itself stood solid and sturdy against the world. Savannah hadn't ever noticed that before, and now she wondered where it'd come from. She studied the door carefully. No, she knew she hadn't seen it before. Where on earth had Dem procured it?

Tristan held up a hand, his ear close against the door. He met her gaze and tilted his chin. Someone, or a group of people, stood outside. She was suddenly glad of the new, solid construction. Taking Tristan's cue, she carefully picked up the baby and passed him to Ailene, who watched silently.

"Has he fussed?" Savannah asked in a slightly louder voice, hoping to keep the conversation normal for any listening ears outside.

Ailene stared at her brother. Dem looked furious at this new intrusion clearly meant to challenge his rule here.

Oh, but Savannah was definitely not dressed for a fight.

"Ailene," she hissed.

"No." Ailene's voice shook. "He's a good baby." She spoke faster now. "I named him Shaw. I hope you don't mind. 'Savannah' didn't quite fit a boy."

"It's a lovely name, and I'm honored." Savannah offered a genuine, happy smile. She steered mother and baby toward the back of the room as Dem stood beside Tristan. Then, slipping her dagger from its sheath, she positioned herself between them and the door.

She was ready.

Tristan nudged Dem, who grunted. "No one else has been around," Dem said in an overly loud voice. "The only one asking questions is you, used-to-be fiancé."

"Don't call me that," Tristan grumbled just loud enough to reach where she stood at the opposite end of the room.

Her lips twitched, but she adjusted her grip on her dagger. Whoever stood outside would also be readying for a fight. Tristan held up three fingers, and as he silently counted down, Savannah turned toward Ailene.

"Anyone after Dem's position?"

"Everyone," Ailene said, her voice didn't waver, and her eyes held a hardness born from the rookery. She had grown up protecting Dem from the gangs, knew how to stand on her own. Cuddling Shaw closer to her, Ailene kissed his head. "The attacks haven't helped."

"I'll see that he gets credit for discovering who did it," Savannah promised as Tristan quietly unlatched the door. "Where'd you get that door?"

"Dem," Ailene said as she turned her back and huddled deeper in the corner with Shaw. "He and a few men took it from one of the ships. Not from Shaw Shipping," she hastened to add. "We don't steal from our friends."

Savannah grinned, dagger at the ready.

CHAPTER 17

Tristan hadn't been in a fight in far too long. He'd always enjoyed a good brawl, but he'd taken his role as captain seriously. If he hadn't wanted his men fighting every other sailor when they docked, then he shouldn't either. It hadn't necessarily worked, but he was still proud of himself for the attempt.

Now, with Savannah at his back ready to defend Ailene, and with Dem beside him, he opened the door. He'd rather have Savannah at his side, but he understood her choice. From the limited interaction he'd had with Dem and Ailene, he knew Dem would kill for his sister. The man was a fighter, not one to take a step back and wait it out.

Tristan hadn't time to plan anything more than this, but he knew Savannah would understand and follow his lead.

"Well, hello," he said jovially to the three men standing in the doorway. It didn't escape his notice that these were three of the same men who had watched Savannah from across the street. "Fancy meeting you here."

"We don't want you, fancy man," one snarled. He was clearly the leader, or someone who desperately wanted to be.

"Fancy man?" He looked at Dem. "What do you think?"

"Too obvious. Not enough insult."

Tristan grinned widely. He did like Dem. "Sorry, but Dem here doesn't like it. I'd ask Miss Savannah, but she's not fond of nicknames at all. Always said that if you can't call someone by their proper name, then you don't respect them."

The man snorted. "We'll take care of her later. The witch can wait."

"Witch?" Savannah's indignant voice echoed back to him. "I object. Besides," she sniffed. "That's too obvious as well."

Tristan's brain spun faster with every heartbeat. These men thought they could unseat Dem. If Tristan opposed them, which of course he planned to do, then he'd solidify Dem's place here, but also his own—these men only saw him as muscle who'd help Dem.

He didn't mind that so much as the fact they were also after Savannah. That made him see red. His temper bubbled beneath the surface, and he tried reigning it in. Unfortunately, with Savannah's safety on the line, that proved difficult.

"Shove off, Roberts," Dem spat. "You have nothing to gain here. Unless you want to die?"

"Let's not be hasty," Tristan said. These men probably believed the stories about demons haunting the street. As if humans hunting each other wasn't bad enough. "If we kill you, Miss Savannah might try and save you, thereby causing more work for her. I won't have that."

"Don't let the black witch touch me," one of the men snarled.

Well, that settled it. Tristan stilled, all humor gone. "Apologize."

The man spat on the ground. When he opened his mouth again, no doubt to hurl more insults, Tristan punched him.

"No one insults my fiancée." He brandished his own khanjar, his wrist moving in the adept way he'd been taught as a boy.

Most people lost all courage in the face of someone who knew how to wield a dagger.

Not this lot.

All three men lunged. They'd clearly been waiting for an invitation. Tristan left the loudmouth so-called leader to Dem. Rather than simply end the man who had insulted Savannah, Tristan tackled him outside, onto the street.

"I understand that you think insulting a woman so far above your station is spot on." He ducked a sloppy swing and jabbed the man in the side, knocking the wind from him. "However, it really isn't the way one courts a lady."

"You don't court a woman like—"

Khanjar forgotten, he punched the man again. Again and again and again—he swung until the man no longer fought back or even tried to block his fists. Tristan punched him until he lay in a heap at his feet. He stood breathing hard, irate over the insults to Savannah, his own careless desertion of her, and all the lost years they hadn't shared. It was all embodied in that single man.

"Tristan."

Savannah's voice shocked him, and he wondered how long she'd been watching. His arms ached, his fists throbbed, and his chest hurt from his labored breathing. Slowly, uncertain what he'd see in her face, he turned.

"Did you mean—" She shook her head. "We'll talk later. Browne and Peters chased off a couple others." Her face remained unreadable in the dim light, her voice even. She didn't give a single thought away. "Come inside."

He did as she requested, brushing his hand down his dinner jacket. He wasn't dressed for a brawl. He'd apologize to Aunt Nadia's staff for the extra work in laundering his clothing. A rip brought his attention back to the matter at hand.

Or perhaps he'd consign his evening wear to the bin.

Without another word, she disappeared inside the dwelling.

Tristan blinked. What had she meant? He didn't spare a look for the man lying in the gutter. But before he could follow Savannah, he saw shadow peel from the wall.

Tristan braced for another fight that didn't come. The street had grown busier, the women off to the theater or other evening work. Most, he noticed, watched the fight, probably trying to figure out who'd come out the winner. Dem had. He now stood over the loudmouth with a triumphant gleam in his eye.

No one else noticed the shadow. Tristan followed the man, not bothering to keeping his distance. He headed not for the church but for Charing Cross, walking as if he knew Tristan followed but didn't care.

"I'm not here for a fight." The man stopped to face him at the intersection, his voice rough.

"Then why are you?" Tristan had a feeling the man smiled, but the roads were dark here, only lit further up, closer to the center of activities. "Out for a leisurely stroll? Want to see the sights?"

"Wanted to check out rumors," the man easily returned.

"I see." Tristan didn't feel threatened by the man. He felt intrigued, and he had a feeling he intrigued the stranger as well. The whole interaction felt more like a ballroom conversation than one taking place in East London, far from any brightly lit room. That strangeness itched down Tristan's spine. "And what have you discovered?"

"That the rumors are true, and you have returned. And that no one here knows anything about what's really happening."

That set Tristan on edge. The man knew him. Otherwise, why say anything about him at all? "That's why you're skulking around? That's all you've learned from your little investigation?"

"It's enough to move on. You should as well." The stranger started walking away.

Tristan let him go, certain he knew the man and equally certain he did not.

"I hear Vauxhall Gardens is a better place for a courtship," he called over his shoulder. "You should take someone up on their offer for a visit!"

Son of a bitch. Tristan glared at Lord Shilby's grandson. Then he headed back for Savannah. Perhaps the grandson wasn't as worthless as he let on.

SAVANNAH DIDN'T KNOW where Tristan disappeared to but waited for him inside Ailene and Dem's house. Dem worked the street, issuing orders and corralling anyone who thought to challenge his authority. His fury over being confronted in his own house, challenged there in front of his sister and Miss Savannah, knew no bounds. Ailene rocked Shaw, who fussed over the interruption of his bedtime.

"Would you have used that knife?" Ailene asked, pacing around with Shaw. She showed no fear, merely curiosity.

"Yes." Savannah looked at the other woman. She tugged off one of her gloves and dabbed at his mouth. Only then, now that the fighting had passed, did her body remember its aches. She swallowed down her hiss of discomfort. "No one hurts those in my charge."

Ailene nodded slowly, bouncing the baby. "Who taught you?"

"My mother." Savannah offered a small smile. "Tristan's mother taught my mother, who taught me and my siblings."

At last, Ailene asked hesitantly, "Can you teach young Shaw? Dem, he's good with a knife, but nothing like yours."

"Ailene, I can teach both of you," Savannah promised. "No one should be unable to protect themselves."

Ailene nodded, looking somewhat stunned, and returned her attention to baby Shaw.

Savannah returned her own attention to the door, listening. It was a good, solid door, and she applauded Dem's innovation, if not exactly his means of procuring it. But those who lived in the rookery hadn't much choice. Which ship had he taken it from? Perhaps she'd surreptitiously repay the owner, though he'd no doubt already put in an insurance claim. Perhaps she'd purchase the row of homes, if not to remodel them, then at least—

The knock interrupted her thoughts. Savannah had strained for it, waiting for the signal as if she and Tristan were once more sneaking around one house or another. One knock, pause, then three in rapid succession. Barely a pause, then a staccato of five knocks.

Savannah opened the door as Shaw quieted at his mother's breast.

"You're bleeding."

Tristan looked surprised. "I am?" He grunted, scowling in annoyance. "I didn't think he'd managed a blow. Damn."

"It's not bad." She reached for her basket but of course hadn't brought it tonight. "What did you discover?"

Tristan's gaze flicked toward the back of the room, but Ailene had disappeared into the kitchen, away from their conversation. "Ran into Shilby."

"Lord Shilby?" Savannah straightened in surprise, her hand dropping from Tristan's lips. He caught it in his own, warm and solid. "He was here?"

"No. Mr. Shilby, the grandson."

Tilting her head as she worked through that, Savannah asked the first relevant question that made sense. "Did you catch his name?"

"I'm afraid we didn't exchange pleasantries."

"Drat." Frowning, she dabbed at his lip again. "No matter." For all that Lord Shilby—George—had tried matching her with his heir, Savannah had never paid enough attention to Mr.

Shilby to even bother learning his name. "What was he doing here?"

"Looking for someone or something, I'd say. He suggested Vauxhall again." Tristan paused, his lips turning downward. "I can't say it had much to do with this particular investigation, but I also can't explain why he was even here."

"This is far more complicated than I originally believed."

"You believed someone trying to kill you wasn't complicated?" Tristan asked in disbelief.

"No. I mean, yes." She sighed and pressed a finger to her forehead. It didn't help the beginnings of a headache. "There are too many players now. Shilby, Baron *and* heir. Crichton. The entirety of Denmark Street." She paused again. "None of this makes any sense."

"I wonder if the Shilbys are muddying the field."

It was possible, but she couldn't figure out why they'd do it. "What would be the point?" She hesitated, but it wasn't as if they hadn't already discussed her lack of socializing. "Until Eliza's picnic, I hadn't seen the baron since you left."

She'd cut herself off so completely, it was a wonder her friends still tried. Grateful they had, she planned to thank Eliza once more. Perhaps extend an invitation to her, since she hadn't had any visitors in three years. Well, perhaps she had, but the staff had followed her strict instructions not to disturb her.

"Let's get home." Tristan shook his head, winced, and placed a hand on his jaw. He moved it gingerly, grimacing, which caused him another grunt of pain. Or perhaps annoyance.

"Ailene?" Savannah called softly, a smile already forming. Tristan wasn't as dramatic as the rest of his family, but he certainly had a way about him. One that tugged at her heart. "I'll return tomorrow. Send Robbie round if you need anything before then."

Ailene returned from the kitchen and nodded, watching her curiously. She placed a cold, work-roughened hand on Savannah's. "I've never seen you this happy. He might be the used-to-be fiancé, but he makes you happy."

Savannah's heart skipped.

Standing at the door, looking both the same and different as he had before, Tristan held out a hand. It was reminiscent of so many times past, but he held himself differently now. Taller, which was ridiculous—she knew he hadn't grown. When she'd kissed him in the theater hallway, every single bit of his body had felt the same against hers.

Savannah took Tristan's hand and let him lead her outside. The night had cooled with a strange buzz in the air, like the calm before a storm. She didn't see Dem or any of those who challenged his authority. She also didn't look very hard.

Browne and Peters materialized from the shadows only two doors from Dem's. Neither looked any worse for wear, but Browne limped slightly.

"I'll take you home," Tristan said as Peters hailed a hackney. "We can talk tomorrow."

Yes, that sounded perfectly reasonable. A good night's sleep after all this. Or not, given she hadn't slept much since his return. Then tomorrow, when she wasn't so tempted by him, by her memories and those long-suppressed feelings, they'd talk.

Browne slammed the hackney's door closed, isolating them in the darkened carriage. The hackney rocked as the footmen climbed onto the back, but Savannah only had eyes for Tristan.

"Stay with me."

Tristan's head shot up. "What?"

As much as her head shouted that this was a terrible idea, that they'd only this evening discussed moving forward together, the words remained spoken. Savannah could dismiss them. She could say she didn't mean it, had spoken in the heat of the moment, or some such.

Except she had meant it.

"Stay with me." She reached across the cab and took his hand.

"Why?"

"I could say it's because I want to talk, but we both know that isn't true. I want you. Even after everything, I still do." That admission burned through her, as hot as his touch.

"This isn't a strange way of getting me alone so you can toss me out the window?" Despite his jesting words, his gaze remained level and serious on hers. He held her hand confidently.

"I'm always tempted by that." She grinned, knowing deep in her bones that this was right. "But I want you anyway."

"You have me." He reached across the cab and traced a finger down her cheek. "Always."

CHAPTER 18

Tristan kept his hand on the small of Savannah's back as Walters opened the door. He ignored the man, who watched him with far less hostility, as Savannah took his hand and guided him up the stairs, toward the family rooms. There'd be words later, he had no doubt. But later wasn't now.

"Are you sure?" The words drifted between them in the silent hallway.

She didn't lead him toward her bedroom, the one he knew as well as his own. Rather, they walked past the door he expected her to open, past the one he knew led to her youngest sister's room, and toward the end of the hall.

"When you left, I didn't want any reminder of our time together." Her hand squeezed his, warm and assured. "I…am not proud when I say I destroyed my room."

"You were angry. Betrayed," he added with a stab to his own heart. Guilt, remorse, a choking sorrow and regret. "I don't blame you."

He hadn't thought about what he'd have done if she'd suddenly left him with a five-line letter about finding himself and needing to explore the adventure he'd so long craved. He hadn't thought about a lot of things when he left.

"I haven't set foot in that room since," she whispered, her voice as soft as a spring breeze. "I never thought I'd sneak you back into my rooms." Savannah turned, her dark eyes unreadable in the dim hallway. "Though I suppose I didn't sneak so much as waltz you past Walters."

"I'll be sure to look for a knife headed into my back." He said the words jokingly but didn't raise his voice or smile. He merely watched her.

Arousal tore through him, the temptation of her lips drawing him closer. His fingers ached to brush her skin, and Tristan slipped his fingers along her wrist. Savannah shivered at his touch, her breath warm over his cheek. His heart raced with need, his cock aching for her touch.

"You jest—"

"I don't," he corrected as she pushed open the door and led him inside. "I know what I did."

Savannah watched him for a drawn-out moment. A fire warmed the room, chasing away the nighttime chill.

"I won't push you. I never would." The words sounded confident, even yet oddly quiet in her room. A room he'd never before stepped foot in. He didn't bother taking in the decorations. They didn't matter. "I know forgiveness is...well, I'm not sure it's possible. Or that even I deserve it."

He lifted her hand to his lips and pressed a kiss against her knuckles. Her fingers trembled, but she didn't pull away, and her gaze never left his. Tristan stepped closer.

"All I know right now is I haven't felt this alive in three years. I don't know if it's because I'm visiting people I once considered friends, or because this mystery involved me."

She closed the little distance left between them, framed his face, and pressed her lips against his.

Tristan ached to deepen the kiss but held himself back. "You're sure, Savannah?"

"About wanting you? Yes. About wanting to feel you move within me? Yes." She breathed out that last and ran her hands over his shoulders, sliding off his jacket. "Make love to me, Tristan."

He thought he should ask about tomorrow, whether she'd regret it then, but this was her choice, and she'd clearly made it. She wanted him, and Lord knew he wanted her. Always had.

"Should I lock the door?" He felt her smile against his kiss, her soft laugh warm against his cheek. "Like old times?"

"No one ever said anything, but I'm sure we weren't as secretive as we thought."

She pushed off his waistcoat and let it drop, then tugged his shirt over his head and let that drop as well. They'd never been careful. Not with their clothing, not with sneaking about. Not even with withdrawing during sex, though they both knew he ought.

"I'm equally sure Hugh talked Sophia out of calling me out numerous times." He turned her around, struggling with the laces along the back of her gown. Slowly he revealed her beautiful dark skin with every freed button.

"You're taking your time," she complained, a slight hint of breathlessness in her words. "You never used to."

"It's been three years," he needlessly reminded her. "I want to savor every inch of your skin. Every touch. I missed it." He pressed his lips against her shoulder. "Missed the taste of your skin." He nipped the nape of her neck, and she shuddered.

Finally relieved of the dress, Savannah faced him and made quick work of the rest of her undergarments. He watched her as he unbuttoned the fall of his trousers and shoved them off. She pressed her body against his, pushing him toward the bed, her mouth on his. She kissed the same, tasted the same.

He hit the bed and sat down, instinctually pulling her onto

his lap. With every kiss, every touch along her naked skin, Tristan knew. He'd never let her go again.

IT CLAWED THROUGH HER, that wild need for Tristan's touch, for his body pressed intimately against hers.

Was this wise? Probably not. Did she care? No.

Savannah wanted this, and only this.

Settling herself on his thighs, his cock hard between them, she rocked lightly. The feel of him so close shivered over her skin. With her fingers tangled in his hair, she absently noted that his soft curls felt the same. She didn't think that would've changed, after all, he kissed the same, felt the same beneath her as she ground her hips against his.

Lust consumed her—only that mattered. Assuaging the ache that had burned through her since seeing him again.

"It was never the same," she admitted. "No matter how I touched myself, it wasn't you."

Tristan scooted back on the bed, bringing her with him, until his back hit the headboard. He tossed pillows aside and kicked the comforter out of his way, but he never released her. "Nothing was the same," he agreed. "I promise, I only ever wanted you."

She believed him. He'd told her that before, and she believed it then, too. "I know."

Still straddling him, she wrapped her hand around his cock and eased him into her. It'd been years, but her body welcomed him. Tristan's mouth closed over one nipple, his teeth grazing the hard nub just as she liked it. One hand rolled her other nipple, tugging until she gasped, rocking hard against him.

"More," she ordered, her body on fire, as if chasing her first orgasm ever.

He kissed along her shoulder, one hand on her hip as she

rocked over him, the other slipping between her folds to find her clit.

"Yes," she hissed at that first touch.

He rolled the sensitive nub between his fingers, tugging on it, scraping a blunt nail along it over and over, until that pleasure she longed for crashed over her. He didn't stop, even as her hips rolled against his, taking him deeper again and again and *oh, yes!*

Savannah chanted his name, her arms wrapped around his shoulders, her nails digging into his back, her thighs tightening around his hips. *More*, she thought, her teeth closing around his shoulder as another orgasm swept her away, over that delicious cliff, pleasure swamping her limbs.

"Savannah." He rolled them both over, shifting her legs over his shoulder, and thrust into her again.

"Yes." She dug her nails into his back, arching to meet each thrust as he pounded into her, chasing his own pleasure.

She wanted another orgasm—it'd been so long—but her clit still tingled, and her nipples ached from Tristan's teeth. Delicious, wonderful, delectable aches that she celebrated for what they were.

He came then, grunting her name as he pulled out, rolling onto his side and breathing hard. Though her own limbs were heavy with pleasure, Savannah rolled onto her side and rested a hand on Tristan's chest.

When his breathing evened out and he opened his eyes, she smiled. "I don't regret tonight."

His hand rested on hers, holding it over his heart. "Good." He raised their joined fingers and kissed hers. "I could never regret our time together."

She lay in silence for a while, weighing what happened with what she wanted. She wanted it all. Wanted the feel of Tristan inside her just as much as she wanted to never feel such abject grief and betrayal again.

"I don't know if this means I forgive you," she said into the darkness of her bedroom, which Tristan had never before set foot in. Did that make this a christening of sorts? Savannah had no idea. She'd never felt particularly attached to this room; it'd been a means to an end. Nothing more, nothing less.

A place to sleep and dress, devoid of any trinkets or memories she'd collected over the years. Tristan's presence changed that. Now, with so much changed in the last week, she wondered if her mother had kept any of the items that had once decorated her room. The memories Savannah had thought she no longer wanted.

"I know." His hand tightened around hers. "I don't know that I could forgive me in your situation." He rolled onto his side and tugged her close. "But until you tell me otherwise, I won't give up on us."

His vow, hot and low with promise and want and potential, slid over her skin like a caress.

"I know my stupid choice broke your trust in me, but I swear I'll spend the rest of my life—the rest of ours—earning that trust again." He kissed her slowly, running his fingers down her back. Savannah sighed and slung a leg over his hips, pulling him closer.

"I know." Savannah sighed and closed her eyes, resting her head on his chest. That, too, felt the same, and she wondered why she'd thought it wouldn't. "When you left, I fell into a deep melancholy. It nearly broke me."

His hands tightened around her, and for one moment, unreasonable or otherwise, she resented that he hadn't felt the same.

"I never meant for that," he whispered, his voice cracking. "When I left, it truly was a spur-of-the-moment decision." He kissed her forehead, and she relaxed against him.

"Your return, our time together now, it's made me see our lives in a new light." She spoke slowly, letting the darkness cocoon them, the fire banish the chill, the silence bolster her resolve. "If we had married then, I'm sure we would've been happy, but perhaps not content."

"How so?" He shifted and tried to tug the bedding from beneath them, but gave it up as a lost cause. They had tangled everything in their haste for completion. "Because of my restlessness?"

She leaned back just enough to watch him. "That, yes. But also, my own. I know now I would never feel content following in Mama's footsteps. That's not who I am. If the past had been different, I might've been happy doing what she does. But now, that's not what I want."

"You know," Tristan said slowly, "I understand better than you might think. Those first days and weeks were…well, hard."

Savannah had a feeling they were more than hard, but she let it slide. Neither did she voice a snippy comment about how he didn't have to leave. That's not what this conversation was about, and they'd moved beyond those angry retorts.

"I regretted it. I missed you, I hated everything, and yet being on the sea, on my own ship, it was…thrilling."

Once more, she didn't say that she would've gone with him.

"Where did you sail first?"

"Rotterdam. It was already on the itinerary; we had a shipment there. Simple, easy." He settled in, drawing her close, and if Savannah closed her eyes she could almost envision this was them before. Except now she realized she hadn't wanted before. She wanted now.

"How did Arnault take all this? It was his captaincy, you said, yes?"

"Better than he should've," Tristan agreed. "But he only laughed. He has this booming laugh you can hear across the Channel. Slapped me on the back and told me to have at it. He'd been sailing with the company for a while. I think when Karl Van den Berg retired from his pirate ways, Arnault missed the sea." Tristan paused, and she heard the faintest of laughs from him. "Or perhaps he was running from something on land. He never said, and I didn't pry."

"Did you enjoy it? Living on the ship, sailing from port to port, being so far from your family?" *From me*, she wanted to add but refrained, proud she'd managed to reign in her pettiness. They'd moved on from that.

"Enjoy?" He sounded like he was weighing the word. "I don't know about that. I missed my family." He squeezed her side. "You. I know it might not seem so, but I did. Terribly."

"Go on," she managed.

"I even occasionally missed land." The humor had returned to his voice, but he didn't release her nor loosen his grip. "Would I sail again? Yes, probably. Things are different now."

"They are." So many things were different, not only his return. He was different, and she was as well. Savannah rolled onto her back but held his hand. "I've been thinking about the man who was shot."

"That's what you think of while we're in bed together?" He sighed dramatically, but she heard the smile in his voice.

Turning her head, she grinned back. "It was when I was on top."

Savannah envisioned it now, shivering at the memory. She'd raised up onto her knees, Tristan's mouth on her breasts, his hand teasing her folds. At the time, for obvious reasons, she hadn't connected that jolt.

"I must be losing my touch," he grumbled.

"Hmm." She stretched in languid aftermath. "Definitely not that."

"You still don't think that rifle was aimed at you?" He sounded skeptical, which she understood now that she wasn't fighting for the freedom she'd craved. The one thing she'd clung to when he'd left, and she felt she needed that new path.

"He was shorter than me." Eyes closed, she envisioned the

poor man who'd died next to her. His features remained fuzzy; she hadn't looked at him that long or hard. And then he'd been shot. "Even if the rifle had been aimed at my heart, he wasn't that much shorter, an inch or so, no more."

"Perhaps they are two separate incidents," he acknowledged.

"Finally," she huffed. "Though I admit that doesn't explain the knife."

"Maybe it was one of those men from tonight." His hand tightened around her, as if he could protect her in the safety of her bed from the attackers. "It's a stretch, I agree. The timing is a little too perfect."

"It was someone, either those who don't want me helping or someone else. I don't know."

"Maybe that knife always wasn't aimed at you," he said slowly, hand still moving rhythmically along her arm.

"What do you mean?" She pulled back and looked at him but could barely see him in the darkness.

"Mr. Shilby's presence. I still don't understand that or his grandfather's interest in anything that happens in the rookery."

"I'll agree with that," she sighed. "Or why either man would discuss it with John Crichton."

"He was there for a reason, and I doubt very much it had anything to do with the murders of those women. He said he was looking for something."

"Something?" she asked. "Or someone?"

"If I were a betting man, I'd say someone." Tristan huffed. "I should've asked him about his interest."

"He didn't seem interested in telling you," Savannah pointed out.

"No, but he definitely showed an interest in me taking you to Vauxhall Gardens." He offered a slight laugh, one Savannah couldn't quite decipher. "If that's the case, and his interest is not in the murdered women—"

"I also agree with that," Savannah added.

"Then we're the ones muddying the field." Tristan hummed for a bit, his thumb running along the backs of her knuckles. "Perhaps *we* brought in too many players, made this more difficult than it should've been."

Looking back at that conversation at Eliza's picnic, Savannah had a feeling that Lord Shilby's interest in Vauxhall Gardens had more to do with her and Tristan's renewed courtship. She'd been so focused on finding the culprits that she hadn't really considered anything else.

"I think you're right. I think Lord Shilby invited us to Vauxhall not for answers to this crime, but more for our courtship." Savannah paused and frowned. "I wonder if he knows anything about the dead man."

"How so?" Tristan shook his head. "It's a stretch, but I'm willing to entertain the idea."

"I agree, and I've no proof or even anything more than a guess. Other than the gangs there, what purpose would Mr. Shilby have in setting foot in the rookery, let alone that specific street?"

"True," he agreed slowly. "Or even in speaking about it with John. Damn it. I should've asked him," he growled.

He'd wanted to return to her, and Savannah didn't mind that one bit. "If Shilby's interest was in the dead man, then he might know something." Before she could follow that line of thinking, a small weight plopped onto her naked belly. "Ooph."

"What?" Tristan was already moving, reaching for his hip, where his dagger most definitely did not sit.

"Jiesha." Laughing, Savannah picked up the small, soft rabbit and lightly stroked her. "Oh, I'm sorry, sweetheart. Did we scare you?"

She felt a pang of remorse for forgetting about the rabbit, but then she'd been utterly focused on Tristan. And his kisses. And most definitely his body.

Tristan reached out, but Jiesha nipped his fingers. He looked highly affronted. "I saved you!" he told the rabbit. "I rescued you from Van Zanten!" He pouted and cradled his fingers, though Savannah knew Jiesha hadn't nipped him that hard. "This is the thanks I get? Hmph."

Savannah laughed, holding the rabbit close and leaning up to kiss Tristan. "She knows who feeds her; she's no fool. I'm clearly her favorite."

Tristan grumbled, pulling Savannah close once more. "Let's not talk about rabbits, not while we're in bed." He pressed a kiss against the corner of her mouth. "Let's not talk about murder, either." Another kiss to the other corner of her mouth. "Let's stay in the here and now."

Savannah kissed him back, still holding the rabbit but letting Tristan's tempting kisses sway her. The future could wait; only right now mattered. Pulling back, she set Jiesha back on the floor on the opposite side of the bed. No sense in stepping on the poor rabbit in the darkness.

Savannah wrapped her arms around Tristan's neck and tugged him down, letting his weight comfort her even as it excited her.

"And how should we pass the evening then, Mr. Conrad?"

"Let me show you." He nipped along her neck, his hands cupping her breasts. "Let me make you scream." He took her nipples and tugged hard, pulling the breath from her and making her arch into his touch. "Perhaps we'll scandalize the servants."

Savannah's laugh turned into a moan as he slipped a finger into her wetness. *Yes*, she thought, already aching for more. *This right here.*

CHAPTER 19

॰⌇॰

The sun barely lit the sky when Savannah opened her eyes again. She'd spent the night in Tristan's arms and though she seriously thought about it, already knew her answer. She wanted that future with him.

Tristan's lips brushed her shoulder, which still stung from her fall yesterday. Savannah ignored it. There were more important things on her horizon than a little shoulder pain. Like making love to Tristan again.

"When I was in Riga, I saw beautifully laid out parks. They rebuilt after the French burned much of the city's perimeter," Tristan whispered over her skin, his hands sliding around her waist and up to cup her breasts. "They were beautiful… peaceful."

His choice of words surprised her, and Savannah decided not to hide it. This was their second chance, as he said. She'd not squander it on keeping her own feelings secret. "That might be the first time I've ever heard you use such a word." Her head fell back, resting on his shoulder. She didn't stop either his kisses or his words. "I know you to be many things. Peaceful is not one of them."

He laughed, a low, soft sound that brushed over her skin, reminding her of all they'd shared. And all they could—and would—again. His fingers lazily tweaked her nipples, teeth nipping the sensitive space between shoulder and neck.

"The only time I've ever known true peace is in your arms." He paused, pressing his lips hard against the side of her throat to forestall whatever protest he thought she might make.

Savannah had none, had no words at all. Her heart thudded so loudly she wouldn't have been surprised if he heard it. If the entirety of the house heard it. Licking her lips, she willed her heart to stay quiet, wishing her mind would speak instead. Once more, he spoke first.

"I've spoke of it before, and I know I haven't been clear no matter how hard I try." He shook his head. His fingers resumed their delicious torture, his mouth kissing along the side of her neck. "My heart missed you every day. I constantly thought of you. Those adventures I craved would've been so much more enthralling if you'd been there."

"But you didn't ask," she reminded him, heartache once more twisting through her. That betrayal. Would it ever stop hurting?

After last night, Savannah had thought so. Hoped so. Now, even in his arms, her blood heating, her arousal pooling hot between her legs, she had no idea.

"It took me three attempts to explain and almost losing you again, but I realize why." He huffed out a breath and rested his hand over Savannah's. He lifted her hand and kissed her palm, turning her so she faced him. "I was scared."

"Scared?" Savannah froze at the admission, half risen on her knees over him. Her head jerked upward, and she stared at him in shock and disbelief. She had not expected that answer. "Of what? Me? Us?"

"Of disappointing you," he whispered.

"I don't understand." Head tilted, she watched him in the lightening day. They hadn't bothered closing the drapery last night, and now the dawn cast him in burgeoning light. It highlighted his eyes, serious as they held hers.

"It's nagged at me." He didn't look away, didn't distract her. He held her hand, solemn and sincere. "When I was fighting that man last night, I kept thinking, *Don't disappoint her. Not again. And definitely don't die.*"

"Good," she quipped primly despite their current position. "I'd have been most vexed."

His lips ghosted into a smile. "I hadn't realized I'd been thinking that same thing for the last three years. Or some version of it. *Don't disappoint Savannah. Don't let her realize the truth about you.*"

Try as she might, Savannah couldn't clear her face of its frown. Nor could she ignore the confusion that seeped into her. "I don't understand. What truth? I know everything about you." She paused and squeezed his arm. "Everything about your family."

The secrets he'd told only her, the ones that his siblings had insisted were meant for the person he trusted most. His mother's heritage as the daughter of an Egyptian soldier and a Turkish sultana. His father's compulsion with the drink and opium.

The reasons he never drank, never gambled.

"I wouldn't spill your secrets," she added in a slight huff, not at all certain where this conversation was headed. "No matter what."

"I know," he said quickly. "Savannah, I know. It's not about that. You do know me best." His lips twisted into a wry grin. "Better than I know myself."

She huffed. Settling on the bed beside him, all thoughts of making love again vanished in the face of his confession. Now that she wasn't near his warmth, she shivered and tugged the bedding around her. "Please explain."

"It wasn't Philip's grand stories about adventure," he began, shifting so he faced her. "Not entirely. Something else pushed me—farther, faster, do more, see more, help more."

Savannah nodded slowly. She couldn't brace for his next words; he'd already surprised her. Something in her shifted, and she had a feeling it was the wall surrounding her heart. Its last pieces falling away. Part of her tried to grab onto them, rebuild that wall that kept her safe from pain.

"I hadn't realized it, not fully, until last night. Even when I rescued—" He made a face, a grimace that turned into a smile—"*stole* Jiesha. When I liberated the two office workers. I know now that same thought raced through my mind. *Don't disappoint Savannah.*"

"If you had stayed, do you think you'd have disappointed me?" she whispered, the words pulled from her syllable by syllable. "That us being together, building a life, would have disappointed me?"

"I think I was afraid that if I had stayed, if the life we'd planned came to fruition, then I'd still have disappointed you. Somehow, some way."

"You can't have known that," she snapped, more confused now than when they'd started this conversation. "No one can know the future."

"No, you're right." He looked away, over her shoulder at the wall behind her, and shook his head. "Was I scared of marrying you? No. Of a life with you? No." He took her hand again and held it tight in his. "I always wanted to be your knight in shining armor. The perfect man for the woman I loved and worshipped."

"There's no such thing as perfection," she said quietly. Savannah felt as if the words echoed around the room.

"I know that now. I know that the only thing that disappointed you was me leaving. That any conversation we would've shared about this before would've been smarter, far more preferable to me sailing away for three years in a stupid attempt at finding myself."

"And have you?" She tilted her head, watching him carefully.

He was different. Changed. More at peace, though until he'd used that word, she'd never have herself. Not when it came to Tristan. Constantly on the move, constantly learning, implementing his knowledge. He was the smartest person she knew; at one time he planned to study law. He read all the journals—astronomical, farming and horticultural, veterinary, medicine, even the newly expanding area of natural science.

He rarely slept, always telling her there was so much to do in this life.

"Have you found that peace?"

"Yes, I think so. Finally," he added with another twist of his lips and a squeeze to her hand. "Now that I'm back here. With you."

TRISTAN DIDN'T KNOW how much of that conversation made any sense. How much sounded like a rambling attempt at putting emotion into words and how much sounded cohesive. If any of it had.

"I can see the change," Savannah said as she shifted again, tugging him onto the bed beside her.

She wrapped her arms around his shoulders but instead of kissing him, nodded slowly. Whatever change she saw, Tristan felt. Pulling her closer, he kissed her jaw and rolled onto his back, settling them comfortably together.

"At first, I thought it was because of the distance between us. Three years is a long time. I thought perhaps I hadn't known you as well as I'd assumed, given—well, given you left with barely a word." Her hand squeezed his shoulder, and her voice softened. "But yes. That peace you speak of, that's what's different about you. What are your plans now?"

"They haven't changed," he said. "I still love you, perhaps more now than I did before." He chuckled, low and warm. "And if you're in doubt over whether I still want you, I hope last night put those worries at ease."

She laughed, a light breath of sound that banished his own worry. "Consider me put at ease."

They stayed like that in silence for a while, and Tristan once more felt that sense of peace.

"When you returned, I most certainly didn't want to give you a second chance. I'm not entirely sure what's changed since then, but something has."

She paused again, and he let her have this time, focused entirely on Savannah. She was, and always had been, the only person who mattered.

"We have this life to do with as we please." She met his gaze in the brightening dawn, which flickered enticingly in her dark eyes. "I don't wish to squander any more of our time together. I don't know if I still love you or if I have fallen in love with you again—but I know that what I feel for you now is stronger than I ever thought it could be."

"I love you, Savannah," he whispered. "More than I have words to express. More than any apology can say."

Tristan moved then, rolling her beneath him and kissing her. He wanted to ask her to marry him. Again. Wanted to plan a future—a new future—together. For right now, with her naked body beneath his and the morning lightning the room, all he wanted was to taste her. Feel her shudder around him, hear her breathless cries as she orgasmed.

He urged her higher onto the bed and knelt before her, dancing his fingers up her legs. Kissing her bare skin, he smiled when he felt her thighs tremble and her breath catch. His fingers teased closer, and he nipped the sensitive skin on her inner thigh. She'd always loved that.

Savannah shuddered beneath his touch, and his tongue darted out, caressing the light bite. Hands curling into the bedding, she opened her legs and urged him closer. Kissing along her inner thigh, he lightly teased her folds, rubbing lazy circles around her most sensitive place.

She whimpered, a low sound in the back of her throat.

"That's it, my Savannah." He slipped a finger into her, kissing along her thigh. She gasped and clenched around him, hips arching into his touch. "Let go for me."

He loved teasing her, tasting her. He knew the pace was slow and playful, that she wanted more, craved that orgasm he kept just out of reach. But Tristan wanted to hear her scream.

"Yes," he whispered against her belly, fingers pressed harder against her clit. "Scream. Go on."

He scraped his nail over her clit, circling it as his fingers thrust into her. She gasped his name, and Tristan thought he'd never heard a more beautiful sound. She tightened around his fingers, nails digging into his shoulders as her orgasm crashed against her.

Tristan didn't say a word—he didn't have to. Instead, he gently kissed her hip, up her belly. Her chin, her cheek. Savannah opened her eyes, panting. He wanted to grin at the dazed look on her face, but then she nipped his throat and drew him closer until he settled between her thighs.

His nudged her throat, pressed soft kisses along her skin, inhaled the beautiful scent of her orgasm. His fingers brushed her core again, easily slipping in, and he teased her once more.

His beautiful Savannah arched against his touch, and she kissed him hard, nipping his bottom lip with a hint of desperation.

"Tristan," she moaned, wrapping her legs around his waist. Her fingers danced down his chest, teasing just above his cock.

His breath caught in a growl when she caressed the tip of him. She ran her fingers over the head of his cock, then scraped her nails down to his balls.

Tristan shuddered against her, breathing deeply into the crook of her neck. Savannah guided him into her, humming breathlessly when he thrust hard. She rocked against him, nails trailing along his hips. When she raked them across the small of his back, his control snapped.

Steadying himself on his arms, he watched her as he thrust into her. Her head fell to the bedding, and her breath caught, fingers pressed hard against his sides. Tristan moved, thrusting hard into her welcoming body, his blood on fire, his entire being focused on her and her alone.

She met his every thrust, pressing her fingers to her nub, her lips parted, and she breathed his name, her hips meeting his with every thrust.

Tristan groaned even as she gasped something he didn't hear, and moved faster, thrusting harder into her. His teeth nipped her throat, found her lips again and kissed her hard.

Her nails dug into his back, hips meeting his as her orgasm crashed through her, and she cried out, eyes closed, his name falling from her lips.

He kissed her, a sloppy, bruising kiss, and pounded into her. It wouldn't be long—he was already on the edge—then he shattered, pulling out and shuddering in her arms.

Savannah caught him. She always had. Holding him tight as her own breathing evened out, Tristan knew he'd never let her slip away again.

"I love you," he whispered against her cheek. "Always."

CHAPTER 20

"Where is he?" Lyneé's voice, louder than it should be considering her question, burst into the room with the same vigorous anger she did.

The door slammed against the wall, no doubt smashing a hole in the plaster. The sound reverberated through the room and along Savannah's nerves. Her sister looked fierce, like an Amazon warrior hunting for a Roman soldier.

Forcing her lips not to curve into a smile, Savannah smoothed her hands down her day gown and met her sister's gaze. "He hasn't snuck out, if that's what you're thinking."

Lyneé looked carefully around the room, as if she might spot Tristan in a compromising position. "He left you?"

"Are you angry that he was here, or that he no longer is?" Savannah couldn't hide the humor in her voice and grinned at her sister. Lyneé didn't seem amused. Pity. "He's under the bed."

"Hiding from Mama?"

"No." Tristan's muffled voice grunted with effort. He wiggled out, arse in the air and looking most becoming in his evening trousers. "Rescuing Jiesha from the upstairs maids." He held up the rabbit, who looked less than pleased with her so-called rescuer. Lucky for Tristan, he held her head motionless, so she didn't nip at him. Again. "Or the upstairs maids from Jiesha. Take your pick."

Lyneé looked skeptical. Clearly Tristan had spent the night, but Savannah wasn't worried about the gossip. The household staff had been hired and retained for their discretion. And while Walters might've threatened Tristan, he wouldn't talk about her bedroom goings-on with any of the street's other servants. Not even Aunt Nadia's household.

"I heard there was a brawl." Lyneé closed the door behind her but didn't look entirely mollified. She eyed Tristan's ripped clothing with a raised eyebrow.

"Bah, a mere scuffle," Tristan countered.

Savannah remembered the hateful look on that man's face the moment before Tristan tackled him. That was why she carried her dagger. That was why she took Browne every single time she ventured outside the house. Why she'd retained Dem's protection.

"They didn't like my being there. Or Dem's leadership," Savannah said tiredly. Then she gestured for the small table on the balcony.

"Dem said there were rumors about demons killing the women," Tristan added. "It's possible they were the ones who started those rumors."

The sun had just barely risen. It was far too early for all but a small stream of servants and the hardiest of gossips. With her room closer to the rear courtyard and the gardens, she doubted anyone could see them. Specifically, that Tristan had joined them for an intimate breakfast.

"I do so enjoy when people claim they want answers without trying to discover those answers themselves." Lyneé sighed and sat opposite her, her eyes flicking between Savannah and Tristan. Thankfully, her sister kept all her questions to herself. For now.

"Have you had the chance to speak with Lord Shilby?" Tristan asked, still holding Jiesha.

"No." Lyneé sounded surprised. "Why?"

"We think," Savannah said slowly, "that the man who was murdered in front of me is the reason the baron and John Crichton are interested in the St. Giles murders."

"What makes you say that?" Lyneé reached for a cup of tea, but of course no setting graced the table yet. She scowled.

Savannah agreed; it was entirely too early for this sort of conversation without fortification. "I'll call for breakfast."

As loathe as she was to leave Lyneé alone with Tristan, Savannah stood and rang for her lady's maid. Coyle, well used to the early hours, appeared a moment later, and Savannah requested breakfast. Yes, for three.

The quiet of the table did not ease Savannah's tension. She and Tristan had settled more than she'd expected last night: they still very much wanted each other, still loved each other.

Even now, attired in a fresh morning gown that he'd helped her dress in, and *quite* satisfied, she wanted to reach across and touch him. She'd laugh at her improperness, but nothing about her relationship with Tristan had ever been proper.

"At Eliza's picnic, Lord Shilby mentioned the murders," Savannah began, if for no other reason than to break the tension vibrating over the table.

"How did he know of them?" Lyneé drummed her fingers on the table as Tristan moved his chair closer to Savannah's.

From the corner of her eye, she saw his lips curve a heartbeat before he rested his hand on her leg. Even through the layers of her gown and undergarments, she felt the heat of his touch.

"That's the question," Tristan agreed. "Why would a baron, even a forward-thinking one such as Shilby, care about the murders of poor women from the rookery?" He shook his head as his hand moved up her thigh. Savannah clamped down on her reaction but had a feeling she failed to hide it completely.

"If the stranger was targeted by someone else, that would explain Shilby and Crichton's interest." Tristan's hand moved higher, and she lost her thoughts in the heat of his touch.

Luckily, the scratch at the door that indicated breakfast brought her back to the matter at hand.

"Thank you," she murmured to the maid, who wheeled in trays of food. No meat today, which surprised Savannah. Not that the kitchen staff didn't know that Tristan didn't eat sausage or bacon, but that they didn't hold the last three years against him and "forget" that part.

"That would make sense," Lyneé was saying when Savannah returned.

"It's the only thing that does," Savannah added as she took the hot kanaka and poured the coffee into her cup, stirring in the cardamom with a quick flick of her wrist. "Otherwise, there's something else about these murders we're missing."

"What about the cravat?" Lyneé held her teacup against her lips, eyes closing as she inhaled the fragrance and heat.

"Arnault insists it's some sort of satin silk, incredibly expensive." Tristan looked at the toast in his hand, head tilted. "He was investigating which shops sold such fabrics. I had my cabin boy, Little Ricky, eavesdropping in them, but as of yesterday, he hadn't learned much." He met Savannah's gaze. "I'll return this morning and find out what they discovered," he promised.

She nodded and bit into her own toast and blackberry jam. "Even if they list every person who bought a black cravat, it's still a whole list of suspects to go through."

"The attacks are still happening in daylight?" Lyneé asked.

"Yes, which only means they think they can get away with it." Tristan scowled.

"They have thus far," Savannah reminded him. "But if the stranger's death had nothing to do with the murders or me, then that means there is more than one killer in the rookery." She paused and realized the absurdity of that comment. "More than one that we're looking for," she amended. "I realize people are killed every day."

Tristan's hand returned to her thigh, so very close to the juncture of her legs that Savannah nearly moaned.

Lyneé rolled her eyes, clearly aware of what was happening between her and Tristan. "Have you asked Shilby or Crichton about their information?" Lyneé asked rather than comment.

"Not yet. We only realized the connection recently." Tristan's smooth deflection made Savannah choke on her yogurt and berries.

She swallowed hard. "I'll send a note round to Lord Shilby about a meeting."

"Include his grandson," Tristan added.

She nodded and met Lyneé's gaze. Her sister watched them through narrowed eyes but remained silent about any reconciliation—true reconciliation, not merely the pretense Savannah had once insisted upon—between them.

The anger that had simmered inside her for so long hadn't exactly dissipated. It had lessened, not so heavy, not so onerous and demanding of her energy. She might never absolutely forgive Tristan, and she'd definitely never forget what happened, but she knew she wanted to start anew.

WHILE TRISTAN WENT off to Bond Street to inquire about the cravat, and what his cabin boy had discovered, Savannah returned to Denmark Street, on the opposite side of the wealth coin. She might never be fully accepted in either place, but at least in the rookery, there were people who needed her and respected her.

"You've forgiven him then?" Lyneé asked, her tone nothing but skepticism.

"Forgiven?" Savannah repeated as she thought back to their breakfast together. "It's more complicated than that. I hadn't realized it would be," she admitted.

Lyneé sighed. "What have you done then? Besides," she added with a sly grin, "sleep together."

"Besides that," Savannah agreed with a wink.

Tristan had managed to slip out the side door before most of the street had awakened. He'd kissed her breathless, warm hands cupping her face, and promised to see her in time for luncheon. Only perhaps at Aunt Nadia's, so he needn't worry about the servants' revolt.

"I hadn't thought I'd ever see him again. When he returned and I slapped him—"

"Which you did," Lyneé reminded her with a smirk.

"Which I did," Savannah agreed. "That'd be that. I wouldn't see him again."

"If Nell hadn't been murdered, would you have?"

Savannah hadn't thought about that. Now, she took her time answering, looking around the familiar street with its boarded-up windows and rubbish everywhere. Browne followed her, unwilling to leave her alone after the previous days. Peters had melted into the street, blending in so that even Savannah couldn't see him. Thankful for that added protection, Savannah stopped several houses from Dem's.

"I think so, yes." Savannah felt that deep in her bones.

Not as if fate had a hand, necessarily, but that no matter what happened, she and Tristan would always find a way to each other. She started walking again and let the certainty of that knowledge spread through her.

"What happens now?"

"Now we solve these crimes. Whether it's all connected or not, this street and its people are important to me." She stood before Dem's door now, the heavy wooden one he'd stolen. She couldn't be too indignant about that; the thick, heavy door protected Ailene and little Shaw, too. "After?" She shook her head. "After is for after."

"Savannah." Lyneé rolled her eyes. "That isn't an answer."

"I have no answer," she admitted. But her voice remained calm, and, oh, that lovely feeling of calm and even keel washed over her for the first time in a very, very long time. Since even before Tristan left, Savannah now realized. "I have only feelings, and right now my feelings tell me that things have changed. I've changed."

Tristan had as well. If they'd married before he left, would he have eventually left her to seek out those adventures he craved? She hadn't an answer to that. However, the last three years had taught her that no matter her heartache, she could survive.

She didn't necessarily need Tristan in her life, as she'd once thought before he left. Did she want him? Yes. That much was obvious given their night together. And she loved him— whether she still did from before or had fallen in love again didn't matter. She loved him.

"I find it interesting how a person can change over time." She held Lyneé's gaze. "Some for the better, some not so much."

"I always loved the woman you were," her sister whispered. "I love her now, and though it fills me with rage I want to take out on Tristan, I'm glad you aren't hiding away so much."

Savannah sighed. "I hadn't realized that until Eliza's picnic."

That freedom of release made her want to dance down the street in joy. One more thing she hadn't done in three years. She used to love dancing. Maybe now, it wouldn't be such a bad idea.

"Where did he find this door?" Lyneé asked, eyeing the structure with suspicion and curiosity.

"Best not ask," Savannah mumbled. "I believe he and a crew liberated it."

Lyneé choked on a laugh, and Savannah grinned at her as she knocked. She was unsurprised that Ailene answered, though Ailene looked shocked at her early appearance.

"I brought fresh food," Savannah said as they stepped inside. "Is Dem awake?"

"Aye, Miss Savannah." His voice echoed from the back of the small living area.

"Good. Breakfast first, then you can tell me who sent those men."

Lyneé snorted and set her own basket on the table. "It's early yet, but have there been any more attacks?"

"No, Miss Lyneé." Dem frowned at the yogurt and berries. "What's this?"

"It's for Ailene, so she can build back her strength." Savannah slid a pot across the table. "We brought meat for you." She paused but held back her other offering. She needed to hear what Dem had to say about last night first. One bribe at a time.

"They were a bunch of ruffians," Dem said, digging into the feast. "Nobodies who thought they could grab my power."

She'd thought as much, but the timing bothered her. Or perhaps it was the revelations she and Tristan worked through last night that made her even more suspicious. "No one sent them?"

Both Dem and Ailene stilled. Shaw fussed in the bassinet, and Lyneé went to soothe him. Savannah looked between brother and sister and knew they hadn't lied. They truly believed that.

"Who would've sent them?" Ailene asked slowly, frowning at a blueberry. At least she was eating. "Other than a rival gang, and they wouldn't have kept quiet about it."

"None of the other gangs have said anything," Dem admitted. "Is that odd?"

Dem nodded. "Aye. They like to brag. If they'd anything to do with this, the entire rookery would know of it."

That made sense. It was what she'd long assumed. She still didn't understand why this street, why here? Chance?

"The man who was killed last week," Savannah said slowly, not certain how much she should reveal. "Any news on him?"

"Nothing." Dem sounded surprised. She knew he hadn't forgotten, but a lot had happened since then. "You think it's connected?"

Too smart by half. "I think everything here is connected, Dem. The question is how."

"He didn't have nothing on him," Dem reminded her. "Just another poor bastard in the wrong place."

In the wrong place, yes.

Before Savannah could ask any more questions, a commotion outside distracted her. Ah, Tristan. She stood, but Dem beat her to his feet.

"I know you can use that fancy dagger, miss, but let me first."

Nodding, she allowed him his moment. She didn't care about earning power on this street; she carried her own and knew its worth. Dem, however, fought for every scrap every single day. Savannah turned toward Lyneé, who handed a now sleeping Shaw to Ailene.

"Tristan?" Lyneé asked, her voice neutral.

"Oh, no doubt." Savannah sighed. "He was supposed to be on Bond Street." Then again, it was a mere mile from here. A quick horse ride would've seen him here in less than fifteen minutes.

"Ah, the used-to-be fiancé." Dem's voice drifted through the open door, along with the stench and noise of the street beyond.

"Dem," Tristan called in a strong voice. "Just the man I wanted to see."

Savannah stepped toward the door, so Tristan knew she was safe inside, though he'd have seen Browne standing guard at the door.

That was when all hell broke loose.

CHAPTER 21

One minute Tristan was dismounting his horse, nodding at Browne and wondering where Peters had disappeared to, and the next the mood shifted. The already noisy street didn't scream; there was no cacophony of outrage. Tension simply raced through the people, as if they knew what would happen next.

Tristan turned, drawing his dagger, his feet braced wide. Scanning the street, he waited, listening for movement, that shift in the air. That wrongness wasn't around Dem's house, but close. The tension built like a wave, cresting higher and racing closer.

Browne appeared next to him. Tristan didn't know his entire story. All he knew was that Browne had grown up as a poor tenant farmer near one of the coaching inns Savannah's great-grandmother had purchased a few decades ago. He hated farming, preferred fighting, and had somehow found his way into Hugh Shaw's employ. That was enough for Tristan to trust both the man's ability with a knife and that he wouldn't stab him in the back.

"Peters," Tristan shouted, facing the street and this strange

THE LADY'S COURTSHIP

unknown quality that rushed along, cresting along the street.

"Aye, sir. I've got them."

"They can take care of themselves." Savannah's voice drifted from behind him.

"Savannah," Tristan sighed, forcing his attention from the street to her.

"Don't look at me." She spared him a glance, her eyes fierce, her mouth set. "What's happened?"

"I don't know. I can't see," he admitted.

Dem had already disappeared into the crowd, head high, shouting orders into the storm about to break. Lyneé stood on Savannah's opposite side, and Tristan heard the door close and latch. At least Ailene and Shaw were safe.

"I'll start her lessons next week," Savannah muttered. "After we settle this."

Tristan had no idea what that was about. But this…it crawled over his skin, an open wound on a street full of them. Tristan stepped into the street, ignoring the overflowing gutter and the rubbish flying freely in the wind. He looked down the street, watching Dem, listening for that break.

"He's too late," Savannah muttered, walking beside him.

Tristan felt that, too. That no matter what Dem did, it was already too late.

"There's going to be a war on this street," he murmured, moving slowly along the center, where people cleared a path. They felt it, too. "Stay back."

"Tristan," she protested in a voice that sounded both tired and annoyed.

"Savannah, please." He paused and met her gaze. "I can't lose you again."

"And you think I'm ready to lose you?"

That gave him pause. He'd never considered himself invincible, but he did know his strengths. Law and philosophy and natural sciences—and fighting with the best of them. He hadn't necessarily set out to beat either of his brother's number of fights at Harrow but had never backed down from one, either. Savannah could handle herself, but he knew he needed to keep her safe. At all costs.

"I'll let this entire street burn before I let anything happen to you," he snapped. "I'll start the fire myself if it means keeping you safe."

Before she could say a word, Tristan closed the short distance between them and kissed her hard. He didn't care about the public street, rookery or not, about Lyneé's presence or the very real danger sweeping closer.

He pulled back much sooner than he wanted to. "I love you."

"If you die," Savannah threatened, "I'll come after you."

His own lips quirked into a smile. She would, too. Not to tell him she loved him, but to berate him for dying and not giving them a second chance.

"I promise I'll be careful." He caressed her cheek and stepped back. "Stay safe."

He hadn't even had the chance to tell her about the silk, about who had purchased it. Of the dozen names on the list Arnault had discovered. Of course, right then, it might not matter.

Tristan wanted to tell her again that he loved her, but he disappeared into the crowd instead. She didn't follow but remained on the fringes with Lyneé. Browne walked beside him.

"Have you a plan?" Browne asked.

"Walk in, find the problem, handle it." Tristan sighed. "I realize that isn't exactly what one might call a plan."

Browne snorted. "Are you letting Dem take the credit?"

"Yes."

He had to. Tristan didn't care if this street knew about his fighting abilities; he didn't care about credit or accolades. For Dem to stay in power and protect Ailene and the baby, as well as

Savannah when she visited the women here, he needed the perception of strength.

"Find Dem," Tristan said. "See that he keeps at the head of this. Whatever this is."

Browne hurried ahead, following Dem's voice. Tristan slipped around the side, walking through the crowd. He wasn't certain this was a better idea. It gave him minimal room to maneuver, but at least no one would see him coming.

He hated not knowing what the problem was, or if it was simply a fear the street carried now that it had woken. Still, Tristan couldn't forget the attempt on Savannah's life. He stilled, torn between returning to her and moving forward.

The scream made up his mind. Even as he ran forward, he worried he'd made the wrong choice. He cared about the people here because Savannah cared. Given the choice between her and them? Her. Every time.

Tristan skidded to a halt just as Dem arrived. The woman lay on the ground; he couldn't do anything to help her. And he knew Savannah would already be on her way. She had to have heard the scream.

Turning in a tight circle, he scanned the area. The locals were easy to spot. Some went barefoot, others in clothing too large or too small, all of it threadbare. If the murderer was smart, he'd have dressed in similar clothing. But if the cravat Tristan still carried in his pocket was any indication, their perpetrator was not that smart.

He looked for something unusual, out of the ordinary in the rookery. A hat, as foolish as that would be. Shoes—though Tristan didn't blame anyone for not wanting to walk barefoot in this street. He focused, ignoring the crowd, pushing through them as they gathered around the poor, dead woman.

He searched for any telltale sign. The flash of a knife, the glint of the blade as he'd seen when Savannah had been attached. Anything that marked the person as different.

A well-made greatcoat.

"Got you," he muttered.

He raced after the suspect, pushing people out of the way. The person didn't turn, just kept walking at a slow, even pace through the gathering mass. Tristan watched him as he casually walked toward the intersection, where fewer people crowded the street.

Now that he saw the killer, dressed in an old, worn greatcoat but a well-tailored one nonetheless, he couldn't unsee it. The garment looked as if he'd beaten it with a rock and rubbed dirt over it, but the quality stood out here. Tristan easily followed the man through the crowd, not daring to look away from the fine material.

"If you hadn't dressed in such fine clothing, I never would've found you." The figure continued his unhurried pace as if he hadn't heard. "You stick out quite obviously, I'm afraid. You'll never leave here alive."

That stopped him. Tristan grinned.

"How did you know?" The voice, male, calm yet oddly excited, called back.

Rule number one: never admit to anything. Tristan shook his head slightly.

"Franklin and Sons." Tristan inched closer. He knew the man carried a knife, his weapon of choice, but he didn't know how truly proficient he was with it. Using it on unsuspecting women was hardly a testament to his skill.

The man snorted but still didn't turn. Tristan inched to one side as silently as the filth on the street would allow. Just in case the man also carried a pistol. No sense standing in the line of fire.

"I admit, most people wouldn't have put it together," Tristan continued, taking another sidestep. "But I'm not most people."

He had friends who knew their textiles. He had Little Ricky, who definitely knew the value of spying on shop owners. And bribing their assistants.

"It doesn't matter. No one will care." He was so blasé that Tristan wanted to throw his khanjar at the man's back.

Reining in his anger, his blind fury over the man's unconcerned tone, Tristan loosened his fist from around the bone hilt of his dagger. Anger wouldn't give him the upper hand. All it'd do was make him sloppy.

"That's where you're wrong."

"Ha. The black witch?" The man dismissed Savannah with a flick of his wrist. Tristan stepped closer, his hold on his temper unraveling too fast for him to regain control. It beat through him, protect Savannah, keep her safe at all costs, no matter what. "That wasn't me."

"I'd be careful if I were you," Tristan said between clenched teeth.

"No one cares about these women." The man turned. Tristan didn't recognize him, but that didn't mean anything—he'd been at sea for three years. Little Ricky had said something about the men, several of the dandies, who'd purchased the cravats, but Tristan also hadn't recognized any names. "And no one will prosecute me."

He held up his knife, a long, serrated thing that looked wickedly deadly even in the scant light of the crowded street. In the moment before Tristan moved, he noted three things: the man held it far too sloppily for any sort of prolonged fight; Dem made his way toward them; and he wasn't certain he'd let the man live.

"That's where you're wrong."

"Stay with Ailene," Savannah ordered Peters.

"Sorry, miss, I'm to follow you at all times."

"Peters," she said through clenched teeth, "I need her safe. Her and the baby, little Shaw." He startled at that. "If something happens to me, I promise I'll let my father know it was my fault."

"If you die, miss, I'll be right behind you," he muttered unhappily.

"I promise I won't die." She grinned. "I have too much to live for."

Peters nodded, looking miserable. "At least Browne is with Mr. Tristan."

Savannah glanced at Lyneé, then raced after Tristan.

She wasn't ready to lose him again.

It wasn't hard to find him. The street gave him and the murderer a wide berth as they fought. The crowd kept back, though she noted several were placing bets.

Browne appeared by her side as she stepped into the circle surrounding Tristan. The suspect moved well enough, with the grace of a fencer or a well-off pugilist who had years of proper lessons behind him.

Tristan fought like his father, his form far from proper. He fought to disable, incapacitate his opponent by any means. Oh, but she loved watching him fight. The grace with which he moved, the hard, knowing smirk on his beautiful lips. The knowledge that he waited for his opponent to make a mistake. They always did, always underestimated his lean body as a sign of leisure.

Gripping her dagger, she forced her gaze from the beautiful sight of Tristan moving around the street, dagger drawn, easily sidestepping the man. Instead, she glared at the man who had killed her women. Savannah didn't recognize him.

"See anyone?"

"Dem is gathering the troops, so to speak." Lyneé kept her back to Savannah's, her own dagger gripped in her hand.

"This is the only suspect?" She couldn't hide the surprise in her voice. "There aren't more?"

She'd expected a group of men, like the one that had attacked Ailene. Savannah had thought the violations were related to the attacks. Perhaps they'd been wrong. If so, what else had they been wrong about?

Tristan tackled the man, and his knife clattered to the street. Its teeth stood out in stark contrast with the smooth blade. Where had he found such a thing?

The entire street had shifted from where poor Orla now lay in the filthy gutter. Savannah had sent word to Mr. Christie at St. Giles Church before racing after Tristan. Apparently, Orla's death hadn't hindered the crowd's morbid interest in Tristan's fight. Or maybe the street wanted to see the end of these attacks as desperately as Savannah did.

"Do they travel alone?" Lyneé murmured from behind her.

"I have no idea. I've never tried to murder anyone and cover it up." From the corner of her eye, she saw movement that didn't belong.

Reaching around for Lyneé's hip with her free hand, she slowly turned them until they stood back-to-back, ready for a fight. Another man stood there, his greatcoat collar pulled up to hide his face, but she recognized it. Rather, she recognized the quality. Solid, well made, tailored. New despite the obvious attempt at making it look worn, as if he'd stomped it with his horse.

"Lyneé," Savannah hissed from the side of her mouth.

"I'll find Dem," her sister agreed.

"Miss Savannah." Browne sighed but followed her. She'd owe him for his dedication, he and Peters.

As much as Savannah didn't want to leave her sister, she wanted to confront the second man. He watched the fight like all the others, yes, but he clearly stood out. Even those standing beside him stood a little bit farther from him, no matter how he tried to fit into the crowd.

"Looking to help your friend?" Savannah asked casually.

She watched the man, who stiffened, unable to stop his gaze from swinging from the fight, where Tristan clearly had the upper hand, to her. Savannah didn't need to watch to recognize that annoyed grunt. Tristan had had enough, and this was the end of the fight.

The man ignored her and looked back at the fight, as everyone else did.

She nodded. "If you wanted to fit in, you should've worn something else. Stupid."

That got his attention. The anger in his eyes at such a mild insult eclipsed his impasse of whether or not to acknowledge her. She had a way with fools.

"I should've killed you when I had the chance."

Browne stiffened at her side, bracing for a fight. Part of Savannah had expected that admission, but she had never expected the chance to confront her attacker. She wasn't the only one who heard that admission. Those around him had as well.

Not everyone here accepted her. Many of the women did, because she was the only one who offered them help during childbirth, who saw to their sick children in hopes they'd live past their first birthday.

It happened all at once.

Dem appeared, Lyneé right behind him. The crowd stepped back from the man who had threatened her, leaving a wide circle to show everyone that the killer was in their midst. Tristan grunted behind her as she heard the body of his opponent drop to the ground.

"You threatened someone under my protection." Dem stepped up, his voice ringing out over the now buzzing mob. She had the feeling his words were the only thing that held them back. "You came here with your notions of trying to take over my territory." He sounded almost sorrowful, as if the rage that always boiled just beneath the surface wasn't about to explode. "I protect Miss Savannah, and you attacked her. You attacked the women of my street."

Savannah stepped back as Dem stepped forward. This was his fight.

Tristan's hand touched her shoulder. "Savannah."

She turned to him just as Dem brandished his own knife.

Her heart pounded, but relief swamped her, making her knees weak. She turned her back to Dem and focused on Tristan.

"You're bleeding." She eyed him critically as Browne and Lyneé joined them, leaving Dem to his work. Savannah reached into her pocket for the gloves she'd shoved in there when she unsheathed her dagger. She pulled one out and dabbed at his bleeding lip, at the cut on his face. "I'm going to ruin another pair of gloves."

He caught her hand and kissed the inside of her wrist. "Not on my account. You're safe? Unharmed?"

"Dem's taking care of the partner. Let him have his moment. He needs it after these last few weeks."

Tristan watched the fight over her shoulder. Then he took her hand, held out the other for Lyneé, and nodded at Browne.

"Where's Peters?"

"Watching Ailene," Savannah said as they returned down the street, far from the fight Dem was clearly drawing out for the benefit of the crowd. "Don't tell on him. I promised he'd be safe from Papa's wrath."

Halfway back to Dem and Ailene's ramshackle house, another crowd parted for them. Savannah nearly gasped at the sight. Ailene, who hadn't left the house since her attack, knelt by Orla's body, holding the dead woman's hand as a small group waited for Mr. Christie. Little Shaw lay swaddled against her chest, and Peters stood over her, holding a pair of knives and looking fiercely at anyone who ventured too close.

"Ailene."

Ailene looked up from her kneeling position, angry and sad and, yes, shaking. Savannah squeezed Tristan's hand and knelt beside her.

"When you teach me to defend myself, can you teach me healing, too?" Ailene whispered, her voice thin and cracking.

Lyneé knelt on Ailene's other side, bracketing the shaking woman, and together they helped her stand. Savannah gripped Ailene's hand.

"Any bit of knowledge you want," Savannah promised her.

Ailene nodded, her other hand cradling little Shaw. "I won't let them take anything else from me."

Lyneé guided her away, and Savannah turned for Tristan. "Did you want to check on Dem?"

"And ruin his moment of triumph?" Tristan laughed, then winced. "I'd never be so callous."

"All right." She looked behind him but couldn't see anything through the mob. She did hear the cheers, and the barking of a bet maker.

Tristan cursed. "Browne, do me a favor and place a couple shillings on Dem. Make sure the street knows which way the wind should blow."

"Aye, sir." Browne offered a slight bow and disappeared back up the street.

"Did you recognize the man?" Savannah asked as they drifted into the shadows that veiled side of a building, away from prying eyes and eavesdroppers.

"I recognized his clothing," Tristan said, drawing her close. He kissed her forehead. "Too tailored for this area."

"When Mr. Christie arrives, we'll send for the magistrate." Savannah paused, frowning. "I didn't look at your opponent after your fight ended. You restrained him, right?"

"Of course." He sounded insulted. "What sort of Conrad do you take me for?"

She laughed and leaned her head against his chest. The words crowded her throat—*her* Conrad. The steady thump of his heart lulled her eyes closed, and she breathed deeply of his scent. She could stay like this, Savannah realized.

"Would you care to accompany me to Vauxhall Gardens this evening?" His voice ghosted over her skin, and she shivered from the intimacy.

"We already solved the murders." Savannah pulled back just enough to meet his gaze, the blue-green lay in the shadows of too-close buildings.

"Not for the murders," he corrected, his fingers brushing her cheek. "For a not-scandalous, perfectly chaperoned evening together."

She did. Of course she did, and, oh, her heart longed for such an evening.

"Not scandalous, eh?" she repeated in a vain attempt to give herself a moment. Her brain had scrambled at his question, and she couldn't sort one thought from another.

"I admit, our previous courtship was unconventional." Tristan's lips brushed her cheek. "And our renewed courtship scattered convention on the four winds."

Previous courtship. Current courtship.

His lips brushed her other cheek, his fingers warm on the nape of her neck. His touch didn't help her scattered thoughts.

"Is that what this is?" Savannah asked, cursing her breathlessness. "A courtship?"

"A second chance." His lips hovered over hers. "Our second chance. A second chance for me to show you how desperately I love you. More than that, how much I care. Not about adventure or seeing new lands, but about enjoying life with you."

Savannah swallowed hard. "And if I wish to remain in London?"

"If you wish, and you want me back in your life, then we can create a new life here."

Savannah didn't know. She didn't mind sailing. She'd gone with her parents several times on trips to Copenhagen, Oslo, and Stockholm. It wasn't the ship travel that gave her pause, or even staying here in London or someplace else in Britain.

"I don't know," she admitted.

"Let's enjoy Vauxhall," Tristan tempted, his lips gentle on hers. "And see from there."

She kissed him back, enjoying the rush of need, the familiar ache of desire. Savannah pulled back from the kiss and nearly laughed at herself. She'd already made her choice.

"Miss Savannah." Ailene's hesitant voice broke through her fog of arousal.

Stepping from Tristan's arms, she smoothed her hands down her skirts and smiled politely at Ailene. "Has Mr. Christie arrived?"

"Aye. I sent your Peters round for the magistrate. Do you mind?" Ailene's voice wavered, but her eyes remained fierce.

"Good thinking," Savannah told her.

"Has Dem returned?" Tristan asked, placing his hand on the small of Savannah's back and leading her from the building shadows.

Savannah didn't stretch like a cat into his warm, comforting touch, but it was a close thing.

"Not yet, but the crowd is thinning out," Ailene said.

"I'll speak with him about the magistrate and the two men. This ends today."

Savannah hoped so. Though she would never abandon her women here, she thought perhaps it was time to start yet another new path in life. Tristan nodded, held her gaze for another moment, and crossed the street to speak with Dem.

"Thank you, Miss Savannah," Ailene whispered.

Savannah's eyebrows rose. "For what?"

"Keeping your promise," Ailene said. "Not many do, but you did. You and Miss Lyneé." She paused. "And your man."

Her man? Savannah's heart flipped at the sentiment, and she smiled.

Yes. Her man.

CHAPTER 22

She and Tristan had to sort out their future, but right then Savannah watched him speak with Dem about the magistrate and handing over these men to the proper authorities. She wanted to know why those two men had chosen their path. What reason could they have had for murdering the poorest of the poor women?

They hadn't talked when Tristan questioned them. They hadn't said a word when Dem threatened them, as they hadn't a reason. Savannah didn't believe that. Everyone had a reason for their actions.

Half the street had just watched Dem exert his control. Dem proclaimed they'd start their own Bow Street Runners to protect themselves, a proclamation that was met with cheers from the crowd. Savannah thought that a was good idea. But, more importantly, his speech offered her the opportunity to slip past, unseen.

Tristan held out his hand and she took it, smiling at his touch, at their future laid out before them. Ailene had returned to the house, Lyneé with her, Browne following them. Peters, Savannah knew, followed her.

THE LADY'S COURTSHIP

"I don't understand," Savannah admitted. "Why did those two men choose here?"

"The magistrate will find out," Tristan promised. "I'll go round in the morning and see what's happened."

Still frowning, Savannah nodded. "I have a bad feeling that we were right about them, that it was a mere wager—the life of those women in exchange for something fleeting. Like money or prestige."

He didn't respond but pressed a kiss against her temple. They walked in silence for a few steps before he peered down at her with a grave, serious look that made her frown deepen. "Do you mind?"

"Mind what?"

"The scandal." He sighed. "I should protect you from that, but all I seem capable of is creating more. I promised to protect you, then I kissed you in the middle of the street."

Savannah returned her head to his shoulder but only for a moment. "I never cared about scandal. Everything the Shaws do is scandalous. Buying the house in Grosvenor Square? Scandalous. Building the shipping business into an incredible empire? Scandalous. Not staying in our place?" She sighed as they moved around the crowd still listening to Dem. "Scandalous."

"No more scandal," he promised, pulling her again him just before the solid door of the house. "Well..." He kissed her softly. "Maybe one more."

Her need for him still buzzed beneath her skin. Her nipples hardened, and her body ached for his touch. Savannah pulled back, smoothing her hands down her gown.

"You always make me feel scandalous," she muttered. Standing outside, a sudden mist surrounding them like a curtain, Savannah felt as if they'd traveled back in time. To when they'd run off together, uncaring about what people thought. "But at least we didn't compound it."

Tristan laughed, unrepentant. "I'll scandalize everyone with the way I feel about you," he promised.

"What was that about Vauxhall?" she asked, remembering his offer.

"I want to take you to all the places we never managed to go before." He brushed his fingers along her cheek. "Vauxhall, Covent Garden. Hell, we can stroll Hyde Park if you like."

"Where else?" She tilted her head, unwilling to leave this moment.

"Where else do you want to go?"

"I don't know," she admitted as he tugged a lock of hair into place and fixed her comb. Savannah was shocked it'd survived the last hours. And Tristan's hands. "I never thought about it. I was always so focused on us, on the business, on—everything." She frowned at him, but he was focused on her hair. "I never thought much about pleasure."

"What was last night then?" he asked, affronted. Tristan picked up her hands and kissed the backs of both of them. "I probably have a mark on my shoulder from where you displayed your pleasure rather forcefully."

She laughed, even as a shiver of need tingled from where his lips had touched her skin. "I never said I didn't want you," she corrected with a sly grin.

She'd always wanted him. Even that first day, when he'd returned with Jiesha as a gift as if he hadn't disappeared from her life for three years. Now? Now, Savannah saw a future with him.

"Let's walk." She shook out her skirts. This wasn't the most ideal place for the conversation she wanted, but they were here, in the moment. One thing she'd learned was that she had to make her own future. "I'm afraid my skirts are a bit muddied." She sighed and smoothed them ineffectively. "First the cloak, and now this. Coyle might never forgive me."

"The cloak was hardly your fault." His tone heated with anger as hot as his passion.

"I know," she soothed. This was the moment where they stepped onto that new path. And that knowledge made her step lighter, her heart sing.

Before Tristan could say anything else, a laugh interrupted them. It startled her but didn't prickle over her skin in any kind of foreboding.

"The pair of you sure do pick the most unusual places for a courtship."

Savannah stared in surprise as Mr. Shilby appeared in the middle of Denmark Street. She'd believed Tristan when he said the man was there, of course, but hadn't thought Shilby would return. Why would he? Yet now he stood before them. If she believed in such things, Savannah would've said their words had conjured him.

"Shilby." Tristan nodded. "Out for another enjoyable walk through rubbish-covered streets?"

"I'm here to see to the men you found." His voice hardened, no longer the affable, almost foppish tone she remembered. He smiled at her, bowing slightly. "Miss Savannah."

She returned the greeting with a quick curtsey, then cursed herself. This wasn't the place for such pleasantries or formality.

"How did you know about those men?" she asked, surprised at this turn of events.

Shilby stepped closer, eyes serious. He glanced around the area, but people had already wandered off now that the initial excitement had dissipated. "I wasn't here for the scenery," he said, tone slightly mocking.

"Well, I know there isn't a garden," Savannah snapped, testily. She cared about these people. "But the place isn't that bad."

Shilby bowed again, face losing some of its hardness. "My apologies. I simply meant I searched for something else."

"The man who was shot with a rifle?" Tristan asked but they'd already figured as much, even if they had no proof.

Shilby didn't look surprised at Tristan's deduction. "Clever."

"It was the rifle," Tristan continued, sorting through what they'd started to figure out last night. "Unusual for the area."

Again, Shilby nodded, his gaze wandering over the area. "He was a hired man, no one of consequence."

Savannah snorted, but it was Tristan who said, "Enough of a consequence that a peer of the realm ventured here."

Shrugging that off, Shilby stepped closer. Clearly, he didn't want anyone overhearing their conversation. Savannah wondered why. He was dressed in older clothes, not new ones forcibly worn to make them look old. Truly frayed clothing.

"However, the knife was my fault." He bowed low again in her direction, eyes holding hers. "I do apologize for that, Miss Savannah. I aimed for him, but someone shot him first."

"You—apology accepted," she said, quite at a loss with this new information. "Why did you aim at him?"

"Are you familiar with Mr. Wilcox?" he asked.

Savannah shook her head. "I've never heard the name."

"No," Tristan admitted slowly. "In what context?"

"I believe he's the man who murdered my parents." Shilby's gaze, hard as flint now, belied the ease with which he uttered those words.

"And you think you found him here?" Savannah asked.

"No, I found Jeffers." He nodded at Tristan. "The man who was shot beside you, Miss Savannah."

She wanted to crow that she'd been right all along, that that man's murder had nothing to do with her. Savannah did not. This wasn't a moment for levity.

"I'm sorry," she said sincerely. "I hadn't realized that—please accept my deepest condolences."

Shilby nodded, light blue eyes softening. "Thank you." He stepped back, a mischievous grin on his face now, erasing the

THE LADY'S COURTSHIP

anger and grief that had bled through his tight control. "I still say Vauxhall Gardens is a better place for a courtship!"

Savannah watched Shilby disappear into the crowd, blending as seamlessly as if he'd always lived on this street. "The world continues to surprise me," she admitted.

"Indeed," Tristan muttered. Then he shook his head and looked down the street, but Dem continued holding court.

"It occurs to me," she said, bringing his attention back to her, "that in all our time together, we never made love outside." She kissed him softly. "Whatever happens in the future, I want to make love in a field of flowers."

"Your wish is my command, my lady." His hands were warm and sure against her back as he held her close.

"Definitely a meadow of flowers," she managed, willing her heart to slow and her breath to even out.

"I love you, Savannah Shaw."

She grinned, her heart light. "And I love you, Tristan Conrad." She turned from him, intent on letting her sister know she was safe. That they should probably all leave before something else happened. Instead, hand on the door handle, she turned back to Tristan. "I want a future with you."

"Good." He grinned. "I very much want one with you." He lifted her hand. "Will you marry me, Savannah?"

"Yes." If she thought her heart was light just moment ago, now it soared. "Yes, I will."

"I'll marry you next Tuesday if you want. Though I suppose I should at least give my parents and your grandmother time to travel to London, give me a proper tongue-lashing for leaving the way I did and a suitable congratulations on our upcoming nuptials."

"It only seems proper," she agreed with mock solemnity.

"Or we can elope to Gretna Green." He knocked on the door, alerting those inside that they had returned.

"I wouldn't mind, but after all this?" She shook her head as

Lyneé opened the door, dagger at the ready. "I think a proper ceremony would be best."

EPILOGUE

For her and Tristan's first foray into Vauxhall Gardens, and their attempt at maintaining propriety now that they were truly engaged—again—both her parents and Aunt Nadia and Uncle James chaperoned them. Savannah didn't know whether to laugh at the absurdity of both couples in a chaperoning position or scowl over the fact that they seemed intent on maintaining propriety.

For the first time ever.

A beautiful, star-filled night twinkled overhead, with only a bare breeze off the Thames. The warm June day had turned into a much cooler evening, but Savannah didn't care. Tonight was perfect, with its vast array of stars shining in contrast with the thousand lanterns illuminating the gardens.

A perfect atmosphere for her first real, respectable outing with Tristan. She didn't count the theater, though Savannah supposed she ought. Still, that had been when they'd pretended to have reconciled. This, this felt different. Real.

They hadn't ever courted previously; it was more like they'd drifted together, enjoying whatever life offered. An unorthodox courtship, perhaps. Until tonight, they'd never enjoyed a proper one. Even with eagle-eyed chaperones, it was lovely.

"Thank you." She smiled up at Tristan as he helped her from the boat that took them across the Thames. She seriously debated sneaking off into the privacy of the gardens.

"Would you care to visit the pavilions first?" he asked, his head close to hers despite everyone watching. In the cool evening, his voice brushed warm and promising over her cheek. "Or the buffet?"

"The pavilions," she said, not hungry for whatever meager offerings the gardens provided.

For Tristan? Yes. For a chance encounter with him in the darkened hedges? She'd definitely try to arrange that despite his promise to see things remained respectable.

Smiling at her scandalous thoughts amid their very serious attempt at decorum, Savannah rested her hand on Tristan's arm.

He lifted her hand to his lips and kissed her gloved fingers. "Once the fireworks begin, let's sneak away into the hedgerow."

"What happened to dignity and no more scandals?" She grinned mischievously up at him.

"I changed my mind," he growled.

"You read my mind." She laughed freely. She had everything she wanted.

"We can still elope." He watched her seriously.

"Ah, Miss Savannah." Lord Shilby's voice cut through whatever else Tristan was going to say.

Tristan cursed under his breath at the intrusion. She noticed that Tristan didn't drop her hand nor move to a more respectable distance. A quick look showed her parents and aunt and uncle waiting along the rows of seating for the later fireworks.

"Lord Shilby. Mr. Shilby." She offered a brief curtsy. "I had not expected to see you this evening." She tilted her head, her smile widening. "Though I suppose I should have."

"I often enjoy the gardens, my dear," Lord Shilby said, glancing around the crowd.

Beside her, Tristan stiffened at the familiarity, though he didn't utter a disparaging word.

"They're a quiet place to enjoy a bit of privacy," Mr. Shilby agreed in that same bland tone Savannah expected of him. The one she remembered from the few times they'd been introduced. Not the strong, hard, confident tone from earlier today. The younger Shilby offered a quick, wicked grin that did not befit the dandy he portrayed. "Do you know who the men were?" he asked.

"No. I planned on paying a visit to the magistrate in the morning." Tristan didn't look at her, but she knew they thought the same thing: they'd had more important things on their mind. Like ravishing kisses in the middle of the street.

Dem, Robbie, and a couple others had watched over the bound-and-gagged men while Dem proudly proclaimed the men who attacked their women had been captured—that justice would be served. Savannah remembered Dem's speech about patrolling themselves, and Savannah had assumed the magistrate had arrived and had some of the Bow Street Runners take the men away.

"Lord Davon, heir to the Marquess of Balrath, and Mr. Mooreland, third son of the Earl of Ainwick," Mr. Shilby said.

Savannah's anger burned through her. These were wealthy men, their titles old and distinguished. That was why they had claimed nothing would come of any arrest.

"They wanted for naught," Savannah seethed. "Anything they wished; they could've easily bought. Do you know why they committed the murders? A wager, the so-called thrill of murdering an innocent woman?"

"They didn't say, I'm afraid."

Tristan's hands curled into fists. "Did the magistrate release them?"

"Not as yet," Mr. Shilby promised. "Though I'm certain it's only a matter of time."

"What happens then?" Savannah demanded, fury coloring her words.

"I'll bear witness," Tristan promised. "I won't let them slither away from their crimes."

Shilby shifted, and the dandy's bland voice disappeared. "I promise you, Miss Savannah, they might be released, but they won't get away with murder."

"How can you guarantee that?" Savannah demanded, but she kept her voice low, so as not to be overheard. "Will you also bear witness for those women?"

She looked from Lord Shilby, mouth set and determined, to Mr. Shilby. There she saw the hard determination of a warrior. Not the layabout heir to a barony from King Edward III's time.

"I don't make promises I can't keep."

His words about finding his parents' murderer echoed through her, and Savannah believed him. His set face, his precise words, belied his stance, the loose-limbed look of a man with naught better to do than spend his days sleeping and his nights socializing with the prettiest of women, drinking the most expensive wine.

"Have you heard of a Mr. Edward Worth?" Mr. Shilby asked, his voice returning to that of the dandy. Lord Shilby snorted, and even in the lantern light flickering over the lawn, she saw him roll his eyes.

"He has part ownership in Sharpe Imports," Savannah offered. "I believe he's engaged to Mr. Sharpe's eldest daughter, Ivy. I also believe Sharpe is in financial straits," she said slowly. Tristan leaned in, too. "Worth has investments in a great many businesses along the wharves. You should speak with my father and Mrs. St. Clair about it."

"His business investments are all more than a little fishy."

Shilby shook his head. "Have you heard anything about his connection to the gaming hells?"

"You should ask Dem about that," Tristan offered. "I never frequent them, but he'll know every person who sets foot in one."

"Dem," Shilby repeated slowly. "The man from earlier who claims to control Denmark Street."

"If you want answers, it's best you find the source," Tristan stated. "Dem knows more than he lets on."

"George." Lord Shilby nudged his grandson and nodded toward the rear of the crowd that had begun to gather for the fireworks.

"Ah." Shilby nodded at Tristan, bowed at Savannah, and walked away.

Savannah watched him. In a moment, the proud stance of a nobleman disappeared. Shilby had transformed into a hunter, all grace and focus as he slipped into the crowd, easily blending in. Savannah shook her head in awe at the change. This man was on the hunt.

"May I join you for supper?" Lord Shilby watched his grandson walk away for another moment, his face creased in worry and fear. In the next breath, he shook off whatever concern he carried and smiled airily at them. "My grandson has other business, I'm afraid."

"Perhaps you can tell us about Davon and Mooreland," Savannah offered, gesturing for their small group. "I'm most interested in the outcome."

"Miss Savannah, I'd be happy to." Shilby bowed in her direction, his eyes twinkling again. "If you'll regale me with news of your own?"

Savannah laughed. "However do you discover your information?"

Shilby merely smiled and walked toward her parents.

Savannah shook her head and rested her hand on Tristan's arm. He was hers and nothing could take that from her.

"I love you," Tristan whispered, stopping her several paces from the group. "Are you sure you don't want to elope?"

"The idea has more appeal with every passing moment." She grinned up at him as they walked for their group.

ABOUT THE AUTHOR

Thank you for reading, interested in reading more of the Conrad family? https://amzn.to/48ksDOr

If you enjoyed this book, I'd really appreciate it if you helped others enjoy it, too. Reviews are precious and help persuade other readers to give my romances a try.

Sign up to my VIP list for a short story, One Day with You. This story, along 3 additional short stories about Louise and Malcolm, are only available to my list. https://bit.ly/ 3kSzMjI

I send weekly newsletters with things like new releases, special offers, pictures of my dog, recipes, and other exciting news about my stories, preorders, research, and travel that I hope you'll enjoy as much as I do.

Stay Connected
CKMackenzie.com
Facebook.com/ckmackenziebook
instagram.com/ckmackenzieauthor
tiktok.com/@ckmackenzieauthor

Thank you for reading, interested in reading more of the Conrad family? https://amzn.to/48ksDOr

If you enjoyed this book, I'd really appreciate it if you helped others enjoy it, too. Reviews are precious and help persuade other readers to give my romances a try.

Sign up to my VIP list for a short story, One Day with You.

This story, along 3 additional short stories about Louise and Malcolm, are only available to my list. https://bit.ly/ 3kSzMjI
I send weekly newsletters with things like new releases, special offers, pictures of my dog, recipes, and other exciting news about my stories, preorders, research, and travel that I hope you'll enjoy as much as I do.

Stay Connected

CKMackenzie.com
ckmackenzieauthor@gmail.com

Milton Keynes UK
Ingram Content Group UK Ltd.
UKHW020955220724
445981UK00004B/248

9 798990 159914